THE MERCHANT OF PEARLS

P. J. Mann

ISBN 978-952-7415-02-3 (Paperback)

i

ACKNOWLEDGEMENTS

I wish to thank Barbara Gerig for the great job she did in the developmental editing and polishing of the first draft. I wish also to thank Elisabetta Emilia Mancini for the final polishing during the translation of the manuscript. My reader's team for the suggestions and support also for this novel.

Intro

There's an old shop on Merrill Street. Precious gems and finely chiseled jewels are exposed in its ever-changing windows. Throughout the year, you can find the cozy atmosphere of the Christmas period.

Although it's not located in one of the busiest or fanciest streets of the city, it attracts customers from every corner of the world.

People coming to Mr. Sherwood's shop are never alike. Many of them come inside, attracted by the beauty of the products displayed like artwork on their windows.

Others are driven by the fame of the owner's family, Mr. Sherwood, being one of the most talented jewelers around. Their creations always amaze the people who receive them as a present.

Mr. Eldridge Sherwood first opened the shop back in 1802. Since then, the tradition of jewelers, crafty stone traders, and charming salesmen had been passed down for generations within the family.

Not a single scandal or gossip has ever marred the owners' reputation, who has always enjoyed the respect of the city's social elite.

Nevertheless, some rumored in that shop were also selling unusual objects, such as cursed precious stones.

How they came into possession of those famous, or infamous, jewels is a secret. But those willing to defy the fate of buying a cursed jewel or gem know how to find Mr. Sherwood's little shop.

Chapter 1

It was almost closing time. Herman glanced at his thirteen-year-old son, Edward, who silently studied in a corner behind the counter. A couple of tourists came through the door, looking lazily around without anything clear in their mind.

He followed them with his eyes, being confident they would leave without purchasing anything. His experience and his father's teachings had taught him how to best run his business and to distinguish when to offer assistance to customers and when to let them browse undisturbed.

Generally, when a person is interested, they find the courage to ask, he thought.

Suddenly the door opened, and a middle-aged man, dressed in a light brown camel hair coat, entered the shop.

With a quick glance around, he took off his hat and gloves.

"Good evening, sir." Herman greeted him with a charming smile.

The man stiffened his muscles and turned his glance at him.

"Oh, good evening." He replied, peering at the end of the eye the couple who was touring the shop, whispering comments about one or another piece of jewelry.

"How can I help you?" Herman asked as the man reached him at the main counter.

"Err... well, I'm looking for a pearl that was sold at an auction a few days ago." The man spoke nervously.

Herman understood and knew they needed to speak in private. Swiftly turning his head, he glanced at his son.

"Edward, I need to show this gentleman a particular item in the back room. Would you please take over for a bit?"

The boy almost jolted in his chair and gasped, turning to look at the man. He knew what they would talk about—days before, his father had bought the most beautiful pearl he'd ever seen for a ridiculous price. Only a few people were known to be interested, perhaps because of the sinister story that came with it.

"Dad, can't I come with you?" The young boy pleaded.

"No, we cannot leave the shop unattended. Besides, our customers might require your attention and service," Herman answered quietly.

Edward pouted and, eager to know the outcome of the negotiation, he kept staring at them, holding his breath as they walked away.

***

When the two men entered the room, the lights automatically turned on, revealing a spacious living room old-fashioned furnished with dark-brown bookshelves and antiquities collected during the centuries. A reddish leather couch faced two armchairs in the same style and was divided by a small sofa table over a red and orange Pakistani rug. A large window offered a view of the street.

4

"I do believe you referred to the pearl I purchased at the auction in Hong Kong, Mr...?" Herman began.

"Milton. My name is Jason Milton. I had planned to participate in it, but my flight was canceled. I arrived just as the hammer fell on your final bid."

Herman smiled and offered to take his coat, gloves, and hat to the wooden stand in the corner.

Having been one of the few bidders hadn't made him savor the taste of victory. "People still believe in curses and fear them. Please, take a seat. May I offer you something to drink? Perhaps a whiskey," he asked on his way to the liquor cabinet to show him his selection.

Jason smiled as he let himself be wrapped in the embrace of the soft leather of the couch. "Yes, please. This winter gets colder every day, and something to warm the spirit is more than welcome."

Herman brought him the glass of whiskey, "I'll get the pearl."

He approached a large safe built into the wall. Deftly dialing the combination, he retrieved a small jewelry box. Latching the safe once again, he returned to the couch and opened it to Mr. Milton.

In a cloud of dark velvet lay the most extraordinary pearl nature had ever produced. Depending on the direction of the light to illuminate it, its color changed from dark violet to pink and yellow tones, making it seem almost alive.

Mr. Milton fell silent, and he barely could take his eyes off it.

"Such an amazing...natural wonder." His voice was hardly a whisper. He raised his gaze to Herman, "Is it true that this is... 'The *Silent Rainbow*?'"

"The auction house has certified its authenticity, and I have done some research on my own. You are holding a 2000-year-old pearl. One of the oldest existing which so far has brought nothing but death and misery to the previous owners." Herman leaned on the couch, entwined his fingers on his chest, and scrutinized Mr. Milton through narrowed eyes.

"It was lost during a cruise, along with its last owner, Lord Mitchell, about 100 years ago. Since then, people forgot about it until a team of amateur scuba divers found relics of a ship. Further research found out to be that of Lord Mitchell," he explained as Mr. Milton continued to stare at it.

"You are not afraid of the curse?" Mr. Milton asked, finally peering up at Herman.

"Curses make for great marketing material, but they're not real. When people end up in trouble, it is easier to blame an item for their disgrace, rather than their poor decisions or an adverse fate, which is something beyond their control." His voice remained calm as he scrutinized Mr. Milton.

Mr. Milton placed the jewel box on the table in front of the couch. He sipped his whiskey, appreciating the pleasing aroma and the velvety smooth, smoky taste.

"What I'm wondering is whether you would accept offers." A slightly sarcastic tone coarsened Mr. Milton's voice.

Herman smiled and paused for the deal of his whole career, "I am a businessman. Everything has a price and, with the right one, you could be the lucky one who returns home with this precious pearl in his pocket." He slowly opened his hands' palms up without taking his eyes off of Mr. Milton.

"So, it's a question of the price," Mr. Milton responded. "What would you say if I offered you the same amount you paid for?"

Herman chuckled, amused. "As a dealer, this is an offer I must decline. The price for the pearl, curse included, is five hundred thousand dollars."

Mr. Milton sputtered his whiskey, "You didn't pay a fraction of that!"

"Of course, but this is because people like you were not present. Had you been in time for the auction, I can assure you, you wouldn't have gotten out of it with the pearl at a lower price. I had planned to spend a maximum of seven hundred thousand dollars-consider this a fair discount from me."

Herman didn't need to sell the pearl right away. He knew it wouldn't be long before many others would bid their offers.

Mr. Milton's expression revealed that he didn't expect to pay such an extravagant sum. "Can I make a counteroffer?"

Herman closed his eyes and shook his head, "No, Mr. Milton, I'm sorry, but this is my final price. Even without the curse, such a large pearl is a rarity. I'm left wondering about the poor mollusk which produced it. Either the oyster was an animal of extraordinary dimensions itself, or the discomfort of that sand grain was unbearable."

Mr. Milton chuckled, "That's indeed true, to say nothing about the light reflections on its surface."

It was a rarity, a marvel that nature itself would hardly be able to create again, and that was the reason why he wanted to possess it at all costs.

Herman remained silent. Mr. Milton would most likely purchase the pearl. The way he twisted his fingers as he looked at the pearl in the jewel box was a clear sign of his inner torment.

"I wasn't prepared for anything above the final auction price," Mr. Milton muttered, exhaled deeply, and took another sip of the whiskey. From an inner pocket on his blazer, he extracted a checkbook.

"I'm sorry, we don't accept checks—cash or cards only," Herman stated tactfully.

Mr. Milton narrowed his eyes, pursing his lips as if he didn't appreciate when his honesty was questioned. Still, he needed to remember he was in a shop. "You can't expect me to carry such a sum with me."

Herman smirked, "Certainly not. If you want, you can come back tomorrow or next month. For the moment, an advance is enough. I'll give you a receipt for it, and you can be sure that I won't show the pearl to other clients or accept any other offer for it."

Mr. Milton nodded, "It's okay. I can pay with my credit card right away."

"Of course." He moved away from the couch. "Please, forgive my diffidence, but I have had quite a bit of trouble with people who didn't have enough funds in the past. I just prefer to play it safe."

Mr. Milton raised his eyebrows in agreement, "I understand completely given this line of work."

Herman stood, gathered Mr. Milton's hat, gloves, and coat, and then guided him to the front counter to complete the purchase. "Forgive my curiosity. Do you already have plans for the pearl?" Herman handed him the printed receipt.

"I don't have any set plan at the moment. For now, I think I will keep it for my pleasure. But perhaps one day..." Mr. Milton said and left the shop.

***

"Did he buy it? How much did he pay?" Edward asked, once the door of the store had closed behind Mr. Milton.

"It was easier than I thought." Herman ruffled his son's hair. "But perhaps I should have expected as much. Sounds like Mr. Milton was after the pearl for a long time, and he would have given me a hard time at the auction if only he reached it in time."

Herman began to close the shop, shutting off the window display lights, and continued with the shop's security routine, which would ensure a good night's sleep.

"Doesn't he care about the rumors connected to the pearl? The fact you were the owner made me nervous," Edward said as they began their walk home.

"Don't listen to all the gossip you hear. Those who came into possession of the pearl did die in tragic circumstances, indeed. However, you need to remember people die every day with or without cursed items." His father smiled as they walked the streets in the light mist, which started to rise.

"But what if they are true?"

"Then we will probably get the pearl back." Herman laughed.

They continued walking on their way home in silence until Edward spoke up, "Dad, how old were you when grandpa started to teach you to deal with all aspects of the business?"

"It took a long time to convince him." There was emotion in his voice as he recalled the times when they used to work together before his retirement. "He was a demanding teacher and remembering the efforts and challenges he had to face early on, Dad wanted to be sure I was able to take the reins of the family business."

Raising his glance at the clear night sky above, Herman wondered whether he was making the same mistake of not trusting his son yet.

He glanced over at his son. Edward was thirteen years old, and maybe it wouldn't be a bad idea to get him started now. He's a brilliant boy, and he won't have any difficulty learning the necessary skills. Plus, his help might give me the chance to travel for more auctions.

"So, does that mean you don't trust me yet?" Edward asked.

A grin appeared on Herman's face. He still remembered when, at the same age as his son, he had asked his father that question and how much his answer had hurt him. *I just need to be sure he's ready.*

This isn't an easy task and running any business requires skills achievable only with experience.

"Of course, I trust you. That isn't a question. I just need to evaluate whether this is the right time for you. One day, you will understand."

Edward remained quiet as he thought about it. Indeed, he was not to be considered an adult, but he was sure he was ready. *Besides, I need to start from somewhere, and the earlier, the better.*

***

They were finally home, and their thoughts were interrupted by the inviting scent of food coming from the kitchen.

"We're home!" Herman called from the doorway.

"You're in time," Josephine, his wife, answered. "Did anything happen? You two are a little later than usual."

They took off their coats and walked in toward the kitchen.

"Only good news…." Herman started.

"Dad sold the pearl!" Edward spoke up excitedly, desperate to be the one who was going to reveal it.

She turned to face them with a bright smile, "Well, that was fast!"

"I know, I was waiting for this buyer to show, but I didn't expect him so early." Herman greeted Josephine with a kiss, holding her tightly to himself. "I remember seeing him at the auction. The way he glared at me was that of a man who doesn't accept defeat."

"How much were you able to sell the pearl for?" Josephine asked as Herman helped her to bring the food to the table.

He waited for everyone to be seated, and then he turned his eyes at her, "Half a million."

Josephine gasped open-mouthed, "What? You didn't even spend half that, and even I thought that was too expensive. How did you manage that?"

"The best part is I didn't have to do anything. I brought him to the backroom, offered the most expensive whiskey I had, and talked about the auction. When I saw the look on his face as I showed him the pearl, I knew that I would be able to push with the price."

He stopped as he served himself the food, smiling at the familiar scent coming from the pot: veal stew. Josephine's cooking was so close to his grandmother that he could still see her hunched over the steamy pot. The scent of thyme was the one that first reached his senses, followed by the richness of the broth and vegetables, paired with the perfectly cooked meat.

"So, you just said that amount and he accepted it?" Edward was puzzled. He was looking at his father with wide-opened eyes, eager to know the story of how he had managed to convince the customer to close the sale.

Herman finished chewing a bite, "He needed an explanation about the price. Sometimes you only need to show the beauty and perfection of a gem to persuade a potential buyer. Today, I also had the benefit of a good story to make it more intriguing."

"You mean the curse?" Josephine asked. "I didn't think people were still buying into those fantasies."

"Well, they make a great addition, you have to admit."

"The pearl brought luck to those local divers and Dad. So, if the curse is real, maybe it got reversed," Edward offered.

They all laughed amusedly, but Josephine turned a thoughtful expression. Glancing at Edward, her thoughts shifted to how fast he was growing and perhaps the time for considering his place inside the family business had arrived. She'd been talking to her husband a few years ago as they had started thinking what Edward's life would be. *It was for his tenth birthday. It only seems like yesterday when we placed the possible deadline on his thirteenth or fourteenth birthday.*

She turned to look at Herman, who kept eating his meal and perhaps he'd already forgotten their discussion. "You need to think about Ed's future too. This is the last year of school before starting junior high school—remember we talked about this. Before you will realize it will be the time to think about his place in the family business."

Edward held his breath, spoon halfway to his mouth, waiting for an answer from his father.

"Is it so?" Herman smirked jokingly. "I underestimated the way time is passing by."

He turned his eyes to his son, visibly tortured by the sense of anticipation, clutching his hand on the table as if he wanted to grab it before falling.

Herman brought a clenched fist in front of his mouth, and after a short pause, he smiled, "In that case, over the summer and during the holidays, we can begin training. Then, you can decide for yourself which path you'd like to take."

Edward jolted up, "Really?"

"Yes. Although there are still a few years before choosing further education, it's wise to think about your path for the future."

Chapter 2

After school, Edward walked with Alan, a friend who shared half of the way back with him.

"What are you going to do this weekend?" Alan asked.

"Not sure, probably just working at the shop. Why?"

"I was thinking about going to the movies on Saturday. There's that scary movie that just came out. Have you heard about it?"

"Yes, I have. It's rated R though, how are you going to get in?"

"Man, you underestimate me."

Alan pulled a couple of fake IDs from his pocket. The one he handed to Edward had his picture and the birth date confirming he was 18 years old.

"You're totally crazy. They'll catch us, call the cops and our parents. We'll be grounded for the rest of our lives!" Edward warned Alan as he scrutinized the ID card.

"Technically, our parents are allowed to keep us grounded until the age of eighteen. Plus, those cards are even better than the real ones. I'll show you, I will go first, and you will follow me after a few other customers. If one of us is caught, the other will get out to help. How about that?"

"Oh man... that sounds crazy," Edward replied, grinning from ear to ear, he raised his eyes to look at Alan. "You convinced me—we're going to the movie Saturday."

"Great, I was almost sure I needed to fight harder to convince you, or maybe my cards are just that good!" Alan raised his eyebrows. "Hey, I know you're most of the time helping your dad at the shop, but why don't you join me online to play? Mom wants me to help her with the house chores, and then I need to study, but in the late afternoon or after dinner, I get online to play Fortnite. Have you ever played it?"

"No, but I heard it's a hell of fun." Edward kept walking. "Well, why not? We generally have dinner at 7:00 pm, so what if we play this afternoon at 5:00? So far, I've played only solo games. It will be fun to try something new."

"Cool! I'll give you a call this afternoon to get you started. You'll see!" Alan replied. "Everybody at school plays it, and I was wondering why you weren't into it. Moreover, it's easy to get good at the game at a satisfying pace."

Alan stopped for a moment and glanced into Edward's eyes. "But I warn you, it's also freaking addictive."

They both laughed and kept walking until the place where they had to part from each other.

After greeting his friend, Edward resumed his walk to the shop. He had only taken a few steps when a dark green sedan stopped at his side. He recognized it being the car of his grandfather, Samuel

Sherwood, and he approached it with a wide smile as the old man opened the door for him.

"Hi, Grandpa!" he said, jumping in and closing the door. Samuel gestured the chauffeur to continue driving, "Good to see you too, Edward. How are you doing?"

"Awesome. Did Dad tell you he decided that it is finally time to start training me to run the shop?"

"It seems I have chosen the right day to ask your parents to bring you home with me," he replied. "So, how is it going at school? Isn't this your last year of primary school?" he asked.

"Yeah, next year I'll start junior high school." Pride filled his voice.

"Time is passing fast, indeed," Samuel replied. "I have a gift for you."

Edward's jaw dropped, "A gift?"

"Yes, it's something I kept aside for you, and it seems like it's time for you to have it."

"What is it, Grandpa?" his feet shuffled in the car, unable to contain the excitement.

"If I told you now, I would spoil the surprise. Besides, I have something very important to tell you, and I wish to have your full attention as it is something you won't learn from your father."

The car came to a stop in front of the large stone home, and Edward stared at it. It was rare that his parents brought him there for a visit. He didn't know the reason, but every time his father and

17

grandfather had been together, he had perceived a kind of hostility and anger.

The chauffeur opened the door for the passengers to be out, and Samuel started to walk toward the house.

Hesitating to have another look at the house, Edward remained behind.

"Aren't you coming?" Samuel asked as he opened the door and realized his grandson was still standing in the yard.

His grandfather's voice brought him back to reality, and with a quick nod of his head, Edward hurried to reach him.

Samuel led him into an elegant parlor and sat down, inviting him to do the same.

"You are thirteen," he began, "and it's time for you to know something about your roots. What did your dad tell you about the family business and the generations of men and women who helped make it a successful one?"

"I know that Great-grandpa Eldridge opened up a small shop as a clockmaker in the same place where it is today. Then worked toward jewelry," the boy recited the story he'd heard many times from his father. "The beginning wasn't easy, and at a certain point, he feared that he couldn't honor his debts. Everything changed when a customer came into his shop to fix his clock. The job didn't take more than a few minutes and, when the man asked for the price, Eldridge declined any compensation. The man was so impressed by his honesty that he gave him a lucky charm, a bright red coral framed in a copper brooch. There wasn't any value in it, but the guy told Great-grandpa Eldridge that he owed his fortune to it."

"That's right," Samuel continued. "That charm actually brought him luck, and soon his reputation as a skilled clockmaker spread even outside the city, allowing him to pay off his debts and collect a small fortune. At that point, Eldridge started wondering if, in addition to lucky charms, existed cursed ones that could bring bad luck and misery to their owners. So, he decided to close the shop for a year and devote himself completely to their search and to the secrets they hid.

"What did he find?" Edward asked. That wasn't the story he had heard from his father and wondered about his reason for having kept that secret.

"Come with me, and I will show you." He stood up and headed for a long corridor, at the end of which he opened the door to a large library.

Edward looked around the room, amazed, trying to grasp every detail of each piece of furniture and rare objects on display.

"This is not simply my collection. In this room are also gathered many items acquired by various generations of Sherwood's." His grandfather walked toward a chest of drawers on the other side of the room.

Adjusting the glasses on his nose, he read the golden drawer labels and chose one to open. From there, he

19

extracted a small velvet pouch and went to sit down on a couch. "Come," he said, amused at the way his grandson turned around, looking at everything with his wide-opened eyes.

"I have never been in this room before...." Edward mumbled as he reached his grandfather on the couch.

"Had your father brought you here more often, this would have been familiar to you, but never mind, let's continue the story," Samuel went on. "Eldridge traveled the whole world, from North to South, from East to West, and came in touch with magic rituals of any kind and from every cultural background. He learned that the market of cursed items had begun with the first explorer who brought to light treasures that had been believed lost. Then, others emulated him, finding ancient gems and precious stones that were considered as something to challenge, something reserved only for the elite who could afford to buy everything and needed something that no one else could. At the end of his travel, he knew everything about cursed gemstones and the attractive power they exerted on people— he wanted it for himself."

"Cursed stones? They do exist?" Edward faltered, unable to avert his eyes from those of his grandfather.

"Sure, just like lucky charms do. But while the latter convey positive thoughts and energies to make the owner realize his dreams and achieve his goals, the others are like hungry beasts who wait in the darkness, feeding themselves with their owner's doubts and fears."

Edward gasped, "So, this means that we are selling items that will destroy the customers' lives? Isn't it wrong?"

"Those who come to our shop to buy these items aren't looking for having their lives ruined but for a chance to dare destiny. Like a daredevil who performs suicidal stunts—he doesn't do it because he wants to die but to challenge and defeat death. Moreover, the cursed gemstones we sell also have great historical value, some of them being around for thousands of years, being owned by kings, maharajas, dignitaries, warlords, heroes, you name it. Owning one of them is like placing yourself in the history books. Therefore, to answer your question, no—it's not wrong."

"Oh, Grandpa, this is so crazy," he whispered.

"After Eldridge retired, he left everything to his daughter Catherine. She was as passionate and determined to find more about cursed stoned as Eldridge was and extended the business, gaining certain popularity. She was also an extremely skilled jeweler, which brought the name of the Sherwood under the spotlight, not only for the chance given to those who could afford to acquire unique items but also to everyone else to buy the finest pieces of jewelry ever made. The rest is history and...magic. This magic is what we are committed to perpetrating, and Sherwood's name should always be bonded with the dealing of cursed items," Samuel concluded. "You will be the next to continue the legacy. Do you understand the importance of your commitment?"

Nodding weakly, Edward couldn't find any words. He realized his grandfather meant each of the words he said, and the weight of the family heritage started to be felt on his young shoulders. Despite that, he was more than ever determined to keep the business going, following the family tradition, learning about those peculiar items, their history, and their power.

His head was spinning, though. "Tell me something, Grandpa."

"Anything you need to know."

"How many cursed items are in the world, and how do we find new ones?"

A smile crinkled Samuel's face, "Whatever leaves the store will return to the starting point. That's the magic of the curse. But that's what you'll have to learn to master--the way it will return to you."

After a short pause of silence, Samuel opened the palm where he had the small velvet pouch. "I talked about a surprise for you, and with that, I didn't mean to tell you about the history of the family business. I have a gift," he said, handing to Edward the pouch.

"What is that?" Edward asked, taking it in his hand.

"Open it and see it yourself."

Gently untying the silk strings, he opened the pouch and turned upside down to his palm when a blood-red coral, shaped like a flame and framed in copper, appeared.

22

"This is the lucky charm Eldridge Sherwood received from his customer. I give it to you, as I see in you the same family flame."

Speechless, Edward raised his eyes at him, "Why didn't you give it to Dad?"

A long exhale escaped Samuel's soul. "Unfortunately, your father refused it. He still kept doing deals on cursed items, but he didn't want to commit to something he wasn't ready for and preferred to focus on the jewel shop. So, I kept this in my possession, hoping that you would have accepted it when the time came. It's a great honor and responsibility to get this charm. It's a seal of our loyalty to the power of the curses and to what binds our family for generations."

He turned his glance at Edward, "Will you accept the charm and its responsibility, giving it full commitment?"

With pride filling every pore of his being, Edward opened up into a broad smile. "I do, Grandpa, I will commit and keep the business, not only alive, but I will make it amazing once again."

"I knew I could count on you." Samuel stood from the chair and walked toward a wall, where a portrait was placed. "That is Eldridge Sherwood, and following clockwise, you find his daughter Catherine, her sons Joshua and Leopold, and so all the people who gave their contribution to the shop. One day, there will be your portrait and those of the following generations." He turned to look at his grandson. "Welcome to the business, grandson."

"Oh boy, wait that I tell Dad...."

"No." Samuel interrupted him severely. "This is going to be a secret you will have to keep for yourself. Since your father didn't want to be included, from this moment on, whatever happens here, it will have to be a secret you will bring to your grave."

Edward nodded, lowering his head and understanding the intensity of his grandfather's word.

He raised his hand, holding the lucky charm Samuel gave him, and a smile chased away the shadows of doubt.

"From today on, you will come once a week here, and I will teach you everything I know about this side of the business. When it is the time to choose your educational path, you will be ready to walk on your own feet, deciding the one that best fits your needs and the ones of the shop."

Edward's glance met the clock on the other side of the room, "I think I need to get back to my father. He might need my help there."

"Of course, do you want my chauffeur to drive you there?" Samuel asked.

"No, I can manage with the bus. Thank you for the trust, Grandpa—I won't fail it," he said as he started to walk away.

Following his grandson with a proud smile, Samuel said with a firm tone of voice. "Remember that life isn't made only of school and work. I hope you take some time to socialize and have fun with your friends."

Shaking his head, Edward turned his eyes to look at Samuel. "Of course, Grandpa, don't worry. Is it OK for you if I come every Thursday? That's the day when we have less traffic at the shop, and I am not busy with school."

"Thursdays will be fine. I will send the chauffeur to pick you up." He stood at the front door.

Edward turned back to him and smiled. "See you soon, Grandpa. Thank you!"

Walking the streets that afternoon, everything seemed brighter, and Edward's head felt on the clouds. He had finally understood the reason behind the tense relationship between his father and his grandfather. Still, he wondered why the first had decided not to accept the lucky charm. He had sold the pearl, and Mr. Milton had seemed aware of the curse, like all the others who had come to the shop to buy those particular jewels. It was true that the jewelry was the prominent side of the business, but the cursed items...

***

"So, you have been with Grandpa today—did you have a good time?" The tone of his voice stirred as if he was making a great effort to maintain calm.

"I did. Why don't we see him more often?" Edward asked entering the shop.

"It's a long story, and it doesn't help anyone to take it out on any occasion." Herman tried to cut it short.

"Dad, please. I feel like I'm in the middle of a family fight anytime I talk about him."

"You know that our shop isn't a common jeweler's boutique. We also sell something that can raise many questions about ethics and fair trade. However, you want to put it, you won't find any explanation that could put that business into clear and bright light. This is because if you don't believe in curses, you know that you are cheating people who instead believe in them and feel as if they're daring mysterious forces. If you believe that there is a curse which will bring misfortune and misery to the owner, then you are profiting on other people's life."

"But you still keep dealing with those items...." Edward grimaced.

"I do because I feel the weight of responsibility toward those who built the business and handed it to me. That's my heritage, and I can't deny it," Herman explained. "Plus, the adrenaline of going to those auctions and thinking about the way I will sell the purchased item is addictive. Undeniably that is also the most profitable side of the business, which is hard to give up. Despite all the controversial feelings, I tried to limit that kind of business, and that is what Grandpa couldn't accept. From his point of view, we have the duty to keep this tradition alive and hand it down from one generation to another." He shook his head and lowered his gaze to the ground.

"Would you be disappointed if one day I decide to follow the path Grandpa wanted? Would you cut the relationship with me if I decided to continue the family tradition of dealing with cursed objects?"

"That wasn't what I said. I would never be angry or upset if you chose a different path from the one I chose for myself." Herman tried to clear up his words. "I would never make the same mistake my father did with me. I won't force you into a decision so important as choosing your career or the way you want to continue the family business. Even if you consider the possibility to give up the whole jewel shop, I will never even think of being upset to you."

The expression on Edward's face relaxed. He knew his father wasn't as strict as his grandfather, and that difference was what kept them apart. "Will you ever fix the stuff with Grandpa? After all, I'm sure he loves you. It's that he's… you know, old-fashioned and stubborn."

Herman chuckled at that description of his father, "You might be right, and keeping the hard feelings alive is like keeping a curse going on. There must be a way to end our disagreement. I will try my best to bring some peace between us."

Edward remained thinking about it for a moment. "What is going to happen once I graduate from high school?"

"At that point, you will have to decide whether you want to continue the education of this business, or you prefer to take a different road," Herman replied.

"I know I want to be a jeweler, and I believe I will get the best training out of you and Grandpa.

However, I would also like to attend a specific course. I checked online, and there isn't anything available around here." He grabbed a pen and flipped it through his fingers, avoiding looking into his father's eyes.

Peering out of the shop in case he could spot someone coming inside, Herman exhaled, "I know about a professional school of goldsmithing in London. I can send you a link about it so that you can look at whether this is something you would like to take." He grabbed his cell phone and searched the webpage. "In my opinion, they offer the best training for a person who wants to learn the best techniques of jewel making."

Edward bit his lower lip, impatient to check the link his father had just sent him. "If you don't need me here, I'd like to go home and take a look at it."

"I was running this business alone before you were born—I think I can manage." Herman chuckled, amused. "Your commitment to this shop is commendable, but you have to focus also on other matters right now."

"OK, thanks, Dad." Edward stood up, grabbed his backpack, and headed for the front door.

As he opened the door, he remembered his discussion with Alan for Saturday. He would probably spend the whole afternoon out.

Despite that, he had no intention of canceling his plans, and he already felt the adrenaline rush. "By the way." Edward turned to look at his father. "Alan asked me to go out this Saturday. I thought there wasn't anything to do with the shop, so I accepted...."

"Of course, go and have fun with your friend, but remember to be back home for dinner, OK?"

"Thanks, Dad—I won't be late." Running outside the shop to reach home, he felt his head light. That was the first time he was doing something illegal and, to tell the truth, the excitement felt intoxicating.

As he opened the apartment door, Edward had the time to get a hold of his emotions. Quietly as usual, he got in and wondered if his mother was already back from work.

"Anybody home?" he asked aloud.

The silence confirmed that he had some time to check what his father had sent him or search for something else to compare it with him later.

"Well, it is pretty impressive. They also can arrange accommodations." He turned his glance away from the screen. For a moment, he stared at the sky outside of the window and wondered whether it was too soon to think about this. "After all, I still need to graduate from high school."

He closed the school's website and opened the page for that weekend's shows at the movies. The horror movie trailer they had planned to see promised to be terrifying enough for plenty of sleepless nights. Still, even at the cost of being traumatized forever, he knew he had to go and watch the whole movie.

For a reason he couldn't explain, the plan and its risk brought to mind the stories his grandfather had told him about Eldridge and his whole family, particularly those connected with the cursed gemstones.

***

The morning after, as usual, Herman reached the shop at 6:30, well in advance on the opening hour. In his mind, he kept on thinking about the conversation he had had with Edward and the fact that he would spend a day a week with Samuel.

He knew that the purpose of those meetings was to convince him to continue the family tradition of trading cursed items. Although there was nothing wrong with the desire to have the family business run as it had been for over a century, he feared a sort of brainwashing.

"Edward is his last chance. If he doesn't carry on the tradition, no one else will," he said aloud as he disarmed the alarm.

Outside it was still dark, but the streets were already as busy as daytime. His cellphone began to ring, and he was surprised to see Samuel's name on the display.

"Good morning, Dad." His tone wasn't the one of a person pleasantly surprised to receive a call from his relative. Nevertheless, he tried his best to sound as such.

"Good morning to you, son. How are you doing?" His father asked to break the ice.

"Can't complain—how about you?"

"Same here. As you know, Edward was here yesterday, and it appeared that he had no idea about that part of the family's history. Why is that? Are you ashamed of it?" Samuel hit straight to the point. It was clear he wasn't in the mood for pleasantries that morning.

"I'm not, and I told him only what was important for him to know. After all, it seems like he hasn't missed anything with your update."

"I did what you were supposed to do. Indeed, this is your business, now, but remember who founded it and to whom you owe its success. I was hoping that you could show a little gratitude by telling your son the reason why Eldridge started to deal in cursed items and how his daughter followed his steps together with her two sons." The bitterness in his voice was palpable.

"Dad, I just wanted to give Edward the time to reach the age when he could make a mature and informed decision about which path to follow. I didn't want to impose on him anything that might ruin his life," Herman justified his choice.

"Did Edward ever mention the willingness to follow a different career?"

"No," Herman replied. "He wants to become a jeweler, salesman, and dealer."

There was a long pause. Herman was tired of their arguments, and Edward was right to suggest ending it before it would be too late. "Dad, I don't want to argue every time we meet. I have chosen a different direction from yours. Edward will choose his own, and his children will. Can't we simply put that difference aside and live our life like a normal family would?"

Samuel paused, and Herman could hear a lighter tone of voice as if he was smiling. "You're right. Besides, there isn't any hurry to tell him everything. It would be good if you all would come for dinner at my place again," he proposed.

"I will talk to Josephine and will let you know." He glanced at the clock.

"Of course, son. Take care," Samuel replied before Herman hung up.

.

Chapter 3

Five years later

The high school years had reinforced Edward's conviction to go and study in the UK. So, after having graduated with honors, he left the States for the *Swinging City*, where he would spend at least a couple of years, determined to get as much as possible from that experience.

Over time, he developed an obsession with the secrets of cursed stones and jewels that prompted him to extend his studies to other fields besides goldsmithing.

He followed courses in anthropology and psychology to find out how the idea of a curse can be conveyed to an individual to the point of becoming a reality.

He'd been learning about different types of curses. The first and most famous one was connected to magic rituals bonding the object to the owner. That was the case of curses written on the tombs of pharaohs or temples, where idols were decorated with precious stones. One excellent example was the *Koh-I-Noor diamond*. For some time, it had served as the eye of a Hindu goddess, and it was believed that nobody should have ever stolen the gem from her.

Others seemed had originated by violent events connected to the mining of the gem, like, for example, the *Star of India.* The *Black Prince's ruby* instead owed its fame to the series of unfortunate events that apparently had cursed it.

According to the legend, it was owned by the British dynasty since the 14th century. Previously, it had been stolen from the corpse of the Sultan of Granada by Pedro the Cruel, King of Castile, who took over the kingdom.

His reign didn't last long, as his half-brother attacked and killed him. The stone was given to Edward of Woodstock, who contracted a mysterious disease and died nine years later. From that moment on, whoever had owned the ruby went through death or misery.

Those legends, whether they came from pure imagination, written curses on the tombstones or temples, or mysterious and unlawful circumstances all had one thing in common, a long list of misery, death, and human ruin.

One person shared the same interests, and that was Sabrina, one of his classmates. They connected immediately, although there wasn't any romance involved in their friendship.

"I'm still wondering about what Professor McGillis said about the concept of suggestion," Sabrina said, shaking her long, copper-colored hair falling on her shoulders in soft curls. "Is it possible to believe so firmly in something, like a jinx, for example, to convey bad luck that it actually alters your statistical probability to misfortune?" she stopped at the pond, glancing at the reflections of the trees in the water.

"Maybe someone helped the curse." Edward pulled a simple one-pound coin from out his pocket. "Let's say I told you this is cursed, and I fabricate a great story about all the people whose lives have been destroyed because of it. Now think about being so intrigued to be ready to pay me ten pounds for it."

Sabrina narrowed her eyes without interrupting what he was saying.

"Of course," Edward resumed. "The curse doesn't exist, but I sell you the coin for ten times its worth. Then, I might be following you until I make sure you will perish in a tragic accident. The coin is nowhere to be found, and people start to create conjectures around this mystery..."

She gasped in realization, "So, you're telling me, a few clever people might have benefited from the tale of the cursed items to gain profit out of them?"

Edward shrugged, "Nothing is certain, but this could be an explanation."

"Those people might be quite wicked to conceive such a plan, and so are you for realizing it."

A laugh escaped him. "I'm not saying I would do anything similar. This is a possibility, and it doesn't mean being evil, but being clever enough to uncover the plan."

"Then you should be a detective, rather than a goldsmith... perhaps working undercover playing the part of a goldsmith." Sabrina patted his shoulder.

"Why not? How about doing a test?" He paused to make sure to have the full attention of his friend. "What if we buy an old object from an antique store, make up a story of a curse around it, see the reactions of our classmates and sell it away?"

"But would the story be completely fake?" Sabrina tried to confirm as if she wondered where he wanted to reach.

"Exactly, but we need to show the mystique lies in the subject owning something reputed to be cursed. A spell cast by the previous owner to protect it from being stolen... Are you following me?"

Sabrina nodded in earnest understanding now, "You know what? This is going to be so exciting unless nothing happens to our target."

"Of course, not—what are you thinking?" Edward elbowed her arm, "We will plan the whole thing this weekend. We need time to prepare everything. During the week, we'll spread some rumors of an auction or a sale we're going to. We'll see who the best person for our little experiment will be."

***

During the weekend, Edward and Sabrina looked all over the internet for curiosity shops, searching for bizarre items, antique rarities, and other unusual listings. They found several shops selling interesting things. In particular, one attracted their attention from the first moment, and it appeared to be the perfect place from where to start.

Without wasting any time, as the store closed earlier than usual on weekends, they hurried to the underground station at Chancery Lane to reach the place.

"What do you think we should look for?" Sabrina asked.

Rubbing his chin, a wide grin opened up on his face, "Traditionally, the best items are old jewels, stones, or small artifacts. Something supposedly cherished by the owner during their lifetime and could have accompanied them to the afterlife."

"Even without a curse written on the tomb, some people believe the emotional attachment of the previous owner to the item might create a sort of magical connection between them."

Sabrina smiled, looking at him with her bright green eyes, "I love the way you can charm people with your tales. One day you will become a brilliant salesman. People will remain silent, holding their breaths for fear of missing something that you say."

Edward continued his explanation, barely noticing what she had said as he continued. "This bond doesn't break with death, particularly when this happens suddenly."

Sabrina gasped, "Do you mean these items are haunted? You don't believe in ghosts, do you?"

"Of course not, but I believe in the power of the mind swayed by suggestion and small manipulations. I can see some serious potential in this little experiment." A wicked smile crossed his face. "This is only to obtain results for our test. Certainly, we won't use this information to harm anyone," Edward said in reassurance.

She shook her head with swift movements. "No, of course not!"

They knew each other well enough for Sabrina to understand Edward's open considerations were not to be taken too seriously. They were primarily freeform ramblings of his brain overthinking every possibility.

These results will provide me hints on how to manipulate the will of customers to convince them to buy.

Silence fell upon them as the train continued along the tracks to their stop. Different from every other day, they were like polite strangers with nothing more to say.

After a short walk, they found the antique store. They wandered around the shelves, looking at every item on display. This was a completely different place than the shop on Merrill Street. The whole place was quite dark, and the spotlights were pointed on the items displayed on the top of antique drawers or other pieces of furniture. It felt like they were shopping in a crypt.

The scents of old wood and incense enhanced the sense of mystery.

Despite the different environment and merchandise, Edward remained entranced as he walked through the aisles. Then finally, one item caught his attention. The label indicated it was an antique pendant made of butterfly wings.

He took the pendant gently in his hands as he inspected it. The glass covering them magnified their shape and the brilliance of the little scales. The light was scattered back from the wings through the polished surface of the glass and reminded him of the hues of a pearl or a diamond.

"How interesting," he said quietly.

"Have you found anything?" The teasing voice of Sabrina surprised him, and he startled.

"Damn, you scared the hell out of me!" Edward kept a low tone of voice, bringing a hand to his chest as if he had a heart attack.

"Sorry, I thought you had heard me coming! I saw how you were looking at that pendant, and I wondered if you had found something for our experiment."

"Yes, actually, take a look at this one." Edward handed it to her.

"It's really impressive. What genius thought to enclose the wing of a butterfly within a lens to magnify its beauty?" Sabrina replied. "Do you think it might be the best item for us to build the tale of a curse on?"

"We can't find anything better, to be honest. I'm also going to buy the other one for myself. I'm wondering what my father would say about it?"

"The crucial part comes now, as to how we're going to show this around," Edward said as they walked out of the shop, beginning to plan the best way to market it. "Obviously, it doesn't have a real value with the frame made from silver, and there aren't any precious stones. We will need to focus on the story and the way we're going to attract the perfect buyer."

Edward began to realize how this could be one of the best ways to test the skills he had learned from his grandfather. A good salesman can understand his target audience and tailor the best marketing strategy for the product.

"What's on your mind?" Sabrina interrupted her friend's thoughts.

With a surprised expression, he turned toward her, "I was thinking about whether I should ask my

39

grandfather for advice. He's one of the best salesmen I have ever met, and his ability to turn the attention of a potential customer into a sale has always impressed me."

"But what is worrying you?"

Edward drew a deep breath. "Like with my father, I see him as something unreachable—he's almost like a god to me, so...."

His words failed him.

"You're afraid of them?" Sabrina was surprised at seeing her friend, who had always been the living portrait of self-confidence, nearly trembling at the simple thought of his relatives.

"No, I'm not. I just don't want to disappoint them..." He stopped for a moment looking around himself. He wondered if he was scared by his family's overwhelming figures, or by the image of them he had built inside himself.

"Edward... You're a grown man—stop comparing yourself to your father or anyone else in your family. They will always be important figures in your life. Still, the only person you have to compare yourself to is the man you were yesterday," Sabrina said, gently touching his arm.

He looked at the sky before returning his glance and a broad smile to Sabrina, "You're absolutely right. I should start tracing my own path, regardless of whether I will continue working in the family business. Still, I'm afraid this will require some time."

***

When he finally got in his room, Edward considered calling his father. Among all the reasons to call him, the most important was understanding why he felt so intimidated by him.

Without a second thought, he grabbed his phone and dialed his dad's cell number. With every unanswered ring, he regretted the idea of calling him at that time of the afternoon because he knew his dad was likely busy at the shop. He closed the call and decided to wait for his father to call him back.

As he was returning to his room from the cafeteria where he had dinner, his phone started ringing.

"Hello?" Edward answered without checking the number.

"Hello." The voice of his father reached him. "I saw you tried to call me today. I'm sorry, but I was busy and couldn't answer. I hope it wasn't an emergency."

He let himself fall onto the bed and stared at the ceiling. "No, not at all. I just need a bit of advice. I got an antique piece of jewelry, and I want to use it to practice my salesman's skills. However, I thought you might have some suggestions about how I should approach a potential buyer."

"Ok, well, not having a physical shop at your availability makes the task more difficult. You need a place to showcase your items. Perhaps you can try some ads online or in specialized magazines. In this case, you need to remember the importance of the first glance, and the pictures must be of high quality." Herman remained quiet for a moment. "By the way, what are you trying to sell? A precious stone, a pearl, or jewelry?"

"It's a pendant. The retail price might not be high, but I'm going to use it for a trial run, see how my skills are."

"Great idea, son. I wish I could offer better guidance for this. Maybe starting with something that doesn't have any real value will make things more interesting. I'd like to know about your progress and the outcome," Herman remarked, intrigued by this initiation.

Edward hung up and considered for a small while how he would be approaching the sale. He wasn't eager to reveal to his father that the test's real purpose was psychological, not economic. *I hate to lie to him, but what if he doesn't understand my reasons. And maybe this will come in handy one day...*

Chapter 4

Edward was waiting for Sabrina in the park. He was turning the pendant in his hands, trying to figure out a story tragic enough to justify the existence of a curse.

If Dad knew about this plan, he would be disappointed in me. He will consider my methods unethical. Still, he's been putting a price on the story whenever a particular item arrives at our shop. That's how he gets such high profits, just like in the case of the pearl.

He bit his lower lip, trying to work out his hesitations and uncertainties, keeping his gaze on the glimmering pendant.

"The jinx starts to work—you're completely under its spell," Sabrina arrived, causing him to jolt on the bench and the pendant to fall on the ground.

"I was just thinking about how to sell the item and the curse. We might find more than one potential buyer, but we need a story." Edward picked up the pendant from the grass, polishing it before placing it back in his pocket.

They started to walk that foggy winter morning. The cold reached their bones, and Edward dug deeper inside his coat. "We must find a way to shorten the time frame. The story needs to be built carefully so no one can see through it."

Slowing their steps, they finally crossed the school's door. The warmth of the closed building relaxed his muscles, and a content smile appeared on his face. Edward hated winter. "Do you think we might end up in trouble?"

Sabrina looked at him, puzzled. "Why would we?"

"Well, it can't be legal include someone in a test without their consent."

"That's your problem—you worry too much. We're not testing a drug. Besides, suppose we tell this person that we're performing a test on the power of suggestion. In that case, we will already have inconsistent results. How can we get reliable results from a person who knows they're being deceived?"

"I don't want to go to jail...." Edward thought about what his father would think if he ended up in trouble with the law.

With a grimace, he narrowed his eyes and grabbed his cell. "I need to call my father," he said, and without waiting for a reaction, he walked away to find a quiet spot in an empty classroom, hoping his father was already awake.

***

Herman left the house and began the walk to the shop. He was surprised by the telephone call from Edward and frowned. "Good morning." He struggled to hide the slight concern arising every time he received an unexpected call.

"Hi, Dad. I'm sorry to call you so early. Hopefully, I haven't worried you." He tried to sound calm as usual.

"I have to admit being a bit taken aback, your calls generally arrive in the afternoon. Nevertheless, with the time difference, I suppose it can happen." He exhaled, relieved that everything was fine, and his son was not at the hospital or in trouble.

"I'm calling you now as this is probably the only time you can listen to me. Later, you might have been busy at the shop or too tired." Edward hesitated, taking some time.

Without interrupting what his son was saying, Herman continued his walk.

"In addition to the goldsmith's course, I am also following one in psychology," he said, all in one breath.

"I want to become a goldsmith. But as a child, I was intrigued by the customer who came to purchase that supposedly cursed pearl. This course has shown me I have a talent that has to be developed and that could help improve my skills as a salesman and dealer." He took a deep breath as his father remained in silence.

Herman remembered the anticipation in Edward's expression, the way he had held his breath as Mr. Milton followed him to the backroom.

"I don't believe in curses. But I have always believed in a sort of psychological factor which can influence our lives. In this course, I learned that the mind tends to associate unfortunate events with a particular item we possess. People buy lucky charms, and as soon as a positive event happens to them, the brain interprets it because of the

45

purchase. The same, of course, can be said about cursed items," Edward explained.

Herman remained quiet for a second to think about it. "Was this the topic you talked about with grandpa?" he remembered how his father had introduced him to that side of the business—a side with many dark spots to make many people cringe and cast a shadow of doubt over the Sherwoods.

"Grandpa told me the story of the family and the way they have dealt with this particular side of the business. But it's something I've been interested in for a while. I hope you can understand how useful this course can be in our business."

"Sure. Nobody in our family ever followed any psychology course. We have been trained by our parents to become salesmen." Herman's lips pursed. "I think I will find a way to come and see you. I'm really interested in knowing more about this course, and I wish we will have the chance to talk about it face to face."

"Let me check on the calendar," Edward said. "What about if I come back home for a short time? It might take a week or so. Next month, I can take a break and we can have a chat about my future."

Herman smiled as he saw someone approaching the shop. "I have customers coming in. Call me tonight, and we can discuss the details. If you can come back home, it will make things a lot easier."

They said their goodbyes and hung up as the door to the shop opened.

***

As Edward returned to his room that evening, his thoughts returned to the call he had with his father.

He put his cell phone on the desk and walked to the window. The '*Silent Rainbow*' and its present owner returned to his mind.

I wonder if Mr. Milton was satisfied with the purchase or whether he found any reason to confirm the curse.

His face displayed an amused smile. The psychology course gave him great insight into people's minds, and he began to understand its potential.

As the room was getting darker at dusk, he went to lie on his bed, observing as the shadows grew longer as the light dimmed.

There was a slight delay between the moment when he could consider the darkness almost total and when the streetlamp outside his window lit up, building a sort of anticipation. That lamp, for some reason, was always the last one on the block to turn on. He often wondered whether it was caused by the power grid connection problem, or it was planned to flick on with a certain delay.

He closed his eyes before flipping the switch, as he knew the sudden difference would hurt. Oversensitivity to light had accompanied him since birth. Usually, passing from a dark environment to a bright one would have caused a terrible headache.

With a slow movement, he stood up and looked at the clock on the bedside table. It was almost time for dinner, and without thinking twice, he hurried outside. He was determined to rid all those thoughts from his mind and focus on better things.

"Everything in its own time, I can think about my father the day when I see him."

Chapter 5

It was on a Friday morning, as Edward browsed on his phone while waiting for class to start when his eyes were caught by an article about an accident.

According to the post, an accident had happened in a field close to New York, a private airplane had crashed, and the only passenger died. Normally, this wouldn't have been the kind of news to leave Edward frozen. However, the man who lost his life was Jason Milton, a multi-millionaire collector, who recently suffered from a financial crisis due to a series of poor investments.

Of course, everybody knows when dealing with money, an investment can be the turning point in both directions, either to increased wealth or ruin.

But Mr. Milton had owned a cursed pearl, which changed the cards in the deck, Edward thought. He knew the misfortune could have been caused by the ancient curse.

Engrossed by the article, he learned the reporter suggested this was not an accident. Either Jason Milton committed suicide to escape with dignity the final remnants of his fortune, or someone he owed money to had sabotaged the plane's engine.

He placed the phone on his desk in the classroom and glanced at the ceiling, "I'm wondering where the *'Silent Rainbow'* is now."

Once again, his mind went back to the words of his father when he had asked him what would happen if the curse were real, *"Then, we will have the pearl back..."*

A sudden doubt came into his mind. *What if Herman, of even Samuel for the matter, were involved in the disgrace and accident of Mr. Milton?* He wondered.

His heart stopped as a sense of fear pervaded his soul. Glancing at his phone on his desk, he wondered whether he should call his father about the tragic fate of Mr. Milton. With a swift move, he grabbed his backpack and phone and left the classroom.

He walked until he reached an isolated corridor of the building. Peering around to ensure he was alone, he took out his phone without thinking about the time difference and called his father.

Nevertheless, as the telephone rang and his father didn't reply, Edward had the time to reconsider he'd been too hasty to conceive a connection between him and the fatal accident.

"My Goodness." His dad yawned, still trying to wake up. "Do you have any idea what time it is here?"

"Dad, I-" He struggled to find a justification for his call - *I cannot ask him whether he has a share of responsibility for the death of Mr. Milton. I cannot accuse him of murder without the slightest proof in my hands, but a sentence meant perhaps as a joke.*

"D-Dad, I didn't think about it. I'm sorry I woke you up at this ungodly time of night."

"Are you in trouble?" his dad asked, sounding more awake.

"Actually not, but I was reading the news and something came up." He tried to find the right way to introduce the accident.

"I'm afraid I don't understand, Edward."

"Dad, do you remember the pearl you bought at the auction in Hong Kong?"

His father remained for a moment to think about it. "Well, yes..."

Edward heard the hesitation in his voice. "The article I came across was about an accident not too far from New York."

"That is terrible, but why are you telling me this?" his dad asked.

"Well, I suppose you recall the man who bought the pearl from you, days after your return from Hong Kong, Mr. Jason Milton." Edward started pacing around, unable to stand still. "He was the man who died in the accident. He was on his private plane when the pilot lost control and crashed into the ground."

"I have to admit you have an amazing memory. I almost forgot his name, and I was the one who dealt with him throughout the purchase." He chuckled, but a light shake in his voice revealed his struggle to grasp the reason why his son so suddenly decided to call him to tell him about the accident. "Are you implying the curse is real?"

"I know I might sound almost crazy," Edward continued trying to explain what was in his mind.

51

"But I wonder if that of Mr. Milton was really an accident, what do you think?"

Herman sighed, "You think someone sabotaged his airplane to make sure he would have died? But who? And how can you think something like this if the investigation hasn't yet begun?"

"I'm simply speculating, and I'm not thinking necessarily about a murder. Perhaps it was a suicide." Edward glanced around. Slowly, students were crowding that place that had been empty until a few moments before.

"According to the article, Mr. Milton lost a big slice of the fortune he'd accumulated. He had been making some bad investments, leading him to financial ruin. Do you have any new information about the pearl?" He hoped his father still had in his possession some knowledge about it.

"Son, are you sure everything is fine with you? You sound a bit too excited about this."

Edward took a deep breath and closed his eyes to regain some composure. He realized he might have sounded like a maniac. He opened his eyes again and smiled, "I am, but I'm just intrigued by this particular story."

"I don't know anything about the pearl. For me, it wasn't more than an investment. A profitable one, too, if I may add."

"But don't you think it's somehow strange that a financial ruin happened to Mr. Milton after he purchased it?" Edward challenged. "I don't believe in curses, but maybe the mindset was cursing him. As he came into possession of the pearl, subconsciously, he became prone to make the wrong decisions with his investments."

"I'm starting to understand what you are aiming for, and I have to admit the theory is intriguing. But we can't jump to conclusions. I'm sure the incident will be investigated, and we will come to know the truth or at least the most accredited one in the next few days. We're still talking about a wealthy person. Whether it's an accident, murder, or suicide, this will attract the attention of the media."

"Ok. I need to go now—class will start soon. I'm sorry if I woke you up at this crazy time in the morning—I just needed to tell you." Edward's voice got lower as he bid farewell to his father.

"Don't you worry, I think I'll survive. I will try to catch some rest but call me this evening, and we can talk about the curse in more detail."

 Edward's eyes lowered to stare at the floor. "Sure, bye."

He hurried back to the laboratory where the professor had already arrived. He glanced at his watch, relieved to not be late.

Sabrina beamed at him as he entered the classroom, "Did you oversleep?" she laughed as he sat down next to her.

"No, I spoke with my father. A plane crashed in a field in upstate New York." He wondered whether it had been wise to tell him about the death of Mr. Milton, the cursed pearl, or his theory.

She gasped. "Did something happen to any of your relatives?"

"No, but I knew the man who died in the accident. He was one of my father's customers."

A strange silence fell between them. Edward knew she wanted to ask more, but her curiosity had to wait as the professor began speaking, bringing the classmates' chattering to a stop.

***

After their lectures, Edward and Sabrina reached a café close to their school in the afternoon.

"Now that we have time tell me more about the accident you mentioned earlier. I've been waiting all morning to hear it!"

"Yes, something was really suspicious to me," he said and told Sabrina the story of the pearl and the way his father was able to resell it for a ridiculous profit.

Sabrina listened to him like a child listening to the tale of Santa Claus for the first time in her life. "So, you tell me your father purchased a presumably cursed pearl and sold it to this Mr. Milton for the crazy price of half a million. I have to say, the curse was already working. That's a completely insane price!"

"Indeed, but that pearl was something extraordinary. The shape was perfectly spherical,

54

something quite rare in natural pearls, and it was also of unusual dimensions. The reflections of the light on its surface changed from yellowish to pink. If you had turned in your hand, you would have sworn it had a life on its own. You could have stared at that light forever."

She brought a hand in front of her mouth. "I'd like to learn more about it. If the pearl has an infamous reputation, perhaps we can find something more about its story and the fate of its previous owners."

He slapped his hand against the table, "That's it!"

"What?" Sabrina asked, a jolt shaking her body.

Edward stood from the chair. "This is what we need for our little experiment. Knowing more about the curse of the pearl, together with those of other gemstones could help us to fabricate a convincing story for our jewel. What do you think?"

Her expression brightened up, "I think we should move to my place, where we can search the internet for every piece of information."

They walked to her apartment, which wasn't too far from the campus. The chance to have a place on her own, rather than sharing the campus dorms, had many advantages. The main one was having a private room to research and study without any interruptions from other students.

Once online, Edward managed to find a few images of the pearl. One was found in the archive of the auction house from where his father bought it. The others were historical pictures taken by the previous owners and collected into a sort of online macabre scrapbook.

"Wow, a lot of people are fascinated by the gruesome tales behind those jewels," Sabrina observed. "That pearl is a real beauty. The price Mr. Milton paid was fully legitimate."

A long yawn escaped Edward and then he spoke, ", That's why it won't be difficult to find someone for our test."

***

For the rest of the day, Herman could not detach his thoughts from the accident that happened upstate. Nobody had witnessed the crash, but the first responders reached the site quickly, alerted by the pilot's SOS.

Strangely enough, he was the only one who had made it out alive to tell the story.

At closing time, he retired to the backroom to read all the updates and if there had already been any speculation about the cause of the crash.

Hmm... According to the preliminary inspection and the pilot's testimony, there wasn't any failure on the engine or the aircraft's structure to justify the crash. So, we'll have to wait for them to carry out more in-depth investigation to find out the truth about what happened.

He creased his forehead and remained listening to the silence inside the shop, particularly in the room. The insulation worked like a charm, but it also allowed the demons of the bloody heritage he'd received to re-emerge from the place he hoped he'd buried them forever.

He glanced once again at the screen of his computer to continue reading about the life and times of Mr. Jason Milton. It was disturbing the attention the tabloids paid to the disgraces that had brought him to the brink of the financial failure.

He stood from the couch and glanced at the clock. It had become late, and Josephine would get worried about not seeing him return home without any reason.

As he switched on the alarm and closed the shop's doors, he wondered whether Edward would call him to discuss the accident.

He shook his head and began the walk home, "He probably realized the news didn't deserve so much attention. Those kinds of accidents happen every day, with or without curses."

***

"You look worried," Josephine said as he finished eating his dinner in complete silence.

With a deep breath, he glanced at her and smiled, amused about the way he might seemed to her, "I'm sorry, darling. I was thinking about the plane that crashed upstate."

"What an unfortunate event. The name sounded familiar. Was he the man who bought the pearl from you?" Josephine asked as she gathered dishes from the table.

"Yes, the press is speculating a lot about the curse. Must be the only way to sell more copies and increase the ratings on their television shows." He stood from the table, helping her put the dining room back in order.

"It's in such bad taste to be making money out of the disgraces of other people. I wonder how his family is coping with the loss. I don't mean financially but on a personal level." She shook her head.

"He had a family of his own, from what I remember." Herman stopped for a second with dishes still in his hands.

He realized he had never considered how a person's death wasn't necessarily connected to one individual but their circle of friends, family, and colleagues.

It doesn't help to know that, at least in Mr. Milton's case, the people who will suffer collaterally from his loss will be restricted to his family. I'm sure as he approached financial disaster, the sharks he considered friends had abandoned him as well. Out of money, they disappear like the morning dew.

 Herman glanced at his watch, "I think I will have to call Edward. He called me last night, and I was too sleepy to understand what he was talking about."

"Tell him hi for me. I talked to him a couple of days ago, he mentioned he might come home a week. Try to get some sort of schedule from him."

"I will do that," Herman replied walked from the dining room to his office.

Chapter 6

For the last few weeks, Edward and Sabrina had been working on creating the story about the curse. Then, Steven, Sabrina's brother, a sort of genius at computers, published fake news completely resembling genuine ones, using the Internet as the stage of an illusionist, targeting the students at their school.

The process had been slow and had to be built carefully. At times, they had been almost sure to be heading towards complete failure. Nevertheless, as soon as the rumor spread, many people were curious to see what a cursed jewel looked like— none of them had any idea what to expect. They were indeed mesmerized not only by its unusual appearance but also because the story could carry their imaginations away.

"How did you find it?" Lorena, a student in one of their classes, asked.

"It was at an auction, and I recognized it immediately. There are many stories connected to it and its previous owners, but one particularly fascinated me." Edward glanced around the group of curious students gathered around him. "It appears that the pendant was originally given to a young lady as a pledge of love. However, her father had plans to marry her to another gentleman, and the contract had been already undersigned. When he discovered the pendant, he asked his daughter about it. To save herself and her lover, she fabricated a story of having found it during a stroll in the park. A servant revealed its real origin to his father, who locked his daughter in a room in the mansion's tower where she lived until her wedding. Her lover was brutally murdered. On the wedding day, the servant who came to get the daughter ready instead found her dead, dressed in black, with a note, asking to be buried with the pendant, and she cursed whoever would steal it."

"But this is not all," continued Edward, *"The Mourning Lady*, as this pendant was named after, brought their owners to such a level of depression, and all committed suicide."

A thick curtain of silence fell among the audience, shocked by the story of that unfortunate young lady who had chosen death to be reunited with her beloved. The lack of any evidence to debunk the legend gave them enough reasons to fear any consequence that would have arisen from the possession of the pendant.

"Was it expensive? How can you be sure that it's exactly the one the articles were talking about?" asked Jeff staring at the pendant. He was a tall and bulky guy with ice-blue eyes able to pierce a soul. Usually, he was kind and smiling, but he could transform into a furious and scary beast in seconds. Because of this peculiarity of his character, the other students learned to call him Hulk. Looking at his large hands, one would think he was more fit for becoming a carpenter rather than a jeweler. Nevertheless, his touch could be as gentle as a feather and create elaborate pieces of jewelry. "May I see it?"

"Of course." Edward handed him the pendant. "It wasn't expensive—I guess most people were scared of the curse and didn't want to place a bid."

"The broker had a certificate attesting to the last owner, and it was almost obvious to connect one with the other." Sabrina's voice became louder to emphasize that detail.

Jeff glanced at them both, then continued to inspect the item closely. "Isn't it quite strange for a pendant, which doesn't cost much, to have such an interesting history?"

Edward knew he wasn't convinced about the story of the pendant, but he was certainly interested in it. Although it wasn't anything but costume jewelry, it was a beautiful item.

"What is it, by the way?" Jeff asked, pondering an eventual purchase.

"The frame is silver, then the wing of a butterfly has been placed under this glass that magnifies the scales and enhances their shine. When I saw it on display, I also had the same thoughts as you, and I'm skeptical about curses, but the pendant itself is stunning—it immediately grabbed my attention."

Edward analyzed every move Jeff was making. The way he was biting his lower lip and his eyes kept staring at the reflected light from the surface of the butterfly wing confirmed that they would be closing the deal soon.

"So, you tell me you don't believe in the curse?" Lorena intervened. She wasn't interested in the purchase, but she was fascinated by the story.

"Those are fairy tales!" Sabrina said.

Jeff returned the pendant to Edward, "I believe we can find a foundation of truth in every legend." A short pause of silence passed over the group. The people gathered were more interested in their debate of whether the curse was real or not than in the pendant itself. Each of them had their own opinion, but the discussion between the two young men and Sabrina was engrossing.

"Oh, come on, you cannot believe everything you read in the newspapers," Edward nagged. "You need to divide the news from gossip."

"I'll give it the benefit of the doubt. If the previous owners had gone through a financial crisis, death, or accident...."

"Those are things happening every day," Edward interrupted. "I'm afraid people give too much credit to legends. Although having an increased number of unfortunate events happening to the previous owners might seem suspicious."

Jeff smirked and appeared to think about it. Once again, he looked at the pendant lying on the table between them and considered asking whether they were interested in selling it.

I don't have any use for such an item, as it's clearly something for a girl. Still, I have to admit it is smart jewelry, and the idea behind the creation is one of the most fascinating. As a goldsmith and jeweler, I'm attracted to it, and perhaps one day, it could be an excellent object to show in the window of my shop. Jeff was lost in his own considerations and didn't see the professor who entered the room. However, as Edward grabbed the pendant to return to his seat, he grunted, disappointed. As if someone woke him up from a dream, he was left with a bitter taste in his mouth.

"I think we got our target," Sabrina whispered.

"I bet he will ask me to sell it to him by the end of this week." A contented smile brightened Edward's face.

***

In the afternoon after his classes, Edward considered the possibility of returning home. He had promised to take a break, but the approaching day of the test and the need to gather data for their experiment had restricted the time at his availability.

Grabbing his calendar, he calculated the time for the lectures at the goldsmithing course, the class schedule in psychology, and the experiment they were conducting.

"I might have underestimated the amount of work I still need to do. Either Dad will have to wait for the end of the semester, or he could decide to come here himself to spend a few days with me."

He hurriedly flipped the pages trying to find a solution, but nothing came to mind. He didn't have the time to take care of everything, particularly his family issues. He brought his hands to his hair with slow movements, pushing it away from his forehead.

"What am I going to do?"

He grabbed his phone and considered whether it was the right time to call his father and ask for advice.

Its sudden ringing caused him to jolt, and as he saw Herman's name on the screen, he wondered whether he had heard his thoughts and come to the rescue.

"Hi, Dad," he answered.

"Hello, I hope I'm not disturbing you. I still find it hard with the time difference," Herman asked cautiously.

"No, you don't disturb me. I was just planning to call you," Edward answered, leaning back in his chair.

"I promised you to return home for a week, to talk face to face about the family business and my education. But I just realized time isn't a luxury I have right now."

Edward hoped his father would understand that his decision to reschedule his journey home wasn't caused by a disinterest in the family or the business.

"No need to be worried. Your educational commitments should come before any other time off, and I'm glad you're taking them seriously." Herman took a short pause, "I called you because in about a month I will attend an auction in Berlin and

64

I will gladly take a longer leave to visit you in London," Herman said.

Edward was surprised that his father was ready to close the shop for any period longer than necessary and wondered whether he had found someone to help him instead.

"That would be great, although I'll miss being home with you and Mom. How long are you going to stay?"

"The auction will take place on a Thursday, so I thought I could take the whole weekend to be with you. This means the shop needs to be closed for only a couple of days," his father explained.

"I have a better idea—why don't we both go to the auction, and we spend more time together? I will have the possibility to learn something more," Edward proposed, as his eyes twinkled with a spark of excitement.

He'd never participated in any auctions. Before he left to go to study in London, he couldn't join his father to any of them either because he had to go to school or remain in charge of the shop. The only chance for training was during the days he'd spent with his grandfather. That was a unique chance to see how his father behaved and learn how to establish connections with collectors and other dealers during those events.

"Brilliant idea! I'm wondering why I haven't thought of it myself."

Edward's expression brightened. He had underestimated the feelings of being away from the people he loved for two years, and lately, he had hoped he could return home at least for a few days. *I thought they would pass quickly, but now I understood we are both missing so many things about one another.*

"I will book the flight to Berlin immediately. Send me your schedule and the name of the hotel where you will stay, so I can make a reservation right away." His voice trembled—he could not wait to be spending some time with his father. The only thing that could make everything perfect would be if his mother joined them. Yet, he knew her job and commitments made his wish impossible.

"I will send you an email with all the details. I'm quite excited to see you again, and we have so many things to talk about." Herman's voice turned suddenly serious, recalling the topic he had to face.

Clearly, Edward was born with the same inclination for the business' side of dealing with peculiar items. Namely cursed ones.

"What's worrying you?" His son's voice interrupted his considerations.

"Oh, no, no," Herman reassured. "Everything is fine—I was thinking about a certain object for sale at the auction. I will also send you a link, so you can familiarize yourself with what I hope to acquire."

"Great! Well, I think every discussion we wanted to have can be postponed to the time we meet," Edward replied.

"We might want to do so. Take care of yourself, son. Remember, your mother and I love you very much."

"I love you too and say hi to Mom for me."

As soon as he hung up the phone, Edward got the email from his dad about the hotel's name and flight schedule. A broad smile appeared on his face, but the light in his eyes betrayed the turmoil caused by the latest events.

***

Herman closed his eyes and recalled the words of his father:

"Curses provide free marketing material. People love to dare their destiny, and we will provide them a way to put it to the test. Always remember, everything you sell in that department will return to you, one way or another...."

A jolt shook his body as if he couldn't breathe anymore. His heart raced in his chest, and a sense of terror crawled up his spine. He felt the presence of a demon behind him, whispering in his ears that the curse didn't only affect buyers, bringing misfortune and death into their lives, but also the salesmen who would live the rest of their lives with the remorse for having been somehow responsible. That was the reason why he decided to step a little aside the dealing with cursed stones.

"Edward is like his grandfather. He has the same interest and determination to become a dealer of those items. Dad certainly trained him for the dealing side, but I need to warn him about the emotional risks this kind of deal involves. This isn't something everybody can handle." Herman's forehead creased as a painful grin contorted his features.

***

Edward immediately started to look for the available flights from London to Berlin. There were a lot of choices, and several flights were scheduled daily toward Germany. His hands trembled at the thought of seeing his father sooner than he could forecast.

"And with such a great possibility of being together at an auction!" He raised his gaze and leaned back in his chair. "I have been waiting for this chance since I was a kid. I remember how I would have given everything I had to have that wish granted."

At those times, perhaps he was too young. His father took some time to decide whether he was mature enough to understand all the nuances of the business. Besides, he wouldn't have had the time to babysit him.

Now the situation was different, and it was time for him to learn the necessary skills to run the family business independently.

Once again, he grabbed his calendar—he had to plan everything, and to do this, he had to compile a list with Sabrina.

Even if I would be away for only four days, we might be working with a tight timetable. Standing from the chair, he paced around the room. *Nevertheless, I'm not going to give up this chance to be at an auction with my father for any reason.*

He let himself collapse on the bed, staring at the ceiling and thinking about everything coming to his mind. The school, the psychology course, the family business, the upcoming auction... and Sabrina.

Until that moment, he'd seen her as his best friend, the one who shared his crazy interest in cursed items. Everything was easier and different than what had happened with the other girls, he never needed to pretend to be someone else when he was in her company.

For a moment, he considered the crazy idea he was almost falling in love with her. "C'mon, there's a rule for friends. And they don't date." He said aloud as if to reproach himself for that thought.

"I believe a girl like her might have already someone in her heart. If I—" He shook his head, trying to forget that silly thought.

Certainly, there were so many beautiful girls to choose from at the campus. "Why it should be her?"

He walked to a mirror on the other side of the room and looked at his image. "Now I tell you one thing, buddy—you keep your hormones far from such a great friendship you have with Sabrina. You need to bring the experiment to an end, and you won't get anything out of it if you two date. You will ruin everything!" He pointed his finger against his reflected image.

He turned his shoulders to the mirror and raised his hands to his head. He'd been infatuated many times in his life and dated several girls. He knew that things could end and all the bullshits of *Let's stay friend* were nothing else but lies. Every time he had quit dating a girl, they had walked their own paths, never to meet again.

He cared too much about his friendship with Sabrina to risk her being another one who had just shared his path for a while. "Moreover, one day I will have to leave, and then we will part...."

With a loud grunt, he grabbed his jacket and got out of his room, slamming the door behind him. He needed to be somewhere else than alone with his thoughts.

Chapter 7

The following afternoon, after the lectures, Edward and Sabrina decided to take a walk. That was a great way to detach from their studies and relax in the many London parks and in Oxford Street, one of the busiest shopping streets. There, they decided to have a coffee.

He didn't want to reveal that he really liked being in her company and would have done everything to keep those moments with her lasting forever. At least not before being sure that she wasn't interested in anyone else. He needed to understand her feelings before risk making a fool out of himself.

That day, the topic of their discussion was focused on relationships and sharing each other's experiences.

"I know you guys consider us girls are a mystery, but maybe you are looking too far, and you don't see what you have around. Are you sure you're not building yourself impossible expectations?" Sabrina tried to guess his thoughts—she believed she gave him all the signals about her interest in him.

"I'm not sure," he mumbled, browsing the menu on the table. "I don't exclude this possibility. I think I keep getting interested in the wrong ones, and I wish I had a sort of crystal ball where to seek for the right one instead."

"So, there is someone in your heart," Sabrina investigated with a cunning expression on her face.

"You ask so many questions about me, but what about you? What's your excuse for wasting your time with a sentimental mess like me?" he asked with a chuckle.

"Fair question," Sabrina admitted, "and I have a crush on the wrong man who doesn't even consider me. I'm also a sentimental mess."

Edward nodded, "May I ask who that fool is?"

She wanted to tell him that to meet that fool, all he needed was a mirror, but she stopped herself, "I won't tell..." she commenced. At that moment, the waitress arrived, interrupting their chat.

"What can I bring you?" She asked with a smile.

"I'll take another coffee," Sabrina answered.

He turned his eyes at the drink list in front of him and lazily went through the choices he liked the most. "I'd like a hot orange chocolate."

"Coffee and chocolate... I'll be right back!" She trotted away.

"What were we saying?" she resumed. "Oh, yes. The name isn't important, but I think I have done everything to show him I'm interested. Still, he's too busy thinking about something else, and for him, I'm nothing but thin air."

She paused for a moment as the waitress arrived with their drinks.

Drawing lazy circles in the cup of orange cocoa with his spoon, Edward wondered about Sabrina. That was the first time they talked about personal issues.

They were always so engaged talking about jewelry, politics, and legends that everything else seemed pointless.

The door of the coffee house opened, and Jeff walked in. Edward scrutinized him out of the corner of his eye.

Sabrina acknowledged it and turned her eyes to Edward. He was looking for them, and as soon as he spotted their table, he strode in their direction.

"Hi, there! I was looking for you two. Do you mind if I sit down here for a moment?" Jeff asked with an embarrassed smile on his face.

"Of course, have a seat," Edward replied and invited him by pushing a chair aside.

"I have been thinking about the pendant you showed us in class. I don't know whether the curse is real or not, but I can't get it off of my mind." Jeff turned his glance around with nervous movements of his head as if to spot someone who might have listened to what he was going to say.

They had been waiting for Jeff to come asking for more information, but the surprise was in the time frame. They were expecting at least another week before Jeff would have reached out to them.

"It's a beautiful piece, despite the low retail value. Silver is the only precious metal on it, and not even the gemstones are adorning the frame. Nevertheless, its simplicity can draw attention," Sabrina explained, trying to keep a casual tone in her voice.

"Would you be interested in selling it?" Jeff asked.

Edward feigned a surprised expression, "Do you want to buy it?"

"Yes, besides being a beautiful item, undoubtedly the history of the curse gives him an aura of mystery that fascinates me."

Jeff blushed, averting his eyes from them. He had no intention to wear it but only to own something unique.

"How about seventy quid?" Edward proposed, after a brief consideration.

Jeff smirked, "We have a deal—will you bring the pendant to class on Monday?"

They shook hands.

"Yes, bring the money. That's more than I could expect to get from it."

Jeff stood from the chair with a satisfied expression brightening his face, "I'll leave you to chat. See you!"

"Bye!" Edward and Sabrina replied together.

They watched him leaving the coffee house and glanced at each other. "Ed, our test has officially started. From now on, we'd better keep an eye on our subject and record any reaction he has to everything happening to him, be it positive or not," she stated.

"We will have to keep a diary." Edward's voice shook, and his breathing quickened. A nervous chuckle escaped him.

He sipped at his hot chocolate and glanced around. People were coming in and out when he spotted a couple entering. He followed them as they went to sit at a table, chatting. They held their hands and shared tender glances with each other. The previous feelings of euphoria subsided as his lips twitched, curling downward.

"What are you thinking about now?" she interrupted his considerations and brought him back to reality.

"I was thinking about the trip I have to take." Edward tried to drown the jealousy that the happy couple inspired him. "Within about a month, I will have to travel to Berlin to meet my father. We're going to an auction to acquire a gemstone he wants to have for the shop. I will be away for about four days, between Thursday and Sunday," he explained.

Sabrina stared in awe. "You're so lucky to have a father who owns a jewelry business. For most of us, following this course means finding an apprenticeship to build our own careers. Not all of us will succeed, but you have a solid starting point."

He was aware of the privilege offered by his family. Still, he also knew what kind of pressure it included. "It's an advantage, but not all that shines is gold, as they say. I will always have to show my worth compared to every family member who came before me."

He rested his chin on the palm of his hand. "The shop opened in 1802 and remains today thanks to brilliant salesmen and gifted goldsmiths. Sometimes I'm overwhelmed."

"Hmm..." she tilted her head. "It might be a difficult heritage to deal with. I suppose nobody has found a pot of gold yet. Don't worry, you won't miss anything here—four days are nothing, and we both need some rest. We can catch up when you return."

"I guess that's what we'll do," he said, taking a final sip of his chocolate. "So, today is Friday—anything going on?"

"Well, as usual, the guys from class are going out to a pub looking for dates or a good time. Do you want to come?" Sabrina asked, surprised. Generally, he wouldn't go out. He would have returned to his room to study or do anything except have fun.

"Sure. I could take a break from studying. I'm afraid one day I'll regret not having enjoyed myself when I had the chance."

With a swift move, Sabrina stood and grabbed her coat. "Then we should get ready for the evening. As for me, I'll go have a shower and get dressed in something more appropriate." She glanced down at herself. This could be her best occasion to win over his heart.

"Do we meet somewhere?"

"Come to my apartment at seven, from there we'll join the others at the pub. We will be a small group of six people, including you, it will be fun!" Sabrina explained.

"Perfect, see you later," he replied.

As he walked home, Edward's thoughts returned to Mr. Milton and the incident that took his life. He hadn't been following the investigation, being too busy taking his life back on his hands, and he wondered if the cause of the accident had already been discovered.

I can't fathom reaching the point of terminating my own life. Although, it might be understandable to escape when a terminal disease guarantees a short future of only pain. On any other occasion, there should always be a solution other than death.

He wandered the streets before returning to his room, thinking about it.

He opened the door and switched on the lights, welcomed by the familiar sight of his dorm. It might not have been as big as a real apartment, but at that moment, it meant home. With a smile, he closed the door behind him.

I wonder where the pearl is now. Mr. Milton could have sold it to fix his problems and perhaps rid himself of the curse.

With a lazy move, he switched on the computer and started to browse for any news about the incident. His eyes narrowed as he found something.

"Interesting," he mumbled, reading about the failure in the engine causing the accident. "The plane had recently passed a routine check. Since then, the aircraft hadn't been used," he read out loud.

Edward averted his gaze from the screen and looked around himself, "Could someone have gotten into the hangar to sabotage the engine?"

He couldn't find any plausible reason to be so interested in that accident, other than the coincidence that the victim purchased a supposedly cursed pearl from his father. Suddenly he wondered whether this kind of news might harm the reputation of the family business.

He stood up and walked to the window, observing the courtyard crossed by the students heading to the various clubs where they would spend the night

He shook his head. *Endlessly mulling about this case will drive me crazy. Accidents happen every day. I just need to have some fun and forget about the curse, business, and school.*

So, Edward began preparing for his night out. It was quite unusual for him to spend the nights out and didn't plan his outfit the way many other guys his age would have. Within one hour, he was ready to leave his room.

At 7:00 pm, as they agreed, he knocked at her door. The door opened, and Sabrina appeared like in a vision. Her red hair sprayed with glitter shone like a crown of diamond, framing her perfect oval face. The dark makeup on her green eyes enhanced their radiance and shine. She wore a black minidress with a tight corset to enhance her décolleté to which his eyes dropped. His heart skipped a beat. He knew he had fallen into the most dangerous trap.

A giggle escaped her, "So how do I look?"

"Honestly? I... You look like a dream. You're gorgeous, and I feel like the frog prince at your side. You should have told me to dress up for a gala." He couldn't take his eyes off of her. She was perhaps the most beautiful girl he'd ever seen in his life.

He offered her his arm, and as she gracefully accepted it, she glanced at him. "If you're going to be nice enough, I might kiss you and transform you into a Prince." She winked.

Chapter 8

The research project began with the new week, and Sabrina had the task of keeping an eye on Jeff, whatever moves he made without being spotted. She found tailing pretty exciting and imagined herself as a detective in a gritty crime movie. Although the task wasn't easy and kept her busy most of the time, she discovered being quite skilled at it.

For his part, Edward would summarize the progress and write the results in a logbook.

According to what Sabrina reported since Jeff came into possession of the cursed object, he's been acting more nervous than his usual, he considered.

Maybe there is a psychological connection between legends and facts. How fascinating.

He closed his eyes and marveled at the beauty and complexity of the human mind. *I wonder if I should pursue more psychology classes or continue my studies independently.* Opening his eyes, he stood up, considering a career as a salesman would still provide him with excellent opportunities to learn more about it.

Someone suddenly knocked on his door, abruptly bringing him back to reality. As he turned, his coffee cup fell to the floor, splattering its content. Muffling a groan, he went to open the door.

Sabrina appeared smiling, but as she saw his darkened expression, her face changed. "Is now a bad time?"

His lips curled into a forced smile. "Come in, sorry. I spilled my coffee on the floor," he added, welcoming her in.

"So, what's the news?" Edward asked as he went to search for a rag.

Sabrina sat on the bed, trying to stay away from his path, "Jeff returned home. I must admit it has been an inconclusive day. Nevertheless, his mood was a bit touchier than usual. When he answered the phone, his tone was less welcoming. It seemed someone was threatening him, or he was expecting to receive some bad news."

Edward finished cleaning the floor and went to sit down on his chair. "We were able to curse him?" A chuckle escaped his mouth.

"So it seems, and it's so fascinating to see how human perception of events can change when given a reason to fear a threat. We should do the same experiment with a good luck charm." She rubbed her chin with her hand. "That would make our research complete, but I'm afraid we might need more than one year. To have consistent results, we should have a targeted group, not simply one individual. Moreover, I think that perhaps we should keep these results for ourselves. We're crossing that ethical border of a grey area between right and wrong."

"You're probably right. When will you go to the auction with your father?" Sabrina wondered.

"In about twenty days." He stood from the chair and stretched his back. "I can't wait. I have never been to an auction before. All I knew was when my dad had to leave for the most exotic destinations in the world, I was left behind, taking care of the shop."

"One day, I wish to establish a business like the one you have back in New York. My parents have completely different careers from the one I'm following. Neither of them is in commerce, and I would die for some guidance..."

She was inspired by his stories about the family business. Sabrina would have given anything for the chance to move to the States to work together. *It would be awesome to share more time with him—I believe we would make a great team.*

A severe expression shaded Edward's face as he recognized the change of tone in Sabrina's voice. *That's the kind of tone aimed to ask for something without saying so. If I owned the business, I would have happily offered her to join me. But at the moment, the only thing I could do is suggest it to my father. He's the one to decide whether to hire extra help.*

"Why don't we go out for a walk?" he wondered, trying to divert the conversation away to other topics.

***

That same morning, Herman reached the shop a bit earlier than usual. After disengaging the alarm and tidying up, he went to the back room where he had his office. He wanted to carefully examine the items that would be sold at the upcoming auctions.

He didn't find any unusual jewel for sale in the coming months. Nevertheless, there were still many gorgeous pieces of jewelry that would be auctioned off worldwide and that he wanted to acquire for his shop.

An extra person to help with the shop while I'm away is something I haven't valued enough. It took Edward being away to appreciate an extra set of hands around here. Several generations of Sherwood had overseen the business and stood at one point thinking the same.

His eyes turned away from the computer screen and browsed the rest of the room,

Each previous owner had brought their personal touch to the room. Although they all had different personalities and tastes, that place kept a harmony of styles.

I wonder what kind of new impressions Edward's presence as the shop owner will leave. A smile brightened his expression.

In Herman's eyes, the most impressive piece was a long wooden plate that reached the roof. It came from India, and the fine carving represented Lord Ganesh in its several forms.

The five-headed god represented the five components that make for the human physique. The four-armed representation was a symbol of his multiple superhuman powers.

The first time he had placed his hands on that plate and closed his eyes, a clear image of the busy streets in Mumbai took form in front of him. The smells, the noises, and the feel of magic pervaded his soul, giving a sense of peace to his whole being.

He turned his eyes to the date on his computer and realized his trip to Berlin was rapidly approaching. Although he had participated in many auctions, his heart raced in his chest for this one, for it would be the first he attended with his son.

There was always a sense of anticipation before every auction. Returning home empty-handed wasn't an option.

If that happened, it meant that either too many people were interested in the same items, or they could draw on more substantial funds to purchase.

It was a strategy game. He needed to understand where he was supposed to invest his funds and quickly give up if he understood the price didn't give any room for profit.

One day, when I will retire, I might keep visiting those auctions. I'm afraid I'll never be able to give up the excitement, not in a hundred years.

He was amused by this thought. Retirement had always been a vague idea in his mind, only a distant eventuality. As he approached his mid-fifties, he realized how time was passing without acknowledging it. He thought he might still have another ten years before he could consider retirement—a sudden frown creased his forehead.

Edward needs to start working here as soon as he finishes school. He stood from the chair, listening to the silence coming from every corner of the shop. *I'm afraid I procrastinated his training for too long. He should have been going to auctions years ago.*

A deep sigh escaped him as if to free his soul.

This auction in Berlin will be Edward's first. I have to make sure everything goes well so he can learn.

The pendulum clock chimed, catching his attention. Nodding to it, Herman opened the shop, ready for another working day.

***

It was almost time to close for lunch when an unusual patron walked inside.

His shop had never been visited by the NYPD, and he wondered about the reason for his arrival. Although he was dressed in civilian clothes, Herman spotted the badge hanging from his neck, barely showing beyond his coat. *I doubt he's here to get a gift for his wife.*

"Good morning. How can I help you?" He greeted with a charming smile.

"Good morning to you. I hope I'm not disturbing you," the detective replied, glancing at a couple who was having a look at some jewelry.

85

Shaking his head, Herman knew those customers were only browsing for something they might want to purchase in the future, "Not at all. If I can help, it will be my pleasure."

"I'm Detective Lars Lindström, and I'm investigating the plane crash that killed Mr. Jason Milton," the detective commenced. "I'm wondering whether you have a place where we can chat in private?"

Herman grimaced, uncomfortable with leaving the shop unattended. "I'm the only one working here, today, but if you come back this evening at 6:00 I will be at your disposal. Otherwise, you can wait half an hour and join me for lunch."

"It won't take long, I just need to ask you a few questions. I can wait for you now." Detective Lindström replied.

"If you want, you may be more comfortable in the backroom." Herman didn't like to have a policeman loitering in the room while customers browse.

"Oh," the detective muttered, noticing the stares of the couple. "I understand, of course. Lead the way."

With a weak nod, Herman walked from behind the desk and guided him to the back room. As the light switched on, Herman welcomed him in.

"You can get comfortable on the couch if you want. I'll be back soon." Although the alarm system would stop a potential thief, he always had an empty sensation in the pit of his stomach when he left the shop unattended.

"Thank you," Lindström replied, walking to the couch.

A million thoughts formulated in his mind about the unexpected visit. *I'm wondering whether he placed me on the list of the suspects. I guess he wants to ask about the pearl, which might be crucial in their investigation. The pearl could be seen as a reason for killing himself or being murdered.*

As soon as the last customers left the shop, Herman hurried to close the door. He strode to the backroom after drawing a deep breath.

"I'm terribly sorry for making you wait. You certainly understand I could not kick anyone out." Herman tried to sound amused, but a storm was brewing in his heart.

The detective raised his gaze to look at him with a kind smile, "'Don't worry, Mr. Sherwood, I understand perfectly."

"Would you prefer to talk here or at the cafe close by?" Herman offered as the situation became a bit awkward.

"If you don't mind, here might provide the privacy we need," Detective Lindström suggested.

With slow movements, Herman took a seat in front of him, "What can I do for you?"

"As I mentioned before, I'm following the case of the death of Mr. Jason Milton. The preliminary investigation of the crash and the black box confirmed a failure of the engine. However, too many questions remain open."

With his eyes steady on him, Herman followed Lindström's every move, trying to guess what he wanted. Herman was sure he didn't come to get the same information he could have obtained from the tabloids.

"What makes me wonder is the fact that the plane departed after a complete inspection following a long period of inactivity. According to the mechanics who performed the check, everything was in perfect condition. They can't explain any reason for the crash," Lars continued.

"Do you believe someone might have sabotaged the plane after it returned from the inspection?"

"That is a possibility, either someone who wanted revenge, someone Mr. Milton owed money to, or someone who wanted to have something back from him...."

"Or Mr. Milton himself, in a final attempt to save his family from the unavoidable financial disaster," he interrupted. "According to the tabloids, the life insurance would have saved them. Perhaps he thought the accident was the only way to maintain the reputation of his family."

Lars narrowed his eyes, "You seem to have known him well."

"Not at all." Herman got more comfortable in his chair. "The only time I met him was in this shop when he came to purchase a rare pearl."

"A half-million dollars pearl..." Lars spelled.

"He wasn't forced to buy it. I told him my price, and he agreed to it—that's how the business goes." Herman didn't like the inquisitive tone in the detective's voice.

"Did you ever mention to him the rumor that it was supposed to be cursed?" Lars wondered.

"He came to my shop to buy the pearl for exactly that reason. People always try to find a scapegoat for their inept investments. I don't believe in curses, do you?"

"Neither do I, but I wonder whether his financial decline was somehow facilitated by someone who wanted to have the pearl for a fraction of the price Mr. Milton had purchased it." Lars entwined his fingers on his lap.

He kept his gaze straight on Lars, "Detective Lindström, are you accusing me of something?"

"I'm trying to find out why the pearl is nowhere to be found, and I'm going through every possible lead until I find the right one."

Lars wasn't impressed by the salesman's quiet temper—he'd seen many killers acting even calmer than he did.

"I don't have the pearl. My relationship with Mr. Milton started when he stepped into my shop and ended the moment, he exited it. I have a business that runs quite smoothly. I continue the tradition of my family in trading particular items. Gems, jewelry, and items with dark histories." He leaned closer to Lars, scrutinizing him. "But I'm not a killer."

Silence embedded the whole room, interrupted only by the regular ticking of the pendulum clock.

Lars smirked, "The pearl is the reason why Mr. Milton lost his life, and he had considered it responsible for his misfortune. Is it possible that you can't feel even a little guilty?"

Herman stared at Lars, "What for? Should a car dealer feel guilty for having sold a car to someone who died in an accident?"

The detective was getting on his nerves. He stood from the chair and walked toward the door, opening it. "I have no intention to stay here and listen to your pretentious accusations. If you have any evidence of my involvement, then I'm all yours—until then, goodbye and have a lovely day. This conversation is over."

Lars knew he didn't have any proof against him.

He came to his shop to get information about the pearl and who might have been interested in it. The way Herman lost his temper and the pulsing of a vein on his temple gave Lars the suspicion that he knew more than he was ready to reveal.

Since they started to talk, the idea that perhaps he had had something to do with the accident to have the pearl back took form in his mind. He needed to pursue that path.

"I'm sorry, Mr. Sherwood, I didn't mean to make you feel accused. I'm afraid I let myself get carried away with my suspicions sometimes. Please, return to your seat. Do you know whether there might have been other people interested in getting the pearl?”

Herman shook his head and tried to relax. “Apology accepted. I need to apologize for my impulsive behavior as well. I should have understood the difficult situation you have to handle. Concerning the pearl, I was one of the few bidders at the auction. It was clear to me that the fairy tales of a curse can still raise curiosity and diffidence. Mr. Milton was supposed to be at the auction for the same pearl, but he arrived too late.”

“Ok, I’m going back to the precinct. I need to reorganize the information I have—perhaps the curse of the pearl is real after all. I hope we can put this incident behind us. I’ll be back if I need your assistance,” Lars replied, trying to smile.

“Of course, whenever you need more information. However, I’m afraid I do not know more than what I have been telling you here.”

With a concerned expression, Lars nodded without saying a word. He glanced one more time at Herman before exiting the back room, “Thank you for your cooperation. I will stay in touch.”

“Have a good day,” Herman replied. The clinging of the bell on the door rang as Lars opened it. That was the most relieving sound.

Herman collapsed on his chair as if his legs had no more strength. He should have been expected the police would have come to question him. Of course, the insinuation that he had killed Mr. Milton came out of the blue and would have done everything to divert the police's attention from his shop.

"That was something I didn't need," Herman mumbled to himself.

He was supposed to go for lunch, but he realized he didn't have much time left for it. He grimaced, exhaling nervously.

"I should at least grab a snack. I can't go without eating until dinner."

With that, he strode out the door where he could see a hot-dog cart on the corner.

Chapter 9

Sooner than Edward had expected, the time to leave for Berlin arrived. Waiting to board at the gates of Heathrow airport, he went through the notes he had collected for the test with Sabrina.

From the day Jeff bought the pendant, things had started to take a wrong turn. He had failed two exams, causing a delay that could have cost him the suspension of the scholarship. Evidently, he hadn't considered this risk.

Edward raised his glance and looked around the terminal full of people waiting to board. *This means he won't receive any money for the next three months. I guess it would be good if he starts to search for some part-time job or he will be in trouble.*

"Adding these two events and other mishaps, the conviction of a curse might have taken form in his mind," he mumbled. "I wonder if he will blame us for having sold him a cursed item."

His heart suddenly raced in his chest—something was trying to warn him of the possibility of the situation slipping from their control. If that had happened, the consequences could have been catastrophic for everyone.

He stood up and started to pace around the hall, unable to sit still and wait. He called Sabrina to understand whether his heart racing had some sort of foundation or was a state of mind caused by the excitement for the research and the uncertainties it held.

"Ed..." she replied groggily as if she was still sleeping.

"I'm so sorry. Did I wake you up?" He glanced at the clock, realizing it was seven o'clock in the morning, and since the lectures wouldn't start before nine, she was most certainly still in bed.

She groaned. "I was... What's going on? Is the end of the world approaching? What time is it?"

"It's 07:00 am," he replied, cringing.

"I was dreaming of the man of my life..." Sabrina giggled, and Edward could hear her roll over and sit up. "Are you already at the airport?"

"Yes, and I was looking at the data we've collected about Jeff. Do you think he will have serious problems with those exams he failed?"

She yawned. "Why do you care? He should have known better that spending his nights at the pub wasn't a great idea during exam week." Her voice seemed irritated for having been woken up for something that could have been discussed later.

Edward nodded, pursing his lips, "You might be right, but I'm afraid he might start to blame us for having sold him a cursed item."

"That's nonsense! He came to us begging to have the pendant. How are we responsible for his bad choices? He should blame himself, not the pendant, especially neither of us."

Taking a deep breath, Edward returned to sit down at his terminal, "Perhaps you're right, and we don't have any reason to be worried, although I'm still sorry for him. He might lose his scholarship if he remains behind in his studies. We don't know about his financial situation, but I guess it might be difficult."

She released a relieved sigh, "I think you're worrying too much. He still has his family to support him, and he can choose between plenty of part-time jobs around here for students. He needs to pick one and stop clubbing."

"Perhaps you're right. But keep an eye on him and be careful of any warning signs of a change in mood toward you. For some reason, I'm not reassured."

"To be honest, I'm starting to worry about you. Take it easy, I believe you need this holiday with your old man more than you think. Have fun and stop thinking about Jeff, okay?"

"I'll try. Thanks. I will call you when I'm back. Don't hesitate to call me in case you need anything. You won't interrupt anything important." He wanted to make sure everything would run smoothly while he was away. He behaved like he was running a business and had to keep tabs on his employees.

I hope this long weekend with Dad will help me unwind from the stress I have obviously accumulated.

"Everything will be fine, boss," she giggled, amused.

As she quit the conversation, Sabrina placed the telephone on the table.

She poured some coffee and went to close a window. In the silence of her apartment, Edward's doubts seemed suddenly to actualize. She decided to avoid the places where Jeff was hanging around, except the classroom, even if she wished she could avoid him altogether.

You're getting influenced by Ed's nonsense, she warned, reproaching herself.

***

Finally, the plane landed at Berlin's Tegel airport. Edward knew his father would have waited for him at the terminal, so with only his backpack, he hurried outside the gate area.

"Dad!" Edward yelled when he spotted him and began running to hug him. He'd never been so happy to see him as at that moment. He couldn't believe how much he'd missed him.

"Edward!" Herman beamed. "Look at you! You're a man—this year away from home did miracles." He scrutinized his son from head to toes. "How are you doing?"

"I'm fine. The semester will end soon, and I'll be ready to return home, at least for the holidays," he replied as they started to walk outside to get a taxi. "I have been missing you and Mom terribly. I can't wait to finish my studies and start working at the shop."

"Home has not been the same without you." Herman's lips twitched into a frown. Averting the gaze of his son, he glanced at the driver. "We need

96

to reach this place, please," he said, showing him the business card of the hotel.

The man simply nodded and opened the doors for them.

"I have to admit it, being alone in the shop has been challenging. This business requires a couple of people. I had to set appointments for high value deals outside the regular hours. Sometimes you need to compromise to accommodate certain clients. One day, when I'm too old to help with the shop, you might consider hiring a coworker."

"What do you mean? You will never be too old." He looked at his father with awe. Since he was a child, he had been waiting with trepidation for the day they would work together. The news that he was considering retiring felt like a cold shower.

"I'm not planning to retire any time soon. I'm telling you what would be more convenient, further down the line." Herman's stare stretched outside the window for a moment.

He turned his eyes once again to look at his son, "One day, when you have children of your own, they might follow in our footsteps, and they'll be there to help you."

Edward's expression froze in response, holding his breath for a second. He recalled the discussions he had had with Sabrina. Particularly the last one. Edward had no idea whether he should have talked to his father about his personal life. In the last months, he had the time to get to know other people and take some time for himself. There were a couple

97

of cute and interesting girls. However, he ended still spending most of his time with Sabrina to the point that he could almost say he preferred her company, but was that what love was about?

"Anything wrong?" Herman noticed the change of expression on his son's face.

"No, Dad. I'm just tired, and the test I'm working at with Sabrina popped into my mind."

"You often talk about this girl. Is she some sort of a special person?"

"Who? Sabrina?" He faltered. "No, she's only a good friend, that's all."

Herman realized something more than stress shook his son's soul and decided not to press until he felt ready.

"You have no reason to be nervous. I was only asking, and it's perfectly normal to want to keep your private life... private," he said, grabbing his son's hand.

At that touch, Edward wondered whether he had neglected something about the friendly relationship with his nowadays best friend.

The trip to the hotel didn't last more than half an hour and went on in embarrassing silence that divided them until they reached Edward's room.

"Ed, I don't mean to be indiscreet, but if you have any worries, I'd like you to consider talking to me about it," said Herman, when they reached

Edward's room. Then he grabbed his son by the shoulders and looked him straight in the eye. "I am your father, you can tell me everything; and even if you think you no longer need me, my experience could be useful to you."

"I know, but nothing is worrying me now. I have been so focused on studying and learning to be a good salesman, I might have forgotten to just live life."

He went to sit on the bed and glanced down at his feet.

"I called Mom because I feared it was weird not being in love or attracted to anyone." He paused as his father took a chair and sat down across from him. "Mom told me I needed to start being social, and so I did, but the result was the same. When I talked to Sabrina...." He wasn't sure if now was the right moment to talk about it or if there would ever be one. "She suggested that perhaps my expectations were too high and that I failed to see what was actually happening around me."

Herman raised one eyebrow. "And?"

"And what?"

"Do you think you have too high expectations?" Herman tried not to chuckle because he already knew that girl had a soft spot for him, and by the way he was always talking about her, that spark was probably requited.

Edward's shoulders dropped. He turned his eyes to look at his father's. "I don't know. I feel as empty as a shell in the sand."

"I guess one day you will have to figure that out, one way or another. Your mother is right—you need to live your life before thinking about work or school. They're both important, but they're simply a way to pay your bills."

"I don't know what to do with my life. I'm so confused, you asked me why I haven't talked about anyone else but Sabrina... What if I feel attracted to her? How am I going to deal...?"

Herman chuckled and patted Edward's leg, "That's called growing up. You will figure it out, don't you worry. And if this friend of yours might be the reason for your internal turmoil, I don't think you should hold back your feelings."

Closing his eyes, Edward took a deep breath. *Perhaps Dad is right. Was I waiting for something like it happens in the movie, and I failed to realize my feelings for her?*

Opening his eyes again, he met his father's smile. "I wish there was a way to figure myself out with a mathematical formula."

For a few minutes, they both remained silent, Edward's head felt light as he thought about Sabrina, and a faint smile arched his lips.

Herman glanced at his wristwatch, "What about getting ready? The auction will begin in three hours. And I would like to be there at least one hour before it starts to have the chance to look at the items on offer tonight. Maybe I can find something else, besides the one I came for.”

That said, he helped his son to stand from the bed. “Thanks, Dad—I should have talked with you about my doubts earlier. If you don't mind, I’ll take a shower and change my clothes.”

“Of course,” Herman concurred. “Do you want to meet me downstairs in the lobby?”

Edward opened his backpack and thought about it for a moment. “It won't take more than fifteen minutes for me to get ready, so you can wait here if you want.”

He sat down on the couch close to the window. “I’ll wait for you. You have a great view from here.”

***

It was early Saturday afternoon, and Sabrina was ready to leave her apartment. At the ringing of her phone, a jolt shook her body. She didn’t make any plans with classmates, so none of them could be the one to call her.

Failing to recognize the number, she answered, nonetheless. “Sabrina.”

“Oh, hi. This is Jeff—I hope I’m not disturbing you.”

Hearing that voice, the blood froze in her veins. Despite the lack of reason, an irrational fear possessed her soul.

“Hi, Jeff. I was actually reaching the bus stop, but what’s up?” she considered lying about her location and promised herself to punch Edward in the face as soon as she had the chance. *I will never forgive him for infecting me with such paranoia.*

"I was wondering whether you were going to meet the guys at the pub later. I don't have anything planned tonight, so I thought we might go together." Jeff's voice was calm, like usual. As Sabrina was more sensitive to every change in his behavior, she noticed a flicker suggesting that he was slightly intoxicated or furious. Whatever the case, she didn't want to find out in person.

"No, I already have other plans. Sorry," she replied, trying to keep her voice steady.

"Oh, and do you know if Edward will be there at the pub?" He pursued, "I haven't seen him in days."

"He's in Berlin with his father. He should be back tomorrow afternoon, I believe."

Jeff grunted.

"If you need him, you might try calling him," she proposed, ready to hang up and leave.

"I didn't have anything important to say, simply wondering whether you guys would have joined us to the pub, that's all," he replied. "But obviously, you both have other plans for the weekend, so see you on Monday."

"Yeah, sure. Have fun," Sabrina replied as she got out of the apartment.

She didn't have the time to place the telephone back in her purse and close the door before someone grabbed her from behind, holding her arms down, making any resistance impossible.

Her heart furiously raced with the fear of being targeted by some thief or maniac.

"What do you want from me? I don't have any money." Her voice was trembling, and her mind tried desperately to find a way to escape the grasp of the assailant.

Whoever it was, he produced a rope and tied her arms together behind her back in a matter of seconds. Sabrina figured out, by the way his body pressed against hers, it must have been someone tall and bulky.

Without saying a word, she was pushed back to her apartment. He grabbed the chair from the desk and forced her to sit down, tying her tightly to it.

Then, the attacker walked in front of her, revealing his identity.

"You should know telling lies isn't nice," Jeff said, extracting a knife from the pocket of his jeans.

She wanted to scream and attract the attention of the whole building. Her heart was beating so ferociously that every word caught in her throat.

"Where is your friend?" Jeff sneered.

Collecting all her strength, Sabrina tried to reply, "I told you, he's in Berlin with his father."

That sentence came out like a barely audible whistle.

Jeff got close and slapped her face hard, "Don't lie to me!" His voice was furious, and her eyes started to fill with fearful tears.

"No, it's the truth," she sobbed. "Why don't you call him?"

"I will call him, and if he cares about your life, he will have to hurry. My patience has a limit." His mendacious voice couldn't hide background of fear and despair.

Jeff's hands were trembling as he pulled a phone from his pocket. He took a picture of Sabrina and sent it to Edward's phone.

Chapter 10

"Pity we have only these three days to spend together," Edward complained as they were walking the street at the Brandenburg gate.

With a deep breath, Herman concurred with his son's feelings, "Although you will be back home within a few months, it still saddens me to leave you. Remember, we will never judge the way you live your life, as long as you follow a righteous path."

The meeting he had with Detective Lindström made him reconsider the meaning of honesty. *Is it ethically correct to use the word 'honest' to define the trade of cursed jewels? Although my customers are aware of the bloody stories behind those items and dealing with precious stones always has a darker side, I don't believe this adjective is appropriate.*

"Dad are you worried or something?" he wondered, noticing his dad's creased forehead.

With a light jolt, Herman turned his glance toward his son. "Oh, no," he replied, relaxing his expression. "I was thinking about the items we purchased at the auction, and I was wondering if they might interest a customer who came into the shop last week."

It was clearly a lie, and he hated lying to his family, but in that case, it was a necessary evil.

"Grandpa probably explained to you the various aspects of dealing in stones and jewels with a particular past and told you about the deep emotional conflict that it involves..." he began, but it was interrupted by the beeping of an incoming message on his son's phone.

"Hold on a moment," Edward said, searching for it in the pocket of his jacket.

As he started reading, the smile he had on his face immediately faded, his mild features toughened as if made of stone.

Edward's heart started to race, he lost his grip, and the phone fell on the hard ground. He tried to scream, but his body remained frozen as thousands of thoughts crowded his mind, making him unable to react.

Herman watched, confused at the sudden change in his son's behavior. He went to grab the phone from the ground, still displaying the picture that had petrified his son.

He glanced at it—the image of a young lady tied to a chair appeared in front of his eyes.

Her eyes were transfixed with horror, pleading for rescue, and her face marred with blood coming from her nose. The message read. *Do you want your friend to survive tonight? Come to her apartment, you know the reason why I want you!*

Apparently, he wasn't the only one who kept secrets. "Edward!" he said with a whisper. "What is going on?"

Without replying, he grabbed the phone from his father's hand and glanced at the image one more time. Toughening his expression, he dialed Jeff's number.

"So, you decided to answer my message," Jeff sneered.

"What do you want?" his voice was calm, but it thundered through the street.

"I want you to come back here right away. Your pendant cursed me, and you have to take it away!" Jeff sounded like a maniac, and Edward understood his worst fears had come true. Jeff was desperate and ready to do anything to have his life back.

"Jeff, I'm in Berlin with my father. I will take the first plane to reach you, and we will figure it out. You don't need to lose your temper," he responded in a desperate attempt to control the situation.

"My life is being ruined, and your pendant is the reason why! You need to come here!" Tears streamed from Jeff's eyes, and even though Edward could not see them, he felt them flowing through his heart and took a deep pained breath.

"I will take the first flight, but I can't arrive earlier than tonight. Please, let her go and wait for me. We will solve this, I promise."

Jeff paused for a second to consider the situation. "Ok," he accepted, with feverish voice. "I promise nothing will happen to Sabrina if you reach her apartment by tonight before midnight. You don't want to test my patience!"

That said, Jeff ended the call and switched off his phone.

Edward stared at his phone for several moments, then looked to his father. "He has Sabrina. I need to leave now, or he might..."

Herman held his son tightly to himself, wanting with all his heart to help him, although he had no idea what was going on.

Edward separated from his father, collecting his thoughts. "I have no time to explain—I need to hurry and jump on the first available flight back. I'm sorry."

"No need to apologize. I'll leave with you, so we have some time to talk," Herman replied as they hurried to the hotel.

They reached the airport and bought tickets for the flight to London that would leave within two hours without exchanging a word.

"It's a long wait, but we should make it on time to save Sabrina." He brought his hands to his face, incapable of thinking straight.

"Then you will have enough time to explain what's going on. Who is this guy, and why is he threatening your friend?" his father's stern voice brought him back to when he was a child and he reproached him for some mischief.

With a nod, Edward chose an isolated bench in the terminal and took a seat. He wiped his hair backward, trying to regain some composure.

"It all started when I was taking Professor McGillis' psychology class," he recalled. "I was intrigued by the lectures about psychological manipulation and the power of suggestion."

His eyes gazed around the hall, fearing to look directly at his father.

"Sabrina and I share the same interest in curses. Neither of us believes in such a thing, yet we know that superstition can alter the perception of reality in those who consider it something real. In the same way that a charm is associated with good luck, prompting its owner to make the right choices, a cursed object can lead them to self-destructive ones."

Herman quietly listened to his son. The more Edward talked about his interest in the items they were dealing with in the shop, the more Herman realized Edward resembled his father. His shoulders tightened.

"Just for testing this theory, we decided to purchase an item from an antique shop. With the help of Sabrina's brother, we targeted a group of goldsmith students with fake news of a cursed pendant that belonged to people who met their fate by simply owning it. We fabricated a story about the origin of its curse and the people who met their fate." He searched one of his pockets and extracted a small blue pendant. "I bought two of them because I thought they were interesting pieces."

Herman took the piece of jewelry in his hand and scrutinized it in silence—he was waiting for his son to finish his story.

"Jeff was curious about the item and its story and asked me to sell it to him. The idea was to follow him, record everything that happened to him and his reactions."

He briefly paused, turning his eyes to the clock. He couldn't help wondering how Sabrina was doing and whether Jeff was keeping his promise not to hurt her.

He turned his eyes toward the clock, wondering how Sabrina was doing and whether Jeff would keep his promise to avoid hurting her.

With a sigh, he continued the story, explaining how Jeff had begun struggling in classes and reacting negatively. When he finished, he finally found the courage to look at his father. "I have never felt so guilty in my whole life. I didn't mean any harm. I don't know what I'm going to do."

Herman closed his eyes, "That was the emotional bond I was talking about," he commenced. "Our family has always dealt with these kinds of objects, but, as you pointed out, there's rarely a happy ending. It doesn't help to know that those who came to my shop were specifically looking for cursed stones, in any case, I have provided them with the means for suicides, homicides, and financial ruin."

Edward's eyes shined with tears he was barely able to contain. "Why have you never told me about this?"

Herman turned to look at his son. "It seemed that you had already made your choice. Pursuing your instincts, guided by fate, you followed the same path traced by your grandfather and those who came before him. It's in your DNA, even if you decide not to deal with those items anymore."

His father was right, he was dangerously attracted to a gray area where the business was legally correct but morally dubious. He took some time to think about it. If Sabrina weren't so deeply involved, he wouldn't have considered it wrong.

Maybe Dad is right. Do I resemble my grandfather? He peered at his father before returning to stare at the floor.

"What I need more than anything else is to make sure she is safe. Although she knew what we were getting ourselves into, I'm afraid we both underestimated the possible consequences."

He almost mumbled to himself, wondering whether, from that moment on, it would have been safer to keep personal relationships separate from business.

"How did Grandpa manage to keep you and Grandma alive and safe? What about you?"

Herman smiled and slid closer beside him. "At our level, there is no risk for our families. When you sell your first piece of jewelry, you will have to clarify the origin, the story, and the possibility that the curse exists. You may put it as a joke, but never forget to mention it. So far, nobody ever returned to the shop threatening my family or me for having hexed them."

Edward's body relaxed, and from the chat with his father, he understood Jeff was driven by despair. *If I offered him my support in getting back on his feet, he might forgive me. Although I have no intention of revealing to him that it was an experiment and the curse never existed.*

Finally, they could board the plane, and within an hour, they left Germany.

"What are your plans?" he asked his father as they sat next to each other.

"I'm going to reach London and change my flight to the next one for New York. I have no intention to come with you. However, I suggest calling the police. This Jeff might be dangerous and threaten the life of Sabrina and yours," Herman recommended, ready to help his son in case he asked for it.

Shaking his head, he looked outside the window. The plane took off and the ground got farther and farther away. "If the police were involved, Jeff's life would definitely be ruined. I feel responsible for his problems. I think it's my duty to try to help him with what he considers a curse. I'm sure I'll be fine, and so will Sabrina."

Jeff isn't a killer. I'm ready to bet my own life on it. He won't consider killing her, not even for a moment.

***

It was about eight in the evening when Edward reached Sabrina's apartment. The door was left ajar and waiting for him to come inside.

His heart began racing once again. His mouth was dry, and his cheeks were wet with tears. He closed his eyes and inhaled deeply, then held his breath until his heartbeat returned to a normal pace.

He opened his eyes and approached the door, opening it with his foot. He wasn't sure whether it was a trap or what to expect once he entered the apartment, so he tried to take all the precautions he could.

A muffled whimper welcomed him inside, and the first thing he saw was Sabrina sobbing desperately through the gag Jeff had stuffed into her mouth. Edward's heart sank at the view of his best friend with her face caked with dry blood and her eyes swollen with tears.

Beside her, seated on a chair, Jeff held a knife. His mouth was nervously twitching while his eyes stared at the door, lost in the nothingness. They had that furious stare of a man who understood he had nothing left to lose and was ready for anything.

As soon as he saw Edward entering the room, he jumped, holding the knife at her throat.

"Close the door!" Jeff ordered.

Edward did as he was told. He gave her an almost imperceptible nod to make her understand he had the situation under control, and soon everything would be over.

"I kept my promise, now it's your turn, let her go," he said, keeping his voice steady.

Jeff shook his head. "First, you need to take the curse away from me."

"How? You don't understand, Jeff, the curse is a hoax."

With a swift move, Jeff stabbed the table with his knife as Sabrina jolted, whimpering through the gag, "Then why is my life going down the drain? Why am I spiraling down more every day!?" He yelled madly.

"You failed those two exams because you didn't study enough. You've been going clubbing almost every night, and goldsmithing is a work of precision. It requires nerves of steel and steady hands. You can't have those with a hangover," he reproached. "But I'm ready to help you out. What if I return your money and you give me back the pendant? That will lift the curse, and you can have your life back."

Jeff grabbed the knife and held it back to Sabrina's throat. "I'm doomed already!"

"Please, you don't want to do this! You're not cursed, but you will be if you kill her." He slipped his wallet from his pocket and took seventy pounds. "Here, this is the money you gave me."

He paced and placed the bills on the table. "Do you have the pendant with you?"

Jeff glanced at the money and nodded.

"Perfect. Now lower the knife on the floor and place the pendant on the table." He tried to talk slowly to soothe Jeff's nerves.

Jeff hesitated for a moment. He didn't want to kill anyone, but he was hopeless.
114

"Desperate men take desperate actions," Jeff whispered as he started to reconsider what Edward had proposed.

He glanced back at Sabrina, who kept whimpering and sobbing. Jeff shook his head, the knife fell to the floor, he searched his pockets and placed the pendant on the table with a deep sigh.

"Now, take the money and get out of this apartment. Everything will be fine. If you need some help, you can count on us. Remember, get a hold of yourself. No more wild clubbing," he suggested, opening the door for him.

Jeff glanced around confused, but as soon as he got the chance to make a clean getaway, he grabbed the money and ran from the apartment, slamming the door behind him.

As they were alone, Edward collapsed on the floor as his strength left him. He raised his eyes to Sabrina and understood his work was far from being done. She was terrorized, and it would take some time for her to recover.

He hurried to untie her and remove the gag from her mouth.

"Sabrina..." he whispered softly as he held her tightly.

They fell on the floor, crying desperately to release the stress. Scared and relieved at the same time, they remained hugged for some long minutes before the sobs subsided, and the warmth of each other's bodies offered a safe feeling that everything would be fine.

She blew a broken exhale. As she was in front of her friend, their eyes met, and their lips touched. Finally, they both understood where they belonged.

For him, that kiss was a confirmation that he was fond of her in a more profound way than the one allowed by simple friendship.

His hands slowly reached the hem of her shirt, pulling it gently up to touch her skin. Uncertain movements guided them into their passion to discover their bodies. As the fear faded away and their newfound feelings to be explored, they stood from the floor and looked into each other's eyes. Her cheeks blushed, and grabbing her shirt, she hid her face against his chest, inhaling the fragrance of his cologne. Edward took her in his arms with a sudden movement and walked to the bedroom. In the semi-darkness of the room, he gently lowered her to the bed and lay beside her. There wasn't any need to rush anything, so they spent a long time kissing and caressing each other, slowly undressing their bodies to find that intimate contact that would have soothed and healed their wounds. Under the sheets of the bed, they held each other, unable to speak any different language than the one between their souls exchanged through their lips and the touch of their hands.

"Don't leave me alone," she whispered.

"Never..." Edward breathed in her ear as cold shivers skated along his spine. The chat with his father had arrived at the right time. "I'm not going to let you go for any reason in the world. I will stay by your side for the rest of my life—I want you to come with me and run the family business together. We can be a perfect match."

Sabrina glanced at him, frowning as the corner of her mouth trembled with fear, recalling what she went through with Jeff. That was an experience she wasn't eager to repeat for any reason in the world. But as she lost herself in his brown eyes, she was sure he would have taken care that nothing would happen to either of them. It wasn't an easy decision, and once it was made, there wouldn't be any coming back.

"I won't let anything like this happen again, I promise," he whispered, sensing the doubts grabbing Sabrina's heart.

She held herself to Edward. "The only place on Earth I wish to be is in your arms."

"Is this a yes?"

With a smile on her face, she nodded. "Yes."

Chapter 11

One year later

On a fair spring morning, Edward and Sabrina landed at JFK International Airport. They walked with fast-paced struts, wide grins on their faces. Some hectic months were waiting for them, as working full-time at Sherwood's Jewelry would have meant the beginning of their careers. Yet, they still had many uncertainties about how they would run it.

"It's a big responsibility to take over a business that has been running for more than two centuries. We'll have to build customers loyalty and broaden the clientele whenever possible," she considered as they reached the baggage claim.

Pursing his lips, he visually toured the familiar environment of the airport. "We won't be alone. Dad promised to supervise us for one year before retiring, and I'm more than sure he will keep an eye on us for the rest of his life. Not to forget that my grandfather is still alive, and he will be of great guidance too."

Edward chuckled, grabbing Sabrina's hand tightly in his.

She had never imagined moving to another continent and going to live at the home of possible in-laws, at least until they could find an apartment for themselves. She wondered how she should behave and if and how that cohabitation would affect her relationship with Edward.

"So, what kind of people are your mother and father? I never met them in person, and I wish to give a good impression." She adjusted her hair, tightening her face. She knew it would be critical and make the difference between a peaceful period or hell on earth.

"Do you worry about living with my parents? I understand it might be awkward for you, but I assure you that they are amazing people, and they will love you as much as I do," Edward tried to reassure her. "I promise you that it won't be for a long time and that by next Tuesday, one way or another we will move. Does this make you feel better?" he asked, as the belt started to deliver the first suitcases.

A smile appeared on her face, but she kept her attention away from him. Silence fell upon them as they moved away from the baggage claim. "I don't want to force anything, and I don't even know how to explain the feelings I am having now. I am happy to meet your parents and grateful for their offer to share their apartment with us. On the other hand..."

"Hey, you don't have to explain anything. I understand, and if I were in your place, I would feel the same. Everything will be fine, I promise."

***

"Here, they come!" Josephine yelped excitedly. "Eddy!" She called, waving her hand.

As Edward saw his mother, his eyes brightened, and tears of joy welled, overwhelming his quiet demeanor.

"Mom, Dad!" He ran to hug them.

Sabrina had a half-smile, wondering what she was supposed to do or how to behave with them, watching as they held each other, sharing happy giggles and laughs. She feared she didn't belong in that scene and wished to be somewhere else.

Josephine glanced at her, sensing her discomfort. "You must be Sabrina," she said with a broad smile, reaching to hug her.

She wasn't expecting to be hugged, and that confidence level was a bit awkward to her. At home, she would have shaken her hand with a general, *How do you do, Mrs. Sherwood?*

Yet, Josephine held Sabrina tightly to herself like she was her own daughter.

"Our son talked so much about you—it's like I've known you forever. How was your trip? Are you tired?" In her enthusiastic way of wanting to know everything simultaneously, Sabrina felt bombed with her questions.

She blushed until her cheeks turned a glowing red, matching the color of her hair. "Thank you, Mrs. Sherwood. I had a pleasant flight. How do you do?"

Herman reached her too. She looked far better than he remembered from the picture Edward had sent him. "Josephine has quite the exuberant temperament—you will get used to her. Welcome to the family, Sabrina."

They shook hands, and slowly Sabrina's body relaxed. "When he spoke about home, he talked about the family business most of the time. I'm pleased to meet you and honored to work in a renowned jewelry shop like yours."

Her voice trembled, and she lowered her glance to her feet. *I wish the floor would open wide and swallow me into nothingness.*

He smiled and placed a hand on her shoulder, "You don't need to be embarrassed or shy. We will not share only the working space—we will be family, and I want you to feel at home. Please call me Herman rather than Mr. Sherwood."

She swallowed hard. "Thank you… Herman, I appreciate your friendliness. I admit being a bit too shy, and I would like to avoid sounding rude out of my introverted nature."

"Nonsense!" Josephine shook her head. "You haven't been rude at all, and we certainly understand your feelings, being so far from home in a foreign environment, surrounded by people you've never met before. We will have plenty of time to get familiar."

"But now, let's move on. I have no idea about you guys, but I'm starting to get hungry," Edward said, glancing at his watch.

***

As predicted by Herman and Josephine, it took only a few days for Sabrina to feel completely at ease with them, and when the next Tuesday she and Edward left to go living on their own, for her it was like moving away from home, again.

A few weeks passed and things progressed steadily for the new couple.

Sabrina and her undisputed talent as a goldsmith had led Edward to think about increasing the services offered by Sherwood's Jewelry. So, when the owner of the adjacent textile shop decided to retire and put the place on sale, Edward bought it and organized a laboratory for her, so as to offer their customers the opportunity to have unique, custom-made jewelry.

****

Life and business went on as smoothly as always. The case of the death of Mr. Milton seemed to be archived as nobody heard from Detective Lindström anymore.

Yet, one day, as Edward was going through the items stored in the safe, he saw a little jewel box hidden in a dark corner at the back.

"You might have forgotten an old purchase," he said as if he was talking to his father. He stretched his arm and grabbed it, curious to understand what kind of treasure was secluded in that little chest. The small child inside his soul was still searching for the loot of some pirate.

He walked to the desk and opened it.

The smile on his face suddenly disappeared.

Just as he had seen it years before, laid on a cloud of dark velvet, the unforgettable shine of the largest pearl he had ever seen seemed to light up the room.

"The *Silent Rainbow*…"

His heart stopped for an endless fraction of a second, short enough to be harmless but long enough to choke the breath in his throat.

Edward placed the box on the desk, unable to take his eyes off its magnificent rainbow-like shine.

Then we will have the pearl back…

Those words resounded once again in his mind. "We have it back indeed, but how?"

Shaking his head and refusing to jump to conclusions without first asking his father, he walked to the shop. There, Herman had agreed to help while he was going through the inventory.

He peeked from the door as his father spoke with a customer who would purchase one of the pieces on display.

His movements were as charming as his smile. The tone of his voice was steady and friendly.

Edward almost forgot why he wanted to talk to him. With a happy expression on his face, the customer left, and the pearl returned to his mind. He paced to the desk, determined to have an answer to all the questions that started to populate his soul.

"Oh, I didn't hear you coming." He greeted. "How is it going in the backroom? Did you find anything interesting?"

A mocking shade colored the tone of Herman's voice as if he had expected his son to find the pearl and come to question him about it.

Edward narrowed his eyes, trying to decipher his father's behavior. "I have found something fascinating, something that shouldn't be in this shop at all."

The slight accusations of his son left Herman unimpressed.

"Why was the pearl you sold to Mr. Milton inside the safe, hidden in a far corner? How did you get it?" his tone started to resemble the one Herman would have chastised his son with.

With a nod, he walked away from the desk and paced toward the room where Sabrina was working. Edward followed him, wondering what he had in mind.

"Sabrina, I need to have a talk with my son. Could you please watch over the shop?" He asked quietly.

She raised her glance from a bracelet she was working on and stood from the chair with a slight nod. "Sure, is he in trouble?" She chuckled as a severe expression plastered on Herman's face.

"I'm afraid this time I'm the one in trouble, but let's not make it dramatic," he replied, guiding her to the shop.

Edward and Sabrina exchanged a fast glance without saying a word. Sabrina had never seen her boyfriend with such a darkened expression and wondered what could have made him furious.

Edward's nostrils were flared, and the corner of his mouth twitched nervously. It meant that he was close to exploding and was doing all he could to keep himself from shouting.

He walked to the desk, where the little jewel box rested and glared at his father. "Now, you must explain why the pearl mysteriously disappeared after Mr. Milton's death is in our shop. I'm sure there isn't a clear story behind it."

"Well, you're wrong. And I'm going to explain you why."

Herman sat down on the couch and invited his son to do the same. As they were both comfortably seated, he started to recall the events.

"One day, you asked me what would have happened if the curse were real, and something would have happened to Mr. Milton. Do you remember?" Herman questioned, being more than confident that his son did.

"Yes, I do, and to be honest, I've been thinking about it ever since," he answered. "You told me in that case, we would have the pearl back. That answer shocked me so much so that I've never stopped thinking about it"

Herman glanced at the clock and strolled to the cabinet where he stored the whiskey he offered to their best customers.

"A few days after the accident, a young man appeared in this shop, introducing himself as Robert Milton, the eldest son of Jason Milton. What they inherited from their father was mostly debts they would not have been able to pay." He poured some whiskey into two glasses and walked back to the couch, offering one to Edward.

"According to his story, a generous life insurance policy could have saved every member of their family. The investigation cast doubts on the dynamics of the accident, so the insurance refused to pay until they received a report from the police."

Herman sipped the whiskey, closing his eyes to recollect his memories.

"The pearl was the only chance to solve everything. If it disappeared as if it had been stolen, the detectives would have followed the murder lead instead of ruling the death a suicide. For this reason, Robert asked me to unofficially buy the pearl, no receipt, and no proof."

Edward's mouth opened at the story—he couldn't believe what his father had told him. "So, you repurchased it? But if you paid in cash..."

"The price wasn't high. I purchased the pearl back for all I could gather: five-thousand dollars in cash, plus another five-thousand dollars' worth of gold."

Edward gasped, "You sold it for half a million!"

"Yes, but I knew I could not spend much more without having the money recorded. Had half a million disappeared from my account at the same time when the pearl got lost, it would have raised suspicions. Particularly because the police have started to ask questions here, too." He tried to justify himself.

"The police suspected you? I can't believe it!"

"It didn't last more than a couple of days, and I came out free and clear. If they checked my accounts and found a withdrawal of half a million with no justification, I would have been in bigger trouble, along with Mr. Milton Junior."

He took a sip of his whiskey—he thought he needed it.

"What's your plan, then? You cannot sell it either. The pearl is supposed to be stolen..."

"You underestimate your old man, and you forget there is another member of our family who is still unofficially active in the dealing of cursed stones: your grandfather. This is why you still need our guidance in this kind of business. You need to learn our network and how it works." Herman placed the empty glass on the table in front of him. He resumed his position on the couch with slow movements and looked at his son.

"The pearl has to be placed back in the market, but we need to wait for some time. I'm handing the pearl to one of our trusted external contractors. He will sell it a few times to muddy the trail. Finally, it will reappear at an auction somewhere, and I will earn the profit."

A long pause of silence was all Edward needed to reconsider everything—he finished sipping his whiskey and got more comfortable on the couch. He contemplated the whole situation, rolling his glass through his fingers.

He raised his eyes to his father. "Sabrina should never be aware of this, but perhaps it's time you finally introduce me to all your business connections and contractor's networks. We're not talking about keeping a shop, we're at the boundary of legality. If those boundaries need to be broken, then I need to know everything involved."

"You are like your grandfather," Herman said as a bitter smirk appeared on his face.

"Have you ever considered repurchasing it? Why not maximize profit?"

He sighed, "Never try to get too greedy."

Chapter 12

For the rest of the day, as Edward continued with the inventory, Herman couldn't think about anything else than the conversation with his son.

Edward had always been as fearless and curious as Samuel, who had tended to push that business side a little further with every deal. His actions had often crossed the boundaries of morality as well as legality, and sometimes Herman had feared his father had ruined the family business's reputation. Nevertheless, his charm and ability had always allowed him to come out unscathed and with no criminal record from every situation.

***

It was almost lunchtime, and alone in the backroom, Edward took the pearl in his hands. "You're not going to our inventory, my friend. There is a better place waiting for you, unfortunately, it's not this…" He kept a low tone as he spoke to it.

He remained for some time admiring the beauty of that product of nature, turning it on his fingers. "Regardless of the bloody history of items like this, some people are ready to pay half a million to own them. Human desires are the biggest mystery, and I'm going to profit on them."

"Wow!" Sabrina said as she came closer. "That is the largest pearl I have ever seen!"

Startled by her voice, he turned to her and had no idea what he should have said.

"Y-Yes, my father acquired it recently, but it has already been booked. He will bring it with him this evening," he mumbled, trying to find a fast excuse to have it soon far from their sight.

"May I take a look at it?" she reached out her hand to observe it from closer.

He smiled hesitatingly, *she might become suspicious if I deny her the chance to hold it.*

With an uncertain movement, he handed her the tiny jewel box.

Sabrina walked close to the window to have a better look at it. "I have never seen anything like this," she mumbled. "Its iridescence makes it look almost alive."

She turned to look at Edward. "How much did the customer pay for it? I guess it was a six-figure sum..."

"We don't know yet," Herman chimed in as he entered the backroom. "I'm going to bring it to an auction house, but it might take some time before it goes on sale."

Edward wondered why his father left the shop. Then, glancing at the clock, he realized it was already time for lunch.

With a nod, Sabrina placed the pearl back on the desk, still keeping an eye on it. "He told me it was already booked. I thought you had a customer who had purchased it."

Herman chuckled. "Defining an item *booked* means that we will not put it on sale in the store, but that it will be given to an auction house."

She nodded, apparently satisfied with the explanation.

"I'm bringing it with me this evening, as tomorrow I'm meeting with my representatives who will bring it to an auction house in Hong Kong," Herman said. "They will take the pearl and wait for the next available auction. This it's the best way to maximize profit."

Herman picked up the jewel box and carefully placed it in one of his pockets, then started to leave. As he was almost at the back door, he turned to look at his son.

"Edward, tonight, after closing, Grandpa and I would like to talk to you. We believe the time has come for you to know our collaborators and our representatives abroad," Herman declared. Without waiting for any reply, he left the shop and headed for the corner cafe.

"I guess we also should go to eat—what do you say?" he asked.

"Sure," she said hesitatingly. "Give me some time to close up the laboratory, then we can leave."

***

In the evening, after Sabrina left the shop to head home, Edward closed the doors and retired to the back room with his father and grandfather.

"Good to see the whole family reunited once again," Samuel commenced as they were all seated in front of each other. "As my son explained to me on the phone today, you found the pearl before he could figure out a way to tell you what's behind the trade in cursed stones. Of course, once again, it's my turn to step in."

"Dad, this isn't the time..." Herman protested.

Raising a hand solemnly glaring at his son, he took back the speech. "This is exactly the time and the reason why you called me to fix your mistakes."

Turning his eyes to look at Edward, he continued. "I hope you haven't forgotten what I taught you about this side of the business. This is a gray area where legality blends with illegality, and morality fades. We're not a charity organization, but not necessarily we pursue this business because of the money. Most of the time, we follow the path of the cursed items for the thrill, the excitement, and the spell they exert to us all. However, now I need to hear your reason from your mouth, in full honesty."

Edward nodded, "I have to admit that since I moved to London and began to take a psychology course, my interest in curses increased." Searching for something in his pockets, he produced the old charm his grandfather gave him when he was still a teenager. "We feel more self-confident, brave and act in a more considerate way when we have a lucky charm. Likewise, our brain can be negatively triggered when we possess something considered cursed. You're right, Grandpa, we don't do this for the mere sake of money—this goes far deeper...."

A satisfied grin appeared on Samuel's face, "That's the way a Sherwood talks, but you also need to understand that this is a lonely road. Although Sabrina showed interest in cursed items and works here, she should never know about our dealing details, I hope you understand."

The room's silence became grave. The ticking of the pendulum clock felt heavier, filling every corner with its steady sound.

"I am ready. Tell me everything I should know about it." Edward stood up and slowly paced the room to focus on his thoughts within the turmoil in his soul.

During the next three hours, Samuel and Herman explained to Edward the *modus operandi* with which they managed the trading in cursed stones, a method that each previous owner of the business had helped to create, by updating and refining it.

They revealed every name, connection, and duty of their cooperators, unfolding an intricate worldwide network.

"How could it be so that despite being here almost every day since I was a kid, I never had any suspicion of what was going on?" Edward needed to understand how his father and grandfather had created and maintained that multi-national team. As he glanced at the list of cooperators, he realized he wasn't inheriting a jeweler shop. He would inherit a complex organization that needed more skills and coordination than he could ever imagine.

"I guess I was good at hiding, but you will have to be better than me because Sabrina will always be

133

working close by. I will organize a meeting with the rest of the team, so you can have the chance to know them all." Herman smirked, "I will make some calls and let you know the date within a couple of days. We may need to go to Hong Kong."

Edward nodded, still staring at the list on the computer screen, "I will have to ask Sabrina to take care of the shop. Hopefully, there won't be any urgent jobs for the laboratory."

***

As he walked the streets to reach home, Edward mentally reviewed the whole evening and the knowledge he'd gained about the business. There wasn't any difference between him and those who had helped make the business the way it was. His morbid interest in curses, all the questions that had swirled in his mind since childhood found explanations and answers in his roots.

With a smile on his face, the doubts he had had about his life faded away like the morning mist. From that moment on, he would follow his own instincts.

***

Sabrina didn't know when Edward would return, so she decided to wait for him and maybe order something once he got home. *I'm not the best chef in the world, and neither is this household, to be honest,* she had thought.

When she came out of the bathroom after taking a shower, the click of the door opening startled her.

"Did I scare you?" Edward wondered, with an amused chuckle, closing the door behind him. "You look like you saw a burglar coming in."

"I just wasn't expecting you back so early," she explained.

He took off his coat and gently placed it on the hook beside the door. With a smile on his face, he scrutinized Sabrina and walked closer, placing his hands on her hips, "But I see you were ready for me to return."

"I'm always waiting for you, baby," she purred with a cunning tone in her voice. He was hungry, but the chance of spending the evening enjoying each other in bed was the best idea he could come up with.

The bathrobe dropped to the floor, and they held each other tenderly, releasing all the tension of a long day. He wanted to forget everything and stop thinking about what would happen in the following weeks. All he wanted was to enjoy the touch of Sabrina's naked body.

His hands ran to her butt, squeezing it and pulling her closer as if to touch her body through the clothes he was still wearing.

As their lips parted, Sabrina's breath grew shallow. "How about going to bed?" he whispered as he unbuckled the belt of his trousers.

They walked to the bedroom, leaving a trail of clothes behind them. As they lay down completely

135

naked, the warmth of their bodies flowing between them felt like a stream of electricity. The intensity of those sensations overwhelmed him, and when the climax had consumed his soul as fire consumes a match, he whispered "I promise no one will hurt you. Never again."

Caught in her own orgasm, she didn't pay attention to those words—she simply held herself tightly to his chest as if to avoid falling into an endless abyss.

They parted and locked their eyes on each other.

"Why did you promise nobody would hurt me?" she asked him.

"I will never stop feeling guilty about what happened back in London, and I would do anything, even give my own life, to save yours." He was dead serious, and his eyes stared steadily at her.

"I have no idea why, but the picture Jeff sent me appeared like a flash before my eyes. I can't describe what I felt as I opened that message. Everything collapsed in front of me. The terror that grabbed me and the fear of losing you dropped me into the deepest pit of despair."

"I might get too emotional sometimes. Having you in my arms means happiness to me, and nothing else matters when we're together."

She blushed, lowering her gaze to look at his hands, gently caressing her legs. She lay down, adjusting her head on his chest, soothed by his heartbeat. There wasn't any other place she'd rather be, and even her hunger seemed to disappear when he was with her.

The silence between them became their world, and their thoughts became loud enough to be heard.

"I might need to go on a trip to Hong Kong soon," Edward said, breaking the silence.

Sabrina raised her brows. "Are you going there with your father to decide when auction off the pearl?" She would have loved to create a piece of jewelry out of that magnificent natural wonder.

"No, I'm just meeting our representatives," Edward replied and sat up on the bed. "We had a video meeting with them, and we agreed to meet in person."

"I wish I could meet them, too, but I'm so busy at the laboratory. We have constant requests for customized creations."

"Besides, someone has to remain and take care of the shop during my absence. We're a team, and each of us has a job to do." He held Sabrina's hand gently. "I hope you don't feel left out for having to work in the laboratory rather than the shop."

"Of course not," Sabrina assured with a giggle.

To be honest, she had never felt so appreciated as she was at Sherwood's Jewelers. She wasn't sure if she would ever consider herself a part of the family, but for any other member it was undoubtedly so.

Herman treated him like his own daughter, and Josephine spoiled her lavishly.

137

She tightened her grip on Edward's hand, and without the need for anything else, she felt complete.

Chapter 13

Two years had passed, and Herman finally retired. It also marked the mourning for the loss of Samuel.

The day of the funeral was something that would have remained forever impressed in Edward's mind. It wasn't the first person he'd lost in his life, but his grandfather was, after his parents and Sabrina, the closest person he had. His death gave him the impression that something inside his soul died too—a connection with the only person who could understand his attraction to the origin and meaning of curses.

He remained in front of the closed coffin of the last person that had incarnated the quintessential Sherwood's Jewelers for a long time, looking at it through his sight blurred by tears. From that moment on, the business would be passed completely in his hands. The fear took hold of him as he wondered if he was prepared enough, skilled enough, or up to the task of carrying the tradition of the Sherwoods, dealers in cursed gemstones. "How will I be sure if I'm growing the business the way it was supposed to?" He whispered.

He turned at the touch of a hand gently reaching his shoulder and saw his father smiling at him. "You will do just fine. That is the magic of this shop. Everyone who takes over is entitled to shape it the way they prefer. You have a white canvas where to write a new chapter," Herman said.

"I miss him so much," Edward replied softly.

"We all miss him. He's been a pillar in this business, as well as for you and for me. We had our divergences and arguments, but I loved him very much. This world won't be the same without him," Herman replied.

Edward nodded silently and thought about the responsibility now left on his shoulders. Their tradition would have reached an end with Samuel if he hadn't decided to carry it forward.

With the time passing by, this detail stopped worrying him. He wasn't even thinking about what would happen within thirty or forty years.

***

It was a cold evening in February, and the shop was ready to close. The late shoppers for Valentine's Day gifts reached him, fulfilling the maximum number of orders for Sabrina's creations. He glanced around, satisfied. Then his telephone started to ring.

He recognized the caller ID of Mikhail, the Russian associate who used to arrange for Edward's security when traveling abroad. He was also the closest cooperator providing crucial information about new items for sale.

With a smile, he grabbed the phone and answered, "Hello, I wasn't expecting a call from you. Any news?"

"I sent you an email about an interesting item. It's a ruby: *'The Burma's Eye.'* As you already know, its history runs back to 1251 when the crown prince of

Burma, Uzana, obtained it for his coronation. However, Uzana's careless behavior and disinterest in ruling the kingdom left the task of governing to his chief minister. The king was accidentally killed in May 1256 while hunting elephants. Some rumors said it wasn't an accident, but those are speculations. What is true is that the ruby mysteriously disappeared, to reappear a few centuries after in the hands of a British explorer, who reportedly died of an unknown disease on his return to Britain. The list of those who possessed it and were killed in unclear circumstances gets longer." Mikhail wasn't the kind of person who wasted time with small talk or pleasantries. He was always getting straight to the point, sounding almost rude. After all, he was not paid to entertain in small talk.

"I haven't had the time to check it, but since you called, give me some information. When and where will the auction take place?"

"It will be in Moscow, three weeks from now. Either you participate or give me the procure to be there in your name. I wanted to make sure you knew about it with a due advance," he replied.

Edward grabbed his calendar from the drawer and flipped the pages, "Hmm... It doesn't seem like I have any urgent matters—I can book the time to attend."

"I might suggest you take precautions for your safety, too. My sources informed me of other people interested in the same ruby. I am afraid they won't give up easily. If they can't outbid you, they might be ready to bury you." His voice was calm like he was simply talking about the previous weekend. The fact that someone could make an attempt on his life wasn't anything new. He was getting used to dealing with such threats with the necessary cold blood. "The name *Kozar* probably doesn't ring a bell to you, but they are one of the most feared Bratva[1] in Russia. If you prefer to try and win it at any cost, I can arrange the bodyguarding service."

"I see," mumbled Edward, thinking about the best way to provide safety for himself and for Sabrina during his absence. "Then you should join me at the auction to watch my back. I would like to have you there personally."

"Wouldn't you prefer to have a backup from the moment you leave your house to the time you return?" Mikhail suggested. "I would recommend you take this threat seriously. I can make sure that nothing will happen to you or anyone you love but don't underestimate the Kozars."

Edward considered Mikhail's words.

"I would be grateful if you could organize it for me because I won't come back without the ruby." He clenched his fist, unwilling to give up on something that might have produced a significant income. "I haven't seen the pictures, but I'm sure any gemstones with a past like that should be something exceptional."

"As far as I'm concerned, I've never seen anything like it in my life," Mikhail commented. "But now, I

---

[1] Criminal organization.

will leave you as I get to work." Without waiting for an answer, he abruptly hung up.

Inhaling slowly, Edward closed his eyes, "I don't think I'll ever understand him. But one thing for sure is I can trust him with my life, and that's the important part."

He finished writing the dates on his calendar. As the closing time arrived, he began his routine to close the shop for the night. In his mind, he reviewed the conversation he had with Mikhail. "I'm not eager to meet a threat to my family or me, but I would like more information about those Kozars," he mumbled as he switched off the lights and locked the doors.

"Are you talking to yourself?" Sabrina asked, appearing from the back room. "I heard you muttering something, and I wondered whether you had a lousy day or there was something more serious bothering you."

At the sound of Sabrina's voice, he Jolted and turned himself to her. "You scared me!" he cried. Then, when his heart returned to a regular beat, he smiled.

"You seem pretty nervous. Any bad news?" She walked toward him, helping to switch off display lights and lowering the security gate.

"No, nothing like that. I received a call from one of my associates informing me about an auction in Moscow three weeks from now. According to what he said, there will be, a ruby for sale that has left more dead than a serial killer behind it, to use his own words: the *Burma's Eye*."

A giggle escaped her mouth, "I would like to see that one, for once."

"I have some pictures of it. Mikhail sent me the information about the item and the auction to look at it together. But now, I want to leave this shop and focus on more pleasant issues."

"How long will you be away?" Sabrina wondered. With Edward abroad she would have to take care of the shop rather than working in the laboratory, thus lengthening the wait of the customers who wanted a custom jewel.

"I won't be gone for more than three days. The auction is on a Friday, so I might leave on Wednesday evening, then return between Saturday and Sunday. You will have to cover for me here. If you're too busy, I can still close the shop for a couple of days. We won't go bankrupt over such a small detail."

She nodded, "I thought that within three weeks, the laboratory's peak period would be over. I could spend some time taking care of the shop. What will be difficult is being away from you." She held Edward's hand tighter in her own.

***

That evening, they decided to eat out at a restaurant to reserve the time at home to go through the email Mikhail had sent him. Looking through the pictures of the ruby on the website when they got home, Edward understood why the local mafia was interested in it.

"Something with those dimensions, depth in color, and perfection won't go for under 250k," she gasped, as the starting price seemed to be astronomical.

"We'll see. With a bit of luck, I might be able to get the stone for a good price," he pointed out. "Nevertheless, for how high it will be, remember there is also the historical value, not to mention the curse. With my father and grandfather, I learned that the retail price of jewelry can become highly inflated when a gruesome story piques the interest of the potential buyers."

"And we both know that's true." Sabrina chuckled as she stood from her seat.

It was impressive that some people were ready to pay even twice the retail price for an item whose story is based on legends. "I hope things won't get as nasty as they did with Jeff. In his case, it was only a matter of seventy pounds. Think about if someone spent one million to discover the curse exists, then they can't get rid of it...." She shivered, recalling what a person in a moment of despair might be capable of.

"I once asked my father that." He brought a clenched fist to his mouth as his stare remained glued on the screen. Drawing a deep breath, he turned his eyes to her, "He assured me when dealing with substantial sums, clients have a clear understanding of the risks they're taking. According to him, he couldn't recall any time his family was threatened. There isn't anything else to do but book the flight and hotel room. Then I'll have to inform Mikhail about my schedule," he added.

"What does this Mikhail actually do?" she sat on the couch on the other side of the room.

Edward turned the chair in his direction and crossed his legs. "He's a sort of fixer, but mostly he takes care of my safety."

"Why would you need a bodyguard? You're going to an auction, not a war zone—that's far from being a dangerous situation."

With a loud yawn, stretching his body, he reached her on the couch. "In case I win that ruby, I don't want to take any chances of being robbed."

He crossed his arms around her shoulders. "I would never forgive myself for leaving you alone. Besides, I would like to live longer and see what life has in store for us."

The ringing of a phone interrupted what was about to become an intense moment between them. Edward walked to the desk with a feral growl, determined to shut down the device for the rest of the night.

His angry expression changed suddenly as he realized the person calling him was his father. He looked back at Sabrina, "It's Dad. This won't take long, I promise."

Sabrina shook her head and smiled, "Say hi to him for me." She walked out of the room.

"Hi, Dad."

"Hello, I hope I'm not interrupting anything." Herman greeted.

"N-No, we were actually taking a look at a ruby for auction in Moscow," he replied.

"That's why I wanted to talk to you. Will you go yourself, or will Mikhail procure it?"

"I'm going myself. Mikhail is going to take care of security. We spoke on the phone this evening, right after he sent me the link to the auction. He was not convinced about my decision. According to his sources, there might be others who don't appreciate being outbid," Edward explained, unwilling to reveal every detail of what Mikhail told him.

Herman grunted in disappointment. "Are you certain you need to attend? Mikhail can be trusted to retrieve the ruby and more so when he questions your safety."

Herman knew Mikhail was not a person who joked around. Whenever he said something, he meant it. If he said there was a good reason for Edward to remain home and allow him to take care of the auction, it was only for the sake of protecting him.

Edward started to pace the room nervously, "Do you think I should listen to his suggestion and avoid going? Has this ever happened to you?" He wanted to know whether there was something else he could arrange besides having the security services offered by Mikhail.

"To be honest, no," Herman admitted.

"Well, when I informed Mikhail about my decision, he didn't object, nor did he try to persuade me to change my plan."

"You know him— he would never try to overrule his employer. His job isn't to change your plans—it's to suggest the best solution. Whether you follow his suggestions or not, that will be up to you. He trusts you as an adult dealing with dangerous business." Herman interrupted.

"I'll think about it. For now, I'm going to Moscow, and he will take care of the security on site. I might call him one more time to obtain more details about the people he mentioned." His heart pumped furiously in his chest. He gasped for air.

"Is everything fine?" Herman asked.

"Yes, I'm nervous, but I'll do my best to keep myself safe." He tried to smile at a situation that started to feel awkward.

"I trust you completely. If you decide to take part in the auction, you can be sure to have my full support."

"Thanks, Dad—I appreciate your concern. I need to get back to enjoying the rest of the evening, or whatever's left of it." Edward glanced at the clock, grimacing as it was already late. He had to go to sleep soon to be efficient at the shop the day after.

As he ended the call with his father, he placed the phone on the desk and raised his hands to cover his face. He had no idea what he was supposed to do. For him, it was more a question of principle.

Likewise, for all the other cursed stones, he needed to have that ruby personally.

"Why haven't you told me about the risks of your trip to Moscow?" Sabrina asked, having listened to that conversation.

He turned to her, biting his lower lip.

"No! I know what you think when you bite your lower lip," warned Sabrina. "You're trying to find an excuse to make me feel better. Now I want the truth because I think I fucking deserve it!"

He could barely recognize Sabrina in that angry woman standing before him, with her arms crossed on her chest and with a hardened expression in his eyes.

"I won't lie, but the situation isn't clear to my father not to me," he began. Then, he told her about Mikhail's warning about the possible risk to his life.

"I didn't want to worry you. I'm not going to lie, but the situation isn't even clear to my father or me."

Edward explained the call with Mikhail, including the warning about the possible risk to his life.

"The reason I'm not sure about what I'm supposed to do is that I can't get a clear idea of the situation. I wish I could tell you more about the risks, but I don't know much about them either."

He walked toward Sabrina, hoping to prove he didn't mean to hide anything—instead, he wanted to know for sure what was involved.

Sabrina exhaled, and her facial features relaxed, melting into the tender expression she always reserved for him. "It would have been better if you had told me everything, uncertainties included. We could have discussed a possible solution." She placed her hands on Edward's hips and lowered her gaze.

"I don't want you to risk your life for the sake of a ruby. It's not worth it. We can find other cursed stones, but if they kill you, you won't return from the grave. I will lose you forever, and I won't be able to forgive you for leaving me alone."

A knot formed in his stomach. "You're right, and I'm sorry. I'll try to consider every aspect, and I promise to share it with you as soon as I have any news from Mikhail. Then we can decide together."

Edward raised his hand to Sabrina's chin and lifted her face to meet his eyes, "You have no idea how much I love you," he whispered.

Chapter 14

The next morning, as often happens, the threat posed by the Kozars didn't seem as dangerous as the evening before in Edward and Sabrina's eyes. Nevertheless, they decided to ask Mikhail for more information.

They reached the jewelry one hour in advance and Edward called him through the speakerphone so that Sabrina could also listen and, possibly, ask questions.

"I have been thinking carefully about your warnings. Do you think there are good reasons for me to step out of this auction and let you handle the bidding?"

"What I meant to say was that that family is not like regular dealers in gemstones. They have a powerful network around the globe, something you cannot even imagine." Mikhail explained, "My advice was to make things easier, certainly not to discourage you. We can set up full safety for you for as long as you're in the Russian territory. You can arrange your own bodyguard for your flight and arrival back in the States. That might be enough."

Edward nodded in silence and glanced at Sabrina, who appeared more concerned than necessary.

"As I mentioned already," Mikhail continued. "If you win the ruby, they may take it personally and either attempt to get it from you illegally or from your dead body."

"I'm ready to give it up for a reasonable price. I'm a businessman, I'm not going to acquire it for my personal collection. If they're searching for an item, I'm more than happy to negotiate."

Edward leaned in the chair in front of his desk. He glanced at Sabrina and nodded to assure her the situation would have been under control from the moment he would step out of the apartment.

A light, nervous smile was the only answer he received from her. Her fingers intertwined, twisting each other, and her creased forehead was all he needed to understand how uncomfortable she felt about this journey.

She didn't dare stop him because she knew how vital the auction was, not only for him but for the shop.

Since they met back in London, there was nothing more in Edward's mind besides returning home and excelling in business. He reached out for her hands and held them in his own, trying to reassure his lover that everything would go smoothly.

"I will arrange for my bodyguards here in the States, with one of them traveling on my plane. I will put you two in contact, so you can coordinate your actions without killing each other."

Unexpectedly, a chuckle came from Mikhail's mouth. "I wouldn't like to be responsible for the death of one of your men. Please send me his contact information—I will stay in touch with him."

Arching his eyebrow, he knew Mikhail wouldn't have any remorse in a kill—he was the perfect killing machine. For this reason, there couldn't be anyone better to ensure his safety.

"Then we're all set. See you three weeks from now in Moscow," Edward said to reach an agreement and end the phone call.

"Sure, I will be there. See you."

Edward placed the phone back on the desk. With a long exhale, he glanced at Sabrina, "Everything will be fine. Nothing is going to happen there. I'm afraid Mikhail is so absorbed in the task of searching for threats that he sees them everywhere."

Sabrina swallowed all her doubts and forced a smile. "I hope so." She stood up from the chair to return to the laboratory and continue working on the orders they'd received.

Three weeks later

Moscow, Russia

When Edward reached the Sotheby's at the Romanov Dvor Business Center, the narrow street where the entrance was located gave the impression that there wouldn't be an easy escape if he needed one. "Don't you worry, Sir, I will be waiting for you here with the engine on," reassured Steve, his bodyguard.

153

Without replying, Edward left the car and glanced at the building. As if to grasp his last hope, he closed his eyes and drew in a deep breath. Edward entered the building and followed the directory to reach the saleroom.

The bodyguards who managed the security for his visit remained at appropriate distances. They kept an eye on those present, positioning themselves strategically to deter any assault attempt.

The hall immediately attracted attention to its elegance. The modern design played games with the old remnants of a distant past, like a brat mocking his elderly grandfather.

Edward inspected the lots that had been slated for auction. Besides the ruby, a couple of other stones caught his interest. He tried to appear unimpressed and browsed past them quickly.

Recalling Mikhail's warnings, he glanced around and found the men he heard about seated not far from him. They were a couple of men dressed in business suits. As they exchanged pleasantries and jokes, they didn't look as dangerous as Mikhail had depicted. Yet, he remembered how appearances can be deceiving, particularly in foreign countries.

I guess even the worst criminal has friends and family who consider him an amiable person. But if we asked the opinion of those who do business with him, I suppose their opinion would be diametrically opposite.

He earnestly hoped Mikhail and his team knew what they were doing.

Finally, the broker arrived, and the auction began. The first item was a beautiful painting depicting an autumn landscape by a famous Russian artist.

Edward felt like he should have known better about those kinds of items.

The painting quickly reached such a high price that he would have never paid.

Then, finally, the ruby arrived for bidding.

By his experiences and what his father taught him, he had to wait until only one bidder was left. Meanwhile, he could use the time to study his opponents and understand what limit they had in mind. The last offer was about twenty thousand dollars.

I can get far more than that. With a swift move, he raised his hand to make his bid.

Immediately, he felt the glances of the whole hall on himself, but he tried to keep his eyes on the broker.

Out the corner of his eye, he observed his opponents. The stares they sent him were far from friendly. They took their chances, but they finally relented as the price reached one hundred and twenty thousand dollars.

Edward scrutinized them through narrowed eyes, wondering why they stopped at such a ridiculous price. They seemed to have enough wealth to push until reaching the limit he placed for himself, which was a quarter of a million.

He stood up without looking at anyone else, keeping his eyes on the door, intending to pay, collect his
155

ruby, and leave the country immediately. His plane would leave within six hours. Still, he felt like he needed to be at the airport right away. His luggage was already in the car waiting for him outside the building.

"Are you leaving so early?" said a voice with a strong Russian accent behind him after he paid and retrieved the ruby. His heart stopped for a fraction of a second—it felt like someone punched him in his guts.

He drew a deep breath and, with a plastered smile, turned slowly in the direction of the voice. The two men Mikhail had warned him about were walking toward him like cheetahs approaching their prey.

"I have a plane to catch, and generally, I'm a busy person," he replied calmly.

"You see, we have a problem. The ruby was not supposed to be purchased by you, as it was mistakenly placed for auction." The older of the two men, dressed in a dark suit, and blond hair, spoke slowly, as if there wasn't any hurry, with the certainty that a man like Edward would have been impressed. The younger man kept his eyes steady on Edward, ready to jump to action.

"I see," Edward said, amused. "Is there any way I can help you with your problem? I'm a reasonable person. For the right price, I could offer it back to you."

The two men glanced at each other, amused. They certainly didn't look like they had contemplated the option of purchasing it back.

156

Well, too bad. I'm not going to give up a deal, and I don't give a shit how badly they want it. Obviously not enough to pay for it.

"And what price would you consider appropriate?" The man sneered.

"Half a million would be quite reasonable, although my client would have paid more."

The expression of the older man turned to stone at the amount. The other on the right pushed away his blazer, revealing a Baikal-442 pistol. "I'd say better you keep your life, and we keep the ruby. How much is your life worth?"

Edward flinched, wondering how they could have gotten their pistols through the metal and body scan at the entrance. Then he saw Mikhail and Aleksey coming from a dark corner, pointing their guns to the heads of the two gentlemen. "We might ask you the same question." Mikhail grinned, hoping for the chance to pull the trigger of his PB pistol.

"Sir, I believe your driver is expecting you outside," Mikhail said to Edward.

He didn't need any other chance and ran to the exit. He didn't even care to know how Mikhail could smuggle the guns inside the building, but he was grateful for that.

Steve, the bodyguard who accompanied him from New York, waited for him with the engine on, and as soon as the door closed, the car peeled away with the sound of screeching tires.

"I have to guess it was an interesting auction." Steve grinned, relaxing as they were on their way to the airport.

"You can say so. For a moment, I thought it was my last day. Mikhail literally saved the day." His heart started to beat furiously as he realized that he wasn't far from becoming history.

He thought about Sabrina. Despite the perfect timing and careful organization of his security, he promised himself that if Mikhail had ever advised him to participate in an auction on his behalf, he would have listened to his suggestion.

As soon as he reached the terminal's safety, he grabbed his phone. There was still plenty of time until departure. The relief of still being alive overwhelmed him.

Allowing himself to regain his composure before calling Sabrina, he drew a long exhale. He knew she would have been scared as hell had she heard his voice so shaken.

***

Sabrina was working on a bracelet and didn't realize it was already time to open the shop. During Edward's absence, she had decided to work at the laboratory in the morning and keep the shop open in the afternoon.

The telephone ringing startled her, and she almost dropped the bracelet she held. Amused by her sensitivity, she grabbed the phone. A smile appeared on her face as she recognized Edward's caller ID.

"Hello, handsome."

"Hello there, baby! How are you doing? Are you already at lunch?" Edward asked, calculating the time difference.

"I had completely forgotten about it. It's almost time to open," she replied.

"I'm at the airport now, and I'm not alone. I have a blood-red friend in my pockets that cost me $120,000."

Thinking about it, he felt proud of himself for having beaten those thugs who intended to have the ruby without paying.

He didn't want to reveal any details of the auction yet. He wanted to face her when he recounted the facts as they were. For the moment, all she needed to know was that he was safe and sound, and he succeeded in acquiring the ruby.

"That's fantastic news! The price is quite high, but I believe that either the story or encasing it in a piece of jewelry will raise the value above what you spent," she suggested.

"I'm not sure I want to enclose it in a piece of jewelry. I'm thinking of trying to sell it based on the story," Edward explained as he went to sit down at a bench. Steve followed him from a distance—he wanted to have an excellent visual of the whole environment.

Sabrina went to open the door of the shop. She lit up the display windows and checked that everything looked pretty. "By the way, when are we supposed to change the arrangement of the merchandise displayed in the windows?" she asked.

A grimace appeared on his face at the realization of having forgotten that detail. *If I can't recall, that means it was too long ago.*

"Would you take care of it?" he begged with a lamenting tone in his voice. He was ashamed of forgetting.

"I'll do it tomorrow afternoon. I guess you won't need me to pick you up from the airport if Steve is going to be with you?"

He peered at the bodyguard with a satisfied smile. "No, there's no need for you to come, better if you focus on the window and wait for me. I can't remember what time I will be there, but I'll call as soon as the plane lands."

He was only away for a couple of days, but they felt like an eternity. He missed the smells and the feeling of home, but most of all, he longed for the presence of Sabrina.

"Oh, a couple of customers are approaching the shop," Sabrina interrupted, "See you tomorrow!" she greeted him, before interrupting the call.

Edward remained looking at his phone as if he could see their home through it. *But will I ever be safe?*

He raised his hand to the inner pocket of his jacket, where the ruby was stored.

Is anybody safe? Who is going to be the next victim of the curse?

With a grin, Edward began to walk around and look at the shop windows in the terminal. Since nobody is ever safe and everyone is subjected to their own fate, good or bad luck, he decided to simply accept its unpredictability and try to find some peace.

When you can't influence your destiny, the best thing to do is enjoy what you have now without overthinking about what life can bring.

He reached the window of a jewelry store and curiously inspected how the items were arranged. As his eyes browsed the displays, a couple of wedding rings caught his attention, and he paused for a moment.

A smile appeared on his face as he wondered whether it would have been the right time for him to propose to Sabrina. They had been living together for long enough to understand they were made for each other.

After everything we've been through, there's no doubt that this is our destiny.

He walked inside the shop without hesitation, determined to buy an engagement ring. Excited to see his fiancée's reaction, Edward boarded the plane.

Chapter 15

The plane landed at JFK the following day, and, within moments of switching on his phone, it started to ring.

Business never sleeps, Edward grinned, amused.

"Sherwood," he replied.

"I was making sure you reached your destination safely," Mikhail said without greetings.

"Yes, the flight went smoothly. I wanted to thank you for your assistance at the auction. I'm impressed with how precisely you organized the security. Without your help, I would have been dead."

"That's why you pay me, and it has been a pleasure doing business with you. Whenever you need my services, you know where to find me. However, you better get rid of that ruby. Those people won't stop until they get it back, one way or another. Believe me, you don't want to discover which way they're going to use." Mikhail warned Edward that although he stopped them at the auction, he could not protect him forever.

"So, I need to quickly find a buyer. What happens to them afterward will not depend on me. After all, the legend may be true, and any misfortune will be attributed to it." Edward chuckled.

"The threat posed by the Kozars is real, but you might be right—there must be a foundation of truth in every legend. People do not invent stories from anything. Anyway, curse or not, I wanted to warn you about the risks and make sure you were fully aware of them to act accordingly."

Edward gritted his teeth and started to figure out how to market the ruby, targeting those who would be intrigued by it. He needed someone ready to spend money. Not to buy a stone, but for the experience of such a crazy ride with death itself.

"I will take care of myself while searching a buyer for it. Meanwhile, I will keep it far away from the eyes of the general public. This isn't an item just anyone can purchase. I need to find the right person," he explained. "I need to ask you one question: how was it possible for you to bring the pistol inside the venue and how the Kozars could. I thought there were stricter rules about gun control than in the US."

A smile appeared on Mikhail's face, "I have a registered bodyguarding business, so I am allowed to bring guns with me when I'm on duty. Concerning the Kozars, organized crime in a corrupted system can also achieve the impossible. That was the reason why I suggested in the first place not to take part in the auction personally."

A long pause allowed Edward to reconsider his future moves and give up the chance to participate in any of the forthcoming auctions.

"Well, let me know when or whether you need me." With those words, Mikhail ended the call.

"Any bad news?" Steve asked as he arrived with their luggage.

"When Mikhail calls, there are always problems. Nevertheless, they were of the kind I was expecting. Sounds like those people at the auction might not give up so easily," he replied, placing his phone in his coat's pocket.

The driver arrived to pick them up from the airport. With his mind focused on Sabrina, Edward leaned in the back seat and closed his eyes, smiling.

***

She stared at the new displays in the window with a satisfied sigh. "Well, now it looks pretty," she uttered to herself as she gazed from outside on the sidewalk. "I would definitely stop if I were to pass by here, and perhaps I might even come inside to have a look."

She glanced at the clock and wondered whether Edward had already reached home. Sabrina hadn't heard anything from him, regardless of his promise. Without even thinking about it, she decided to give him a call.

***

The telephone ringing startled Edward. He realized that he had fallen asleep on the couch immediately once he reached home.

Growling and cursing to find the phone, he finally answered, "Hello!?"

"Good morning to you. By the tone of your voice, I must have woken you up." She giggled, amused.

"Yeah, I might have underestimated the jet lag. I wanted to call you as soon as I arrived home, but I'm afraid I collapsed on the couch," he explained as he sat up.

"No problem, I was taking care of the window displays. I figured something similar must have happened. How was the flight?"

Edward walked to the window, amazed at the night scenery in front of his eyes. "Everything went well, as usual. It was a red-eye flight, so it was easy. Are you close by?"

Turning around, he considered refreshing himself under the shower before her arrival. He walked to the bedroom to get clean clothes.

"I will be there in half an hour—I just left the shop."

"See you soon then," he replied.

Many thoughts were swirling in his mind, and the steaming hot water was exactly what he needed to line them up.

He pondered on the phone call with Mikhail. Undoubtedly, the Kozars still posed a threat, and they would probably try to track him down to have the ruby back. He had to find an acquirer as soon as possible, and once he sold it, he should spread the news.

"The whole world has to know that Edward Sherwood is no longer in possession of the cursed stone. If they must hunt down someone, let it be someone else."

It probably wasn't the kindest thing to do, but he needed to protect himself first. *Besides, whoever gets the ruby will be completely aware of the curse, so if one day they find the Russian mob knocking at their door, they'll know who to blame.*

Coming from the bathroom, he searched for the stone, and under the light of the chandelier of the living room, he started to admire the ruby. The stone was simply stunning. For those dimensions, he felt lucky to have purchased it for only 120k. "It's certainly not as big as the Black Prince's Ruby, but the fine cut, deep dark red, and its luster are enough to tell the story."

It wasn't impossible to believe the reason behind the curse was nothing but envy and jealousy. "The same that put my name on the Russian mob's blacklist," he said, turning the stone in his fingers to appreciate the perfection of its reflections.

Sabrina entered the apartment and smiled at the sight of her boyfriend, carefully observing the new gem.

"I can't wait to see it myself," she considered as she took off her coat, placing it on the hanger beside the door.

Edward dragged his gaze away from the stone. He placed it on the table, and with a broad smile, he approached what he considered his most precious treasure on Earth. "I've missed you so much! Even an hour away from you is like an eternity."

"You have no idea how lonely my nights were," Sabrina purred, holding him tightly. "I want to know all the details about how you got it."

They parted and walked to the table where the ruby lay. "I believe most of the people at the auction feared the Kozars. You should have seen their stares when I raised my hand to outbid them. Without me, they would have had the stone for twenty thousand."

He sighed, knowing the most challenging part of the story had arrived, explaining the need to sell the ruby away without mentioning the possibility of being a target.

"As the broker slammed the hammer on the table, I hurried to get the ruby. I wanted to pay for it and disappear from Mother Russia," he explained, avoiding the gaze from Sabrina's questioning eyes. "As soon as I got the stone, the two men approached, and ordered me to hand it over."" His voice became uncertain as he spoke about this part and turned his eyes to follow every move she made. "Fortunately, things turned out okay, thanks to Mikhail and Aleksey who managed the situation impeccably. So, while they were keeping the two men at bay, I ran away and reached out to Steve, who was waiting for me outside with the car."

"Those people can still be a threat, you know?" she warned, hoping he was aware of some detail that could reassure her. Unfortunately, Edward wasn't.

"Then, we need to sell the stone. I don't want to have it here or even in a bank vault. This ruby could curse my life," he replied in an apologetic tone of voice.

Silence fell between them. It was like they were preparing for a funeral, although nobody had been killed. Not yet at least.

Sabrina held his hand in her own and tried to smile, "Let's not allow a simple thought to put us down. Nothing's happened so far, and tomorrow we can search for the right buyer. Why don't you contact customers you know might be interested in it?"

Edward nodded, and as he recalled the engagement ring he'd bought at the airport, his expression opened into a bright smile. "You're right—we should be happy for having concluded a great deal. This ruby will bring us good luck," he tried to convince himself too. "However, I have something that will undoubtedly improve the mood of this evening."

He was not a romantic man—he had no idea how he was supposed to propose to her.

I'm sure this is wrong, but maybe spontaneous is more romantic than a drawn-out plan.

Almost holding her breath, she watched as he searched for something in his pockets. She was sure he had some sort of gift he'd bought in Russia. Her eyes opened wide when he opened a jewelry box, revealing a gold diamond ring.

She remained petrified, unable to understand what was going on until Edward knelt in front of her.

"Sabrina, you have been my best friend, my reason when I had none, my soul when I thought everything was lost, and my heart when I feel I'm losing it. Without you, my life has no meaning, and I would rather lose everything I have than you." His voice started to tremble as he kept his eyes steady on hers.

"Would you marry me?" Those words came out from his soul like a whisper, as if he said something forbidden and feared being heard.

She could not believe her ears and opened her mouth to say something, but words failed her. Instead, she started to giggle nervously.

"Of course, I'll marry you! There's no other man in this world I could consider spending my life with." She helped him to stand up from the floor. "You're clumsy, Mr. Scrooge. But when I look at you and see the way you look at me, it's like I can hear your heart speaking. I would never be able to refuse you and continue living my life without regretting such a stupid decision."

Without saying anything else, he held her hand and gently slipped the ring on her finger. "I remembered it right. The size is perfect," he said as Sabrina stared at it with an incredulous expression.

"I can't believe it!" Sabrina uttered and raised her gaze to Edward, hugging him tightly, like her life depended on it.

***

Starting from the following morning, he was busy contacting all the clients who were always looking for something unique.

Luck wasn't on his side, as none of those who answered his calls were interested now. Despite the quality and history, the gem wasn't able to attract their attention.

"I need to find a better way, something more persuasive than the beauty and the story behind it. I need a certain detail to convey their curiosity and turn it into a must-have." He continued scrolling through his list of customers.

As if the world was collapsing above him, he grabbed his head between his hands. He inhaled deeply, but calm was fading with every second that passed.

Looking around, he thought it might have been better to put aside the ruby and focus on other issues. When he arrived with Sabrina through the back door, he didn't have time to check out the new displays in the windows, so he decided to go out and look at the arrangement.

He remained open-mouthed at how lovely it looked. It reminded him of one of those old-fashioned candy shops, but instead of candies, there were their best pieces of jewelry. Spring was on its way, and the pastel colors of the drapes completed the decoration, giving the beholder the impression of being on a cloud, watching the Earth from above.

"This is one of the best arrangements I've seen here," a voice interrupted his thoughts.

Edward turned in its direction and recognized Mr. Sean Hopkins, one of his regular customers. He was usually there, searching for the right gift for his loved ones.

Money was never an issue. He arrived, chose an item he liked, paid without questioning the price, and left.

"Good morning, Mr. Hopkins." He greeted, shaking his hand. "Indeed, I was admiring it myself. Sabrina set it up over the weekend."

"I came because of the message you left on my voicemail. I've been busy and didn't have the time to answer the phone," he replied.

Edward's face brightened into a broad smile, knowing this was the best chance he would have to sell the ruby. He opened the door for Mr. Hopkins and guided him to the backroom.

"Please, have a seat. I'll ask Sabrina to take care of the shop while we're talking."

Without replying, Mr. Hopkins sat down and made himself comfortable, and after a few moments, Edward returned and walked to the safe.

"I was at a Sotheby's auction in Moscow last week. There I had the privilege to acquire one of the most beautiful stones I have ever seen, *The Burma's Eye.*" He walked to the armchair where Mr. Hopkins sat and gently opened the box that held an impressive gem.

"That is simply marvelous!" Mr. Hopkins gaped, taking the ruby in his hands.

With an elegant gesture, Edward handed him a loupe to appreciate its tiniest details.

With a light *"Thanks."* Mr. Hopkins took the loupe and inspected the stone. Edward knew he was already hooked by its beauty. He needed to play it smart and charming as his father had taught him.

Mr. Hopkins kept scrutinizing the ruby, murmuring something Edward could not understand. Then he placed the loupe on the table and the ruby back in the box. "It's a remarkable stone indeed. I did some quick research on it before coming here. If I believed in the paranormal, I would be running away from this shop, never to return. Yet you had it, and nothing has happened to you, nor to the people at Sotheby's. Therefore, I must deduce that the legend is merely the result of fantasy and that any misfortune that occurred to the previous owners was caused by the power of suggestion. I'm just wondering whether you're going to charge extra for it."

"I can understand your curiosity. As you guessed, its history does have a price. Similar stones are usually displayed in museums, which was also reflected in the starting price. I was surprised when the broker announced it."

Mr. Hopkins averted his gaze from Edward and pursed his lips. Although it wasn't his custom to bargain, he wondered if Edward was willing to negotiate.

"Hmm..." he muttered, leaning back on the couch and bringing his hand to his mouth, "What would be your price?" Mr. Hopkins asked after a long time lost in his thoughts.

"Considering everything, I was leaning towards four hundred thousand dollars," he replied, keeping his eyes steady on Mr. Hopkins.

"Oh! To be honest, that's more than I expected even if the stone is remarkable!" Mr. Hopkins exclaimed.

"This isn't a common ruby like the ones you can purchase encased in a piece of jewelry. This is a natural, untreated AAAA pigeon blood 23.4 ct. Burmese ruby. This is *The Burma's Eye*," Edward remarked, saying every word slowly. He knew that some rubies could be purchased for a bargain price. Still, what he offered was quite rare for its perfection, color, and clarity, to say nothing of its history. "More famous rubies were sold for millions."

"Yes," countered Mr. Hopkins, "but they belonged to countesses or maharajahs!"

"And so it did the one you held in your hands, which saw dynasties go through all sorts of calamities. If you believe in the curse, you might try your luck and give the stone to one of your enemies. Perhaps Burmese kings aren't as famous and fancy as other dignitaries, but they deserve an honorable mention, at least."

They both laughed heartily at the thought. "You're an entertainer and shrewd negotiator, but can we agree on a smaller price?" Mr. Hopkins asked as he recovered from his laughter.

"Because you're one of my best customers and I value your business, I can come down to three hundred thousand. Though that's my absolute bottom to still make a profit." He needed to consider the money he'd spent for the flights, the security detail, and the import fees.

Mr. Hopkins remained for a moment to think about it. Time seemed to have stopped, and Edward's hands began to dampen with sweat. Nevertheless, keeping a professional demeanor despite the hurricane in his soul was paramount. He absolutely needed to hide his feelings.

He thought about Sabrina and their engagement. That was a sort of consideration able to soothe the turmoil. With a calm smile on his face, he waited for an answer from Mr. Hopkins.

"Well, I think we can agree on the price." With a smile, Mr. Hopkins reached out, and Edward shook his hand.

"It's always a pleasure doing business with you. I hope this stone will bring joy and fortune to the lucky one who wears it." He stood up, ready to guide Mr. Hopkins to the shop where they could have finalized the sale.

"Hold on a second." Mr. Hopkins paused. "Can I have it enclosed in a ring? I think this kind of stone deserves more than a jewel box."

"In this case, we will need to talk to our goldsmith, Sabrina. She will suggest the best solution to enhance the beauty of your ruby."

They walked back to the shop, "Concerning the final price, we will give you a good discount. We want you to be completely satisfied with our service."

"This is why I continue to favor your shop. Besides the quality, you always know how to make a customer happy." Mr. Hopkins chuckled.

As he left, Edward felt like his knees were going to fail him.

"Is everything fine?" asked Sabrina.

"That was one of the most intense negotiations I've ever done," Edward explained, relieved that the mob wouldn't be searching for him anymore.

As the story goes, that ruby will come back home sooner or later.

Chapter 16

Edward bought advertising space in newspapers and websites to highlight the news of the sale of the *Eye of Burma*. In this way, he hoped that they would also reach the ears of those who, presumably, were after him, to divert their attention from himself and his family.

Although he hadn't mentioned the name of the buyer, in actual fact his move had added Mr. Hopkins to the list of victims of the curse, and Edward was left with nothing but a hope that no one would go after him.

I know it might not be fair, neglecting to warn Mr. Hopkins that the Russian mob is after the stone, but it's business, nothing personal.

He wasn't proud of his behavior but felt relieved at the knowledge that neither Sabrina nor he was in danger.

The telephone ringing brought him back to reality. "Sherwood," he answered.

"I noticed your way of putting an emphasis on the sale of the ruby. That's a smart move to protect yourself, but not the fairest." Mikhail still refused to engage in any pleasantries.

"Life isn't fair, my friend. We all need to take care of ourselves and the ones we love," he defended. "If I didn't have Sabrina by my side, I could have taken the risk and seen whether they could catch me. I'm a businessman—I don't purchase any jewels for my personal pleasure. That's a hobby I leave to my wealthy clients."

"It was a simple remark. I didn't mean anything by it," Mikhail replied, acknowledging the bitter tone in his voice.

With a deep breath, Edward nodded. "No harm done. You're not wrong—even if I'm not breaking any laws, my conduit might be morally flawed. But morality doesn't have any place in business. We're all cheating each other to get a better deal for ourselves."

"Anyway, I just called to warn you that if those gentlemen were still determined to get the stone back, you may still be in their crosshairs," Mikhail said. "You made sure the whole world knew you sold it, but if they won't trace the buyer back, they'd come to you. Ask your bodyguard to keep an eye out because these people are unpredictable."

"I've already organized protection for my family. Like I said, business isn't fair, and someone might get the idea of revenge. It happened once before, so I think I learned my lesson," he said.

"That's a good plan. Then there is nothing left to add. You know how to reach me, should you need my services in the future, if I'm still alive."

"I hope to find you well. Take care."

***

"Time to go home!" Edward cheered happily, entering the laboratory.

Sabrina raised her eyes, red and swollen, after a long workday. "Is it already closing time?" She stretched her back on the chair.

"Yes, and you should take care of your eyes. They need to rest from time to time." Slowly, he reached her cheek and caressed her soft skin.

"I know, but there is so much to do. I can't even think about going to the couch and closing my eyes for a moment."

They secured the jewelry in the safe, engaged the alarm, then left.

The days had started to get longer, and the evening temperatures were mild enough for them to consider abandoning their winter coats.

Edward inhaled deeply, "I love when spring returns. It's like the end of a nightmare when you wake up in the morning, and the darkness fades away."

Sabrina smiled and looked up at him. "That's a nice way of saying it. I love it too, but I like summer best."

"I was thinking we could hire someone to help you," Edward proposed. "It would be a great help even when I'm away at auctions, allowing us to keep open both the laboratory and the shop. Paying a salary wouldn't be a problem, and another employee could provide extra income. We should start seriously considering some candidates."

Edward was in a good mood. Despite the omnipresent threat posed by the Kozar family, having the ruby away from his shop relieved him. Of course, Steve and his associates still provided security. If something else happened, he could contact Mikhail for more support.

«I agree, it's a good idea, » Sabrina answered.

They continued to walk in silence. As it got dark the light of the streetlamps replaced that of the sun to light the streets. One after another, shops started closing, while bars and restaurants opened for the evening. It was Thursday, but the mild temperature had invited many people out.

Sabrina scrutinized her fiancé. An almost imperceptible flicker in his voice suggested there was something he was trying to hide. She wanted to find out whether it was related to his trip in Russia or something else.

«What's wrong? » Edward asked. «You're so silent...»

She stopped walking and turned to face him, "I was thinking..." she started. "Are you hiding something?" she asked. Then, taking a deep breath, she stared at him. "When you were talking before about hiring someone, I had the impression you were trying to hide something. I might be wrong, but I'd rather clear it up right now than let it boil inside my head."

I can't tell her everything, Edward thought. *For her own safety, she doesn't need to know all the details behind this business.*

He wanted to find a way to reveal something without giving the whole picture. "I'm not hiding anything, sweetheart. You know how complicated this business can be. Particularly with those cursed gems, there are always more details to be considered. The price is one of them. The retail value of the ruby was nowhere close to three hundred thousand—one hundred and twenty was probably too much. Nevertheless, I always need to find a way to market the stone to get the highest profit, and to obtain it, curses are the best value added."

"Don't you think it's unfair?" she doubted.

"The market rules aren't fair. I always make sure that whoever purchases the goods do not believe in curses. I push the price by placing emphasis on the actual history, not on the legend."

Sabrina nodded thoughtfully, keeping her eyes on the ground. "But there must be a boundary of ethics..."

"... And I'm not crossing it," he assured, finishing her sentence. "Babe, I'm not going to do anything illegal—I promise. There isn't any difference between my marketing strategies and the diner advertising the best burger in the city."

She giggled, amused at the comparison, but eventually, he got a point. Of all the 'best-burgers-in-town' restaurant ads, maybe none of them were good enough to earn that title.

Edward held her tightly as they entered their apartment. "Let's not talk about what is fair or not. I'm not a killer...yet." He laughed loudly at his joke.

"Then I think I can handle your mystery."

It wasn't easy for him to hide the darker secrets.

180

Some gemstones come back to us spontaneously, as in the case of Mr. Milton's pearl. Others need a little help, but this is a detail I must keep hidden. Not only from Sabrina but from my father as this was a secret between my grandfather and me.

Edward was convinced that the fewer Sabrina knew about the deal, the better it would be for everyone. Only a few people were aware of what was going on in the dark side of the jewels business, and they knew how to keep it secret.

Chapter 17

Several months passed, during which Edward and Sabrina were overwhelmed by work. Nevertheless, they decided to marry anyway. It was a simple ceremony, and they renounced the honeymoon, but they promised to make up once they hired more staff and, therefore, with more free time.

It was a warm day in July, and the shop had a few customers coming in to talk with Sabrina about custom-made jewelry.

Edward was checking online for the next available auction and the possibility to acquire new stones from his suppliers. This would take him away from the shop for more than a couple of days, so he would have to rely on Sabrina and the new goldsmith, Janice, they had hired.

The bells above the door jingled, and he raised his smiling face at the potential customer. "Good afternoon." He greeted with a charming expression.

The man with an NYPD badge hanging from his neck didn't reply immediately. He glanced around and walked to the desk. "Good afternoon. Is there any chance to have a chat with the owner of the shop?" He asked.

"You're talking to him. Allow me to introduce myself, Mr. Edward Sherwood."

"I think I owe you an apology, as I was sure to find Mr. Sherwood Sr. still running this business."

"My father retired years ago. I've since taken over as sole proprietor. What can I do for you, Mr....?"

"Detective Lindström, Lars Lindström. I met your father during an investigation into the death of Mr. Milton," Lars said

"I remember the accident. Such a terrible thing." He shook his head sadly.

Lars nodded in agreement, "Yes, it was unfortunate. But the case remains classified as unsolved, as it hasn't been clarified whether it was an accident or a murder. The most curious thing was how the pearl he had purchased from your father mysteriously disappeared after the crash."

"I remember that pearl. It was unique and extraordinary. There was a rumor that it was cursed. Maybe it wasn't all fantasy, who knows!" Edward sighed, with a bitter smile.

"I don't believe in curses," Lars grimaced.

"Neither do I, but you have to admit, there is always a foundation of truth in every legend." His expression tightened, "I don't believe you came here to argue about curses, did you?"

Lars chuckled, "Not at all. I came here regarding the accident that almost cost the life of Mr. Sean Hopkins. Have you heard about it?"

As his mouth opened in surprise, Edward tried to keep his emotions to himself, recalling Mikhail's warnings. "I haven't heard about it. What happened? When?"

"It was a week ago. He's still in the hospital, and his condition is critical. It seems the breaks of his car failed. After an accurate check of the car, it was confirmed there wasn't any sort of sabotage. The forensics described it as an unfortunate accident that could have happened to anyone."

Lars couldn't accuse anyone of what had happened to Mr. Hopkins. Yet, he couldn't help but wonder why two people who had bought supposedly cursed items from Sherwood Jewelers had both met tragic fates.

"You see, what makes me even more suspicious, is that, again, an item purchased from this store has mysteriously disappeared. Mr. Hopkins' wife also reported the missing of a ring where a ruby was encased." Lars tried to explain.

Edward did not like the detective's subtly accusing tone.

"Forgive me, but I don't know what's your point. The last time I saw the ring was the day I gave it to him," Edward replied, quietly.

Despite the apparent calm he had shown, the detective noticed how he paled and the trembling of his hands.

"One accident could be a coincidence," Lars pursued, staring into his eyes. "But two make me think of a pattern that leads directly back to this shop."

Edward shook his head and swallowed hard. "Are you suggesting that somehow, I am responsible for these accidents?"

"Of course not. I just want to find out why, in both cases, the technicians couldn't find any malfunction in the plane or the car. Lars insisted. "I'm also curious to understand what happened to the pearl of Mr. Milton and to the ruby of Mr. Hopkins."

"I see," he uttered, keeping his calm. "Any jewel or precious stone may have a gruesome history, but that doesn't mean they're cursed. The story is full of royals, nobles, warriors who had an object they kept dear; some of them fell into disgrace, others were killed. People are mortal, while the stones are eternal and pass from generation to generation, from owner to owner absorbing their dreams, hopes, love, but also hate, wickedness, revenge. So, for a collector owning one or more of them means to become part of history, a way to perpetuate their name and their feelings over the centuries. In the world there are many ancient jewels and stones, I don't need to kill anyone to satisfy the increasing demand."

He has no idea what he's talking about. Still, I'm afraid he's getting dangerously close to my activity, he thought. He couldn't wait for that nosy detective to leave his shop—he needed to talk to Mikhail and his father. Particularly the latter must have known something about Lars' morbid curiosity toward their activity.

Sensing Edward's discomfort and knowing there wasn't any lead to connect the shop and its owners

185

to the accidents, Lars relaxed his expression. "As I said, I'm not suggesting you or your father are responsible for any of those accidents. I'm trying to figure out the whole picture. Too many pieces don't fit, and I want to understand the reason why."

Lars glanced at him one more time—despite all the efforts to keep his calm demeanor, Mr. Sherwood's forehead glistened with sweat.

"I understand, and whenever I can be of any assistance, you know where to find me," Edward assured, placing his hands on the counter.

They remained looking at each other eyes for a few long moments. Each of them tried to understand the person they were facing.

Edward knew the presence of a detective around his business would bring nothing else but more problems, something he preferred to avoid at any cost.

Lars, for his part, hadn't expected having to deal with Herman's son, and from that first encounter, he didn't have a good impression of the young new owner. Something in the way he looked at him and his movement suggested he was hiding something darker.

Without averting his glance from Edward, the detective took a deep breath. "I appreciate your availability, and I hope with your cooperation we will reach the solution to this mystery. For the time being, I would be satisfied to find out caused Mr. Hopkins' accident and where the ruby is."

That said, without waiting for any answer from Edward, he turned his shoulders and walked away.

As soon as the door closed behind him, Edward grabbed his phone. Since there weren't any customers, the chat with his father couldn't be put off.

"What a surprise to hear you calling." Herman greeted happily.

His face relaxed as he heard his voice, but a storm was brewing in his soul. "Dad, I'm calling because something happened here," he commenced. "Do you remember the case of Mr. Milton?"

"I do remember. You were still in London and called me in the middle of the night," he replied.

"Do you also remember the detective that came to question you about it?" he pursued, trying to keep his voice steady.

There was a short pause of silence. "I could never forget that day. What does it have to do with you now?" Herman asked, with a note of concern in his voice.

"Well, he came today because he's investigating an accident that happened to my latest client. Mr. Hopkins was in a car crash recently. You remember I sold him the ruby?" He drew a long breath to recollect his thoughts and clenched his fist over the desk.

A couple stopped at the shop window, admiring a particular jewelry item. Edward remained watching in silence, holding his breath until they walked away.

"Mr. Hopkins isn't dead, but he's in critical condition at the hospital. The detective is investigating the causes of the incident and the mysterious disappearance of the ruby" he continued.

"According to the forensics, his breaks malfunctioned, but there wasn't any sign of sabotage. It seems Lindström wants to find a connection between this incident and the disappearance of the ruby and Mr. Milton's and his pearl. He came to the shop expecting to find you and was a bit surprised to find out you had retired and left the business to me. Now I'm afraid he's suspecting me of what happened to Mr. Hopkins," Edward finished.

"There's no need to be worried. Unless you caused the accident and stole the ruby, I can't see any reason for your rush. You see, this was the reason why I kept the dealing of cursed items in the background, favoring the main business. At times, we know that cursed items return back to our shop."

A long pause allowed Edward to reconsider his desire to pursue the path traced by the generations of Sherwood before him.

"By the way, how is it going with the laboratory?" Herman wanted to change the subject. Since he retired, he felt like the less he heard about cursed jewels, the better his life was.

"Everything's going great. The demand for custom-made jewelry increased, so we needed to hire another goldsmith, Janice. She finished goldsmithing school and was looking for an apprenticeship. It didn't take long to understand she had a lot of talent, so we hired her."

 Edward's voice relaxed as they changed the topic, "How is Mom doing? I called her last week—she seemed like not herself."

"She's doing fine. She's going through a stressful time, and that was all," Herman said. "She got excited about growing our own vegetables. I believe she got herself a bit too busy with something that was supposed to be only a hobby."

A hint of homesickness veiled Edward's face. Since they moved away to the island of Maui, he missed the presence of his family and seeing them only once a year wasn't enough to bring him the same happiness. "She should take care of herself. I'll call her soon and plan our next holiday to visit you."

"That would be fantastic—we're both missing you. And Josephine would love to see Sabrina again. She's fond of her, and I am too."

"I will let you know whenever we have something planned, and I'll keep you updated about any news that might come from this detective..."

Herman's voice flickered.

"Take care and let me know if there's anything I can do to help."

Chapter 18

As he hung up with his father, Edward wondered whether he should inform Mikhail about the investigations and ask how to handle the detective.

"I need to wait until this evening—now it would be too early," he said, considering the difference in time zone.

The emptiness in the shop was daunting, and never like at that moment, he had hoped someone would come in, even to browse at the items. The noise of the backroom door opening startled him, and he turned as if he were expecting to see a ghost.

He relaxed at the sight of Sabrina and Janice, "You almost scared me. Is it already time to close for lunch?"

"You get scared fairly easily, but yes, we came here to rescue you from overwork," Sabrina smirked as she walked to the front door to lock it.

"I was so caught up browsing the items at the next auction, I lost track of time," he explained, closing his computer, and starting the routine to engage the alarm.

"Besides a couple of customers, it was far too quiet in here," Janice observed, creasing her forehead.

"Days like this happen all the time. We generally get busier in the afternoons," Edward reassured her with a pat on her shoulders.

During lunch at a nearby restaurant, Sabrina and Janice talked about general issues. Edward's mind, instead, was focused on the detective's visit and the future of the shop. He had no intention of ceasing his most profitable trade and those thoughts prevented him from enjoying the meal and following the chatting of the two girls.

The last thing I need is a criminal record to disgrace my family. I can't be responsible for tarnishing the pristine reputation we've developed for over two hundred years, he thought.

***

"You have to tell me what's going on with you," Sabrina commenced that evening as they relaxed on the couch in each other's arms, watching some TV.

Edward pulled away slightly. "What do you mean?"

"Perhaps you hoped nobody would notice it, but I'm not anybody. I know you better than you wish, and I know when something is bothering you."

With a nervous move, he put his head between his hands. It was time to tell her the truth, "I had a visit today. A detective from the police department."

"Really? Is there something I should be worried about?"

"No, I don't think so. He's investigating the accidents that happened to two customers who purchased from us cursed items." Edward began to tell.

Sabrina was petrified. "What does our shop have to do with it?" she whispered, with a faint voice.

191

"I have no idea, perhaps he believes me or my father are behind those accidents to get back the gemstones."

Sabrina stood up, crossing her arms over her chest. "That's ridiculous!"

"That's exactly what I told him. Curses are nothing else than autosuggestion negatively affecting the behavior of people who believe in them." Edward reached her, tilting his head to the side. "Let's not think about this anymore. I'm sorry if I worried you. I shouldn't have allowed such nonsense to put me in a bad mood."

His hands reached her hips, hoping to relax and occupy the evening with more pleasant activities.

Holding her tightly to himself, he didn't think about curses, business, Mikhail, and especially Detective Lindström anymore. *Everything in its own time, and now we need to enjoy ourselves without interruptions.*

As their lips fused into a tender kiss to reach the place reserved only for themselves and their fantasies, life suddenly got easier.

***

A positive feeling welcomed Edward to the new day. The evening spent relaxing with Sabrina allowed him to regain confidence in the future. He turned to look at her.

Reaching her lips, he kissed her to bring her back from a faraway dreamland.

"Hmm... good morning...." She yawned, stretching her body. "I was resting so well..."

"I wish this could be our everyday life...." He stood from the bed, ready to go shower.

He was usually the first to use the bathroom. Sabrina preferred to sleep in, read the news on her phone, stretch out, and resist the sheets' comfort.

Walking through the living room after the shower, Edward noticed his phone blinking. He took it and saw that Mikhail had called him in the middle of the night and, since he hadn't answered, he had sent several messages asking him to call him urgently.

Although Sabrina was aware of the business and the dealings with Mikhail, Edward understood that, in that case, it would be better if she didn't listen to that conversation. Clearly, it was something extremely serious, so, for her own safety, it was better to keep her in the dark.

He decided to reply to the message and buy some time.

-I cannot call you right at this moment. I will go to the shop and find a way to be alone-

He glanced in the direction of the bathroom, where Sabrina was still indulging under the shower singing happily.

He jolted when his phone started ringing.

"Mikhail?" he answered, surprised.

"*Družíšče*[2], there's no time to waste. I didn't call you to ask you about the weather in New York," Mikhail sputtered.

Casting a last glance at the door, he stepped out on the balcony. "What is so important to call me during the night?" he kept a lower tone of voice, knowing they needed a certain level of confidentiality.

"If you're planning on going to Mumbai for the auction, I strongly suggest you not attend yourself. Let us handle the auction," He bluntly intoned.

Edward cringed. The memory of what had happened in Moscow was still vivid in his mind. He didn't want to repeat that experience. "What's the threat?"

"There will be a diamond I know you wanted to have back, '*The Morning Star*. If you're still interested in it, you will need to make sure it won't be under your name," Mikhail warned.

Edward took his time to reply, keeping an eye on the bathroom as Sabrina got out. Soon, they would be ready to go to the shop.

"What if someone else purchased it?"

"Then we will have to keep this person under surveillance. If you want it to return to your possession, that means keeping the secret for another few years before trying to sell it. Generally, four years is enough to avoid raising suspicions.

---

[2] Družíšče it's a Russian word for 'buddy'

However, the police are onto you, and you need to be more careful. This isn't a game."

"I need to go now—I'm not alone. I won't go to the auction, and I'll let you know my decision about the diamond." Without waiting for a reply, Edward hung up the conversation and returned inside.

"Were you on the phone?" Sabrina asked.

"Yes, it was my father. He called me yesterday evening when my phone was switched off, so I called him back."

With a slight nod and an expression he struggled to decipher, Sabrina went to the kitchen, trying to eat something fast.

The conversation with Mikhail had made his stomach churn, and having breakfast was out of the question. He was sure she had caught him in the lie and, soon enough, she would ask him about it.

***

"Next month, there will be an auction in Mumbai. But I'm not sure I will take part in it," he commenced, trying to break the silence between them as they walked to the shop.

"Hmm," she replied without turning to look at him.

"Is there anything wrong?"

Sabrina huffed and stopped, "Are you telling me the truth?"

It was easy to tell when something was boiling in her head—it was a question of minutes before she'd explode.

"W-What?"

She scratched the back of her head, "You know what I mean. That wasn't your father on the phone, was it?"

"It was Mikhail, and he suggested I not to go to the auction. Things might go wrong if I went." Displaying a contrite expression on his face, he went on, "I didn't mean to lie to you—I wanted you not to be scared because it's enough if only one of us is frightened as hell, and that is me."

"I'm not a child, and I don't need you to protect me!" she raised her hands mid-air.

As he was going to reply, Sabrina stopped him. "I know you promised to protect me back in London, but I believe you're overreacting. I need to know what's going on, or there won't be any room for us." She meant it. Despite the love between them, she was not going to condone lies.

"How am I supposed to believe you when you say you love me if everything that comes out of your mouth is lies? Love is trust, and now I demand the truth." She took a short pause to allow her words to sink in, to make sure he understood. Although it would have been painful, she was ready to walk away from his life and start a new one. Perhaps returning to London and opening a jewelry store of her own. Trouble was something she didn't need in her life.

Acknowledging Edward's confusion, she went on, "I know you've been lying to me for a while, and I need things straightened up before I decide to leave. So,

196

I'll ask you for the last time: what is going on?" Her facial features were toughened, and her fists clenched.

Edward looked at her open-mouthed, unable to reply or to think straight. He could lose everything, even his own life, but he could never accept losing her. Tears started welling up from the deepest part of his soul, and the blurred image of Sabrina was the only hope he could grasp.

He tried to swallow his tears and get a hold of himself. When he was sure he could speak without his voice trembling, he took a deep breath.

"We need to open the shop. We can talk there—it will be easier to explain the state of things." He grabbed her by the hand and hurried to the shop as the sun rose and the streets began to be busy.

Not a word was spoken during their trip. Silence filled the space between them until their morning routine was finally completed.

With nothing else in their way to distract them, he turned to Sabrina and nodded, "I'm going to tell you everything that is going on, and I'm sure you won't like most of it. But if you want to leave me, you should do it for the right reasons, not because I've been hiding things from you."

She didn't reply. She followed his words, already suspecting what he tried so hard to keep secret.

Edward averted his eyes from her. He wouldn't be able to look at her without feeling guilty. "Despite bending the business unethically, nothing we do is illegal. For centuries, my family has capitalized on the suggestibility of superstitious people, and they always made sure that the cursed stones sold returned to the shop, in any way."

She shook his head, "Did you family ever play an active role in their customers' misfortunes?"

"No, but they made sure that the customers or their heirs gave up the stone in a final attempt to cast the curse from their lives. I've been taught to keep an eye on customers who buy these particular stones, waiting for the right opportunity to buy them back at a fraction of the price they had paid me."

Telling the truth under the icy gaze of Sabrina made him uncomfortable. He was sure she would immediately go home to pack her things.

"What about you?" she uttered.

Closing his eyes, he reclined his head backward. "Yes, I've been even more active than my father."

"Did you try to kill Mr. Hopkins? I don't care whether indirectly or not—I want to know if you're involved in the accident that almost cost him his life. Have you been responsible for any other accidents in the past?" She gritted her teeth as if she tried to contain the beast of anger rising from her soul.

Edward's heart raced, and his breath got shallow. "I-I haven't tried to kill Mr. Hopkins, nor have I asked any of my associates to step in and kill him. What I suspect is that the Russian family I had the pleasure to meet in Moscow stepped in to get the ruby they believed belonged to them."

There was a long pause of silence—only the sounds of muffled traffic outside and the ticking of the clock on the wall could be heard. Being honest made him feel good, and even his heartbeat returned to normal. *There's only one thing worse than seeing her leave, and that's continuing to live a life of lies. I couldn't go on fearing the truth could get her out of my life at any moment.*

Sabrina glanced at the clock. "I'm going to go make sure Janice doesn't need any help."

With that cold explanation, she left, allowing him some time to think about what he'd done and how to fix the damage he'd caused.

Chapter 19

His eyes followed her, leaving the room feeling the same pain as if she was walking away from his life.

"I'm always struggling to keep you safe, as my grandfather and my father did before me with their loved ones." Edward tried to imagine the perfect words he could tell her.

Less than an hour had passed when the sound of the back door opening startled him. Sabrina approached him once again.

"I took some time to think about it carefully. There's only one thing I don't understand, why you didn't tell me about it earlier," she asked, her voice calm and steady.

"I was afraid that knowing it would put you in danger, or it would get you away from me. I was wrong, and you deserve to know what's going on. I'm sorry, but I know my apologies may not be enough."

She was unsure about what she was supposed to do. But looking at him, considering all the things they went through together, she understood.

"We have been in this together since the beginning. You shouldn't have even questioned whether I accepted." She shook her head and walked to the desk where he stood. "If we want to go on with this side of the business, we need to be together—you can't do everything on your own."

That was something for which he was not prepared. He was ready for an ultimatum, either his business of questionable morality or Sabrina, the love of his life. "Do you mean it? You're not asking me to quit dealing in curses?"

"No! Don't you remember what we did back in London? We both agreed to go on with the experiment because we found it fascinating." Sabrina leaned over the desk, getting closer to Edward's face. "There wasn't any profit out of that deal, but it allowed me to sense the potential of this business. Jeff was the cause of his own misfortune, but it was only a test."

He got even closer to her face, so close he could almost kiss her, feeling the breath on his lips. "I was afraid you got too scared and didn't want to have anything to do with this kind of business..."

She pulled him closer until their lips touched. "You might have misunderstood me," she whispered.

His breath grew ragged. There was nothing he wanted more than to grab her and have her right there.

With a quick kiss, Edward retreated and smirked, "We'll have time to talk about this issue more in the bedroom later this evening. In the meantime, I suggest you return to your laboratory and try thinking about something else."

Once alone in the shop, his eyes turned to look at the clock, showing 9:30 am. He closed his eyes and drew a long breath to calm his restless spirit.

The shop's front door chimed open, and Detective Lindström entered with a grave expression in his eyes. Edward's mood darkened immediately.

Despite this, he kept a smile plastered on his face, "Good morning, Detective."

"We'll see whether it's a good morning or not," he said with a spiteful tone in his voice.

"Excuse me?"

"Mr. Hopkins died yesterday, and this time was no accident. He was murdered, and we both know the first name that came to my mind," Lars explained.

"Then you're in the right place, but not for the reason you think," Edward commenced. "I had no reason to kill Mr. Hopkins. Instead, there are people willing to do anything to get the ruby I sold Mr. Hopkins. They even tried to kill me after the auction, in Moscow. But I couldn't imagine they were so determined to chase to whoever owned it."

Narrowing his eyes, Lars inspected him. "If you have any evidence of this, I ask you to follow me to the precinct to make a statement."

It was evident that Lars didn't like the younger Mr. Sherwood. His mocking expressions and the unnecessary sarcasm grated his nerves. If being annoying was a crime, he would have locked Edward behind bars for the rest of his life.

"Of course. I'll fetch my associate from the laboratory to watch over the shop. I hope I won't have to stay away much, we are overwhelmed by orders," he said, walking to the lab.

His heart started to pace faster. Although he had nothing to do with the death of Mr. Hopkins, he was worried about the possibility of having Detective Lindström investigating the fates of all of his previous clients.

Going more in-depth, it wouldn't be challenging to connect their unfortunate fates and the mysterious disappearance of the items I'd sold them. He hesitated for a moment in front of the door to the laboratory.

From there, he could hear the muffled sound of Sabrina and Janice's voices, the radio they kept on, and the buzzing of the instruments used in their craft.

Gathering his composure, he opened the door. "Sabrina, may I have a word with you for a second?"

She raised her stare from the pendant she was working on and placed it gently on the table. "Is there anything wrong?" A concerned expression forecasted the news waiting for her.

"I need to leave the shop for a while. I have some errands to take care of—could you cover for me?" He didn't want to mention that he was supposed to follow Detective Lindström for the murder of Mr. Hopkins in front of Janice.

"Sure," she replied, standing up from the chair. "I'll be back soon," she added, glancing at Janice.

"Mr. Hopkins was murdered yesterday. Detective Lindström came back to ask me questions. I told him about the Russians who were interested in the ruby,

203

and he asked me to go to the precinct to make a statement," he explained to her, as quickly as possible in the back room.

"Ok, then you'll tell me," she answered.

They didn't exchange a word for the entire journey. Edward had sensed a note of hostility in the detective's behavior, so he preferred to avoid any sort of comment.

I know he's doing his job trying to find who has murdered my customer, but at times it seems as if he wishes it was me. From this moment on, my actions should be more careful—he will keep an eye on me, he thought, looking at him out the corner of his eyes.

Once they arrived at the precinct, the detective made his way to a room and invited him to sit down.

As they sat down, Edward and Lars stared at each other, trying to guess each other's thoughts.

"Mr. Sherwood, tell me more about those people who may have killed Mr. Hopkins." Lars asked briefly.

"Before I reached Moscow for the auction, I was warned about the presence of some Russian mafia members. The security service I hired said they were interested in the same ruby I was there to buy." He took a short pause to recall the events, still shocked at how things worked out. "I outbid them and purchased the ruby for a hundred and twenty thousand, and I soon found myself face to face with their pistols. My bodyguards helped me reach the airport safely but advised me to sell the ruby quickly, as there was a chance I could still be a target."

Lars smirked, "It's like the plot of a spy movie."

"Instead, it's what happened—perhaps you could call the bodyguarding service I was using there—they'll tell you the same story. You could also ask my personal bodyguard who accompanied me to Moscow and back."

"Let me ask you a question, do you always feel so threatened?" Lars asked, surprised at the level of protection surrounding him.

A slight chuckle escaped him. "My business attracts enemies and thieves alike. I spend whatever amount is necessary to protect my life and that of my loved ones—money is not as important as family."

Edward searched for his phone and showed Mikhail's contact information to Lars, "This is the man who organized the bodyguard service in Moscow."

"Would you mind calling him now, so I can talk with him?" Lars asked.

Edward agreed. *There's nothing worse than having a stubborn detective digging in your past to justify an arrest.*

The phone rang at least five times before Mikhail answered.

"*Družíšče,* I wasn't expecting your call." A strong deep male voice replied from the speakers of the phone.

"Hello Misha, I have you on the speakerphone with a detective of the police department and…"

"You've been arrested?" interrupted Mikhail, laughing raucously. "What have you done?"

"It has to do with the ruby I have acquired at the auction in Moscow. Could you tell us about what happened on that occasion?" Edward's voice sounded calm, except for a slight flicker betraying his inner turmoil.

"When you almost got killed by the Kozar brothers?" He chuckled. "Well, Officer, if you're listening, the Kozars were after the ruby Mr. Sherwood won. I'm not aware of their reason, but you wouldn't like to find out if you knew the family. Despite my warnings not to participate in the auction, Mr. Sherwood took the risk. As he was going to leave the auction house, he had the pleasure to meet them." Mikhail took a deep breath. "My associates and I are trained for these situations, and we ensured his safety. Nevertheless, I suggested he sell the ruby quickly."

"So, how do you think they could have killed Mr. Hopkins, the new owner of the ruby?" Lars asked.

"Oh, there's the detective!" Mikhail exclaimed with a chuckle. "You suspected Mr. Sherwood? How far from the truth could you get? Never underestimate the connections and network of a bratva when they are after something or someone. That ruby was a question of honor, and they wanted it back at any cost."

"But the ruby wasn't in Mr. Hopkins' possession. It disappeared, and nobody knows where it is..." Lars mumbled, fearing this meant the possibility of other victims until they found the stone.

"I bet they killed Mr. Hopkins to get rid of a witness. Probably, the ruby is in their hands," Mikhail replied, his voice turning grave.

"Thank you, Mr.?" Lars questioned.

"Orlov, Mikhail Orlov." Mikhail rushed.

"Thanks, I don't have any other questions for the moment, have a nice day," Lars replied.

Without answering, Mikhail hung up the phone, leaving Lars confused and full of questions.

 "I will need all the information about this man. I need to check his background and credentials for the case." He was sure there was something more he was missing.

Without a second thought, Edward gave him Mikhail's business card. "This is all I have about him. You can start checking his credentials from the business he's running," Edward replied. "Is there anything else I can assist you with?"

Lars nodded. "No, not for the moment, Mr. Sherwood, thank you for your cooperation."

Edward stood from his chair, "I'll be available, but now I need to return to my store."

Chapter 20

Walking the streets, Edward called for a taxi to reach the shop. The precinct was far away, so walking was out of the question.

As he watched the blocks passing, a thousand thoughts swirled in his mind, wishing to talk to Mikhail right away. He hoped the bratva was satisfied with having regained the ruby and considered the case closed.

Without even looking at the taxi driver, he paid for the ride and walked into the shop, barely acknowledging anything around him.

Finally, he was in the only place that could give him an apparent safety, enough to subside his internal turmoil.

Sabrina's smile welcomed him, and he felt relieved to have a woman like her at his side, ready to support him no matter what.

"I thought I wouldn't see you before this evening. What was the problem?" She asked.

"The detective needed information about those I suppose are the killers. He asked me to call Mikhail to have more details about them and what happened in Moscow." Despite the good news, a dark shadow obscured Edward's face.

"Then why such a sullen expression?"

With a slight jolt of the head, "I was thinking about something else." He reached the desk and glanced around. "I need to call Mikhail."

Noticing the demurral veiling Sabrina's expression, he understood the need to reassure her. And with the promise of ensuring everyone's safety, he gently touched Sabrina's hand.

"You know perfectly this is a promise you can't keep, particularly when the situation is completely unpredictable," she warned, appreciating his care.

Gazing outside, he spotted a man walking in the direction of the shop. He stopped in front of the window, smiling as he admired some pieces of jewelry. Then, he entered the shop, keeping his eyes on a particular item in the window.

He was a young man in his late twenties, but it was evident by the way he dressed that money wasn't an issue when he went shopping.

Edward's expert gaze hadn't failed. As the man approached the desk, he noticed a diamond piercing in his ear, a large golden ring on his right hand, and the expensive watch on his wrist. It was apparent from the fast glance around that the man was looking for prey as he stepped into the shop.

This isn't a rabbit den—you entered the lion's cage, thought Edward.

"Good morning." Edward greeted him, taking his time to study the man in front of him.

"Good morning, I was passing by yesterday after closing time, and I couldn't avoid noticing a brooch you have in the window," the man explained.

"Of course, would you like to have a look at it?" Edward walked to the window to get it.

"Yes, although, I would like something slightly different," the young man said, following him.

"This is one of our creations, so we can customize it any way you prefer."

They walked to the counter, where Edward placed the brooch on a velvet cloth.

The young man took it in his hand and scrutinized it. He placed it back with an elegant gesture, keeping his eyes on it as if trying to find the words to say or consider the modifications he wanted.

"You see, this is going to be a gift for my girlfriend, and she's interested in the occult and all sorts of odd curiosities," he commenced.

Edward already knew where he wanted to reach. Nevertheless, at the moment, he had only a couple of stones of that kind, but they weren't fit to be mounted on that brooch.

With a deep breath, the man continued his explanation, "Your shop is known for selling items with, particularly gruesome histories. I was wondering whether you have something which could be fitted there."

The way he avoided speaking the word cursed gave the idea that either he believed in the existence of curses, or he considered the topic so ridiculous he preferred not to mention such a foolish possibility.

"Well, I do have a few items your girlfriend might be interested in, but it would be better to create something from scratch to encase it in a brooch or pendant," he elaborated, grabbing the phone. "Hold on, let me call my colleague to attend the shop."

The young man nodded charmingly and browsed around as he waited.

Sabrina arrived immediately. "Good morning," she greeted, then turned his glance at Edward, "Did you want to see me?"

"Yes, I need to show some of our stones to this gentleman. Would you please take care of the shop?"

They exchanged a brief smile as Edward guided his customer to the back room. He would be entertained with fine liquor and tales of the stones available.

"Please have a seat and make yourself comfortable. May I offer you anything to drink? A glass of sherry?" He tried to guess.

"No, thanks, I'm fine," the young man replied with a slight smile.

Without any further questions, Edward walked to the safe where he kept their most precious stones. He returned to sit in front of his customer with three jewel boxes, placing them on the table between them. He opened each one carefully.

211

"I have an aquamarine, a black diamond, and a sapphire. As you can see, their dimensions won't fit the brooch, aesthetically or physically.

The young man looked down at the items, "How do you know they're... cursed?" The last word was barely a hiss coming out of his mouth.

Edward's expression opened up into a smile, "Curses are nothing but legends with grains of truth. Each item has been traded between various museums and collectors. I don't believe in curses, but admittedly, the owners of these stones tended to meet tragic ends. Some of them lost their fortunes, others died in mysterious accidents, or they suddenly decided life was no longer worth living and committed suicide."

His hands entwined on his lap as he took a short pause to recall the stories. "Every stone comes with a certificate, listing the previous owners. But I want to make sure you aren't taking their dark histories too seriously."

The young man twisted his mouth—he didn't believe them, either. Still, the impossibility to definitely debunking the myth added a sense of unease to his thoughts reflected in the way his mouth twitched.

"So then, what about the price?" He wondered.

"Unlike the common gems we sell in the shop, the price of these isn't determined by the mere market rate, but many factors influence it. The uniqueness is one of these."

Taking the black diamond gently between his fingers, Edward raised it between their faces. "You won't be buying a stone that has been taken from a mine yesterday. You're acquiring a piece of history, a collectible item. It's quite rare to have a stone with a certified history, for which you can track its ownership back for centuries."

He took a short pause observing his customer. "This isn't the Black Orlov or the Taylor-Burton Diamond, either of which would sell for over a million dollars. Nevertheless, considering this is a natural 20-carat black diamond, adding the story behind it, I can't let it go for less than two hundred thousand dollars."

The young man remained open-mouthed and blanched. "I'd been reading about natural black diamonds priced around three to five thousand dollars per carat, but this is double the price," he whispered.

"Sir, are you feeling alright?" Edward asked, concerned.

"Yes… but I think now I should accept that drink you offered me before," the young man shook his head nervously.

Edward walked to the cabinet without reply, where he got the sherry bottle and a glass.

"I am certainly interested, and it is a beautiful stone," he mumbled as he took the glass. The smooth warmth and delicate aroma of the alcohol gave him a sense of relief as he sank into the armchair's soft leather. "I'm sure my girlfriend would be ecstatic at the gift, which is precisely the result I'm aiming for. What kind of sum are we talking about if I would like to have it encased into a brooch?" He placed the glass on the table and locked his gaze on Edward's eyes.

"This depends on the design, according to what you wish to spend besides the cost of the stone. I'm sure we can reach a compromise."

Generally, those customers who came to ask for a cursed stone were already aware of the price.

"I hope we can keep it below two hundred and ten thousand," he added shrewdly. "I have no intention to pay any more than that."

"And believe me, you won't. We will ensure you have the perfect gift for your girlfriend. To that end, I believe you should talk to Sabrina, our goldsmith who will design and craft the jewelry." He stood from the couch, ready to move to the shop and close the deal.

"Should I pay for everything now?" He asked.

"You can pay half of the amount now and the other half when you will come to get the jewel unless you prefer to have it delivered to your residence. In that case, we can ship it by courier at no additional cost once the final payment is received."

The young man averted his eyes from Edward and looked around.

With a calm movement, his hand reached out, "I think we have a deal."

They shook hands and walked back to the shop, where Sabrina was talking to a customer in front of one of the displays.

He gave her a brief glance and concluded the deal with his new customer. "So, Mr....."

With a light pat of his hand on his forehead, the young man chuckled, "Where are my manners? My name is Andrew, Andrew Langley."

"No harm done, Mr. Langley. It's quite uncommon to get introduced when going shopping. Our goldsmith is busy with a customer at the moment. I'm going to send her to you, so you can finalize the order together."

With those words, Edward walked to Sabrina. He considered the perfect timing as the man decided to leave before approaching them.

"Sabrina, Mr. Langley here is interested in creating a brooch for his girlfriend." He gently guided her to the counter, where Andrew was busy texting on his phone.

"Here we are, Mr. Langley. Let me introduce you to Mrs. Sabrina Sherwood. She will take care of the design and creation of the jewelry. Meanwhile, if you could kindly give me your credit card, we proceed to the payment of the first tranche."

Sabrina brought Mr. Langley to the back room, where they could discuss in private.

Edward continued his working day without thinking about Mr. Langley. He didn't expect to see him until he came back to pick up the brooch. He

215

wasn't even expecting to see him again until he returned to retrieve his purchase.

The arms of the old clock at the wall, perfectly synchronized with his wristwatch, changed moved with a sharp tick signing the end of the day. With a smile, Edward raised his glance to it, strolled toward the door, and began routine to close the shop after a working day. Walking to the laboratory, he peeked and saw Janice had already left. Sabrina was also standing from the chair, stretching her back.

"Are we ready to leave?" He asked.

"Never been more ready than I am now. I am so tired!" Sabrina whined. "Thank God it's Friday."

"Yep! I'm also exhausted, and I can't wait to be home, so let's hurry!" he pushed her outside the laboratory, engaging the alarm.

As they reached home, she didn't give him time to say a word. As the door closed behind them, she grabbed him and wrapped her arms around his neck. "I believe we have a matter to settle...." Their lips touched as their hands searched for contact with each other's skin.

A light moan escaped her mouth as Edward's hand slipped under her jeans, reaching her butt. "I'm all ears—why don't we bring this discussion to the meeting room?" He breathed, pushing her back into the bedroom.

It took a matter of seconds. As soon as they were naked under the sheets, nothing was more important than the sighs and moans they shared as they kept the discovery of hidden pleasures for as long as possible. Eternity would have been reachable if they believed in it hard enough, and time would have finally stopped, allowing them to enjoy each other's touch.

Life was easy as they lay cuddling. Not even the insistent ringing of the telephone or the fact that for that day they would skip dinner were able to distract them from staring into each other's eyes, losing themselves in each other's souls until sleep conquered them, providing relief from a long day.

The morning after, waking up after the sunrise felt like it had been years since their last free day. That week had been intense, and it was vital for them to spend some time together.

While Edward was watching Sabrina sleep, he realized that working together was not helping to keep them close, in fact, appeared to keep them apart.

I cannot afford to lose you, he thought.

His hand slowly reached her red hair, gently brushing a lock from her forehead. His vision blurred as tears streamed from his eyes, dropping like heavy rain on the sheet. No wealth, diamond, or excitement would have meant anything to him if she were not there.

Twitching her lips, Sabrina's eyes opened up, "Baby, why are you crying?"

Her words released the tension like a switch. "I don't want to lose you..." he whispered.

Sabrina sat on the bed. Edward had evidently reached his limit, so he held him in her arms, to let his anxiety flow away through the tears that kept falling down from his eyes.

It took more than half an hour before he could finally part and get a hold of his emotions. "I'm sorry. The intrusion of the police into my business has put some extra weight on my shoulders." He brought a hand to his forehead and sighed. "God knows I need a holiday."

Sabrina shook her head as her brows knitted, "I'm afraid a holiday wouldn't be of much help. You need to change the rhythm of your business, or you'll burn out." She collected her clothes to reach the bathroom.

As she was at the door, she turned to glance at him, still immersed in his thoughts, "You don't need to be alone in this. Remember, we're together, and we need to share the weight if we want to survive into our golden years."

With a slight nod, he raised his eyes to Sabrina, smiling gratefully, "I'm still wondering how my grandparents dealt with this. I might have underestimated the work involved and the level of commitment."

"Times were different, situations evolve and so your business will. We have a weekend to recharge, and I would like to spend it without thinking about our job."

218

After a shower, Edward's attention was caught by his phone, blinking with a missed call. He grabbed it, and as expected, it was from Mikhail. He thought he should call him, but he preferred to send a message.

It didn't take much time before his telephone started to ring.

"Good morning, *Družíšče*." Mikhail greeted.

"Good morning to you, or whatever time it's there. I saw you tried to call me, and I guess you wanted to know the outcome of the police interview."

"Yes, although we both know you have nothing to do with the murder, it's not a good thing to have the police investigating you."

"Concerning yesterday, I came out clean. As you just said, I had nothing to do with the murder, so that nosy detective can't find any evidence to charge me with it. Nevertheless, I will keep my eyes open." Edward sat on the couch, observing Sabrina going to the kitchen for a coffee.

Mikhail wasn't excited about the detective's interest, "We need to make them understand there isn't anything interesting in following you. One way or another." The last sentence being a muttering between gritted teeth.

"Personally, I would prefer to avoid any casualty. I have better things to do than thinking about Detective Lindström, and I also have a task for you, my friend. Yesterday, a customer arrived and purchased the *Night Star Diamond*. Now, whether this might seem business as usual, he didn't convince me. There was something in his questions and the way he behaved, which made a couple of bells ring."

Mikhail didn't reply—he waited to listen to the whole story. As Edward recalled the episode, the situation sounded even more suspicious. "Hmm," he hummed. "Send me every detail you can come up with, name, surname, address... everything. I will try to retrieve any kind of information to identify your customer. For the moment, I suggest you enjoy your weekend."

Turning around, Edward noticed Sabrina. She stood in front of him with her arms crossed over her chest, impatiently waiting for him to forget about work.

Blowing her a kiss, he hurried to conclude the phone call. As he hung up the phone, he stood from the couch and walked to hug her, determined to forget about everything and spend time only with his wife.

"Aren't you going to tell me who you were talking to and what was the topic?" she wondered, keeping a challenging tone in her voice. She didn't return his hug as if she were disappointed.

With a light chuckle, Edward kissed her forehead. "It was Mikhail—I think he's also suspicious of the last customer we had yesterday. I'm wondering whether he's an undercover cop."

Sabrina retracted her head, surprised, "Why would you think so?"

"Because he was too taken aback when I revealed the price for the stone. No serious client dressed like that would have flinched," he explained as he was going to get his jacket.

"Where are you going?" she wondered.

"We're going out for brunch, and we will try to have a pleasant and relaxing Saturday afternoon. Meanwhile, I'll finish telling you about the chat I had with Mikhail and some other questions that started to twirl in my mind."

They spent that afternoon exclusively enjoying themselves. However, he didn't know whether Sabrina could sense his distance from any activity they were engaging in together. As they reached the restaurant for dinner, he retired to the restroom, and as he was sure to be alone, he glanced at his image reflected in the mirror.

"Can't you forget the job at least for one day?" He asked the reflection. "I hope she didn't read my mind. But now, let's set it aside and enjoy her company."

Shaking his head, he left the restroom and glanced around the place they'd chosen for dinner. A broad smile brightened his face as he approached the table where she was busy picking something from the menu.

"Is there anything interesting?" He said, sitting down at the table.

Sabrina raised her glance from the list and smiled. "I think I will have to decide something random, as everything seems to be the best culinary experience in the world. But I would like to hear about what was on your mind all afternoon."

He closed his eyes and jerked his head to the side. "I know I wasn't supposed to think about anything work-related. Yet since that last customer left the shop yesterday evening, I can't stop thinking about him and what Mikhail will find out."

"Then you have to be patient and wait for his answer. Come on! There's no use in bothering your mind with something out of your control." Her face twisted with frustration.

The arrival of the server interrupted their chat. With a swift move, he went through the whole menu, and the first dish his eyes caught was the one he ordered with a glass of red wine.

"I know, and you're right, but despite all my efforts, I can't get my mind off him. What if, instead of being a regular customer, he is a cop undercover?"

"Then, you don't have anything to fear because you haven't killed Mr. Hopkins, nor you are the responsible for his death," she replied with an impatient huff.

"And what if instead, he's a spy of the Kozars sent to gather information about the people I care? What if they aim to kill you or me?" Edward whispered, glancing around, trying to spot any suspicious presence.

She grabbed his face and forced him to look into her eyes. "You're getting paranoid and acting like a maniac. Get a grip of yourself. Can you hear the nonsense you are saying?"

"I'm so sorry you're married to a man who's already married to his job."

Sabrina lowered her head to hide a laugh, "I know that—I think I can manage it better than another woman."

"Baby, one thing is for sure, I will never have anyone else but you. Besides, I would never have the time to date anyone else."

They both laughed, releasing the stress they'd both accumulated.

Chapter 21

Mikhail glanced at his wristwatch—it was already 10:30 pm. He stood from his computer and switched on the light. It wasn't unusual that he was so immersed in his job not to realize it was already night, and he was working in almost complete darkness.

He needed some fresh air to clear his mind.

Walking the streets, he could not stop thinking about the man he searched for, Mr. Langley. He didn't seem to have any connection with the police, but his senses told him there was something strange.

I wonder whether the American police have developed a new way to protect their undercover identities. I need to get more in-depth data about the new systems. Until then, it would be safer for Mr. Sherwood to keep away from this guy. The slightest mistake and everything might turn into such a twisted mess, it would be almost impossible to get out clean.

Wandering the streets, he reached the Bolshoy Moskvoretsky bridge and stopped halfway to look at the city's lights. Youngsters yelling happily from Zaryadye Park mixed with traffic noises. He turned his head to the Cathedral of Vasily the Blessed. His mother used to go there every Sunday—she was a fervent Catholic and often visited the church. He was sure that, in the past, the reason for her constant visits had been to pray for him and his brother.

From the day we were born, we were lost. Her prayers wouldn't save any of us, nor would they have saved Sergey's life. The corner of his mouth arched downward as he still remembered the day he died. *Then, my family dissolved, and we all went our own ways, disappearing from each other.*

"D'ya have a cigarette?" A raucous, slurred voice brought him back to the present.

As he turned his face, he saw a middle-aged man who probably drank already too much, wandering the streets looking for a way to either sober up or find his way home.

"Sure, *Družíšče*," he replied, briefly searching for the pack of cigarettes from his jacket.

"W-what 'bout a lighter?" the man asked as he brought the cigarette to his lips.

With a smile and no other words spoken, Mikhail lit the cigarette and watched the man wobbling away.

He squeezed in his jacket and strolled in the direction of the church. Right around the corner, he would find an excellent place to warm his spirits without any distractions.

***

Lars raised his head to the wall where a clock was mercilessly ticking time, "There isn't enough time to get everything done. I'm wondering whether we will ever get to the bottom of this case."

225

He stood up, stretching his back and yawning loudly.

Lindsay, one of his colleagues, was leaving the precinct when he saw Lars still lingering in his office. He peeked in. "You should get a life, man!" he said with a chuckle.

"I already have a life..."

Lindsay came inside and turned serious. "And what would it be? When was the last time you spent time doing something else but working? I also bet you're working from home on your days off," he reproached, pointing the finger at Lars.

"I need to solve this case..." he protested, annoyed. He knew Lindsay was right, and he needed to focus on his private life, something to do when he wasn't working. The truth was, he enjoyed working.

"Give me a break!" Lindsay interrupted, throwing his hands in the air.

Lindsay grabbed Lars' elbow and pulled him out of his office without waiting for a reply. "Hey! At least let me switch off the computer!" Lars protested, pulling back his hand.

"The world won't end if you leave it open." With a final pull, he was able to get Lars out of the room.

"So, where are we going?" Lars asked as they were walking in the parking lot.

"First, I suggest we head for a bar. Everyone's there celebrating Joey's anniversary, forty years on the force. We've been planning this evening for at least a couple of months now."
226

"I need to be completely honest with you." Lars grimaced, "I had no idea it was his anniversary, and I haven't heard anything about a party today."

"You're hopeless," Lindsay said. "At least try to have fun tonight and not to think about anything work-related. And try to get some rest this weekend. It might help you with your case."

As they drove, Lars realized it wasn't a question of just that case. It was the fear of having to deal with his life. Being a detective gave him the proper excuse to escape from society and relationships. He felt good when he could decline the company of other people—because he had an essential job to carry out. *But what happens the day you retire? What will you do when you're forced to have free time? Will you find another activity, will you finally start to learn social skills, or will you be ready to commit suicide?* Those questions never came to his mind before and now seemed to pop out from every corner.

Finally, they arrived at the pub. The air inside was already oppressive, but the smell of food, the happy giggles of the people enjoying their drinks, and the clinking of glasses and bottles created a familiar, cozy atmosphere that gave a pleasant warmth to Lars' heart. Inhaling deeply, not merely the scents but also the feelings and the joyous atmosphere, he walked toward the tables where his colleagues were already having fun.

***

It was 1:30 am when Edward and Sabrina returned home.

"I'm afraid we're getting older. I clearly remember starting to feel buzzed by 1:00 am back when we were in London," stated Sabrina, as she slipped off her heels. "I'm heading directly to bed."

"I had the same impression—the good thing is that we don't have to go to open the shop tomorrow morning," he added as he followed her to the bedroom.

Tiredness seemed to overwhelm them, and before they realized it, they fell asleep.

Edward woke up after a couple of hours of tormented rest. He watched Sabrina lying at his side as too many thoughts kept him awake, revolving around the future of their relationship in connection with his business.

He stood from the bed, trying not to make any sound. Despite the tiredness, his brain could not find a way to unwind.

Reaching the balcony, he sat down to watch the streets. The noise of the city felt surreal during the night. It almost seemed another city or even another planet.

He could feel the slight rustle of the breeze, gently blowing through the rows of skyscrapers. He closed his eyes, hoping that the light zephyr would wipe away his thoughts. The morning after he would call his father to have answers to his questions. He hoped that the man who had previously run the business could give him some advice.

He opened his eyes once again and gazed at the other buildings. Most of the windows were darkened, but in some, the lights were still on. He remained thinking about the reasons for those people to be still awake.

Although misery loves company, it makes me feel better to think all those sharing a sleepless night with me are doing it for more pleasant reasons.

He went back into the apartment and checked the time on his mobile phone. It was still 3:20 am. He returned to the bedroom. Sabrina was still lying on the bed like nothing could disturb her inner peace, not even the recent events.

Her ability to unwind was something he also wished for himself, but he lay by her side holding her hand and closed his eyes, hoping to find a way to rest.

He didn't know how much time it took for him to fall asleep. He only realized that when the sunlight filtering through the open blinds woke him up the morning after. Despite the lack of rest, he felt strangely rested, ready to face a new day.

With a loud groan, Sabrina stretched her body, opening her eyes, "Good morning," she mumbled, clinging to his body.

"Good morning. Have you slept well?" With a kiss on her forehead, Edward held her tightly to himself.

"I can't complain—how about you?"

With a grimace, Edward parted from her, "It could have been better, but I guess it was because of the tiredness. I think I'm getting too old to stay up all night long."

"Good thing is that we have the whole day to ourselves, and there's nothing else on the agenda other than to relax," she said, cuddled in his arms.

Sabrina breathed in his ear, sending shivers skating along his spine like a wave of electric shocks rippling his skin.

Most of their morning was spent in bed, regaining the sensations they thought they'd lost in a faraway time. Everything felt easy and careless, like back in London when the only thing they had to be concerned about was their classes.

Neither of them cared about what was going on in the world or whether someone planned to destroy them.

***

Meanwhile, across town, Detective Lindström couldn't follow the advice of Lindsay.

He had enjoyed having some fun with his colleagues, laughing and sharing jokes instead of information about a warrant or an arrest. Yet, as soon as he had been alone at home, remorse had seized him, and he had felt guilty for not having dedicated those hours to his investigation.

Not even the knowledge that nothing had happened while he was having fun was able to lighten the burden that seemed to weigh on his conscience. He was afraid that "stealing" that night at the investigation might cost someone's life.

He should have been out there doing his job.

From the first time he had been dealing with Sherwood's Jewelry, the suspicion that there was something unclear in that business had been increasing. He had never heard about the trade in cursed stones before, and at first, it had sounded like a big scam at the expense of rich gullible people who were willing to pay crazy sums for stones that certainly weren't worth them.

Nevertheless, digging into Herman Sherwood's past, he couldn't find any evidence of fraud. The customers were aware that jinx didn't exist, and Mr. Sherwood himself pushed that it was a legend.

Despite that, people were ready to spend their money on that. It was something that he couldn't explain, but surely, there weren't any laws against it. However, he wasn't after them because of their prices, but he was afraid that Mr. Herman Sherwood's son played an active role in the misfortunes happening to his customers.

He opened the fridge, grabbed a Tupperware container and peeked inside. With a satisfied smile, he placed it in the microwave.

"I could almost stand Herman Sherwood, but not his son." He slammed a fork on the table. "He behaves as if he has many things to hide, and I'm sure the day I start digging, I'll find a whole iceberg."

He started to eat without any satisfaction. Edward could rob him of any kind of pleasure, which he could not forgive. "I'll find what he's hiding, and when I do, I swear over everything I keep dear, I will slam him in jail for the rest of his life," he growled, munching.

That day, despite all his goodwill, he couldn't find any possibility to focus on his duties. It was like the time he'd spent the previous evening with his colleagues opened new chances in his life.

He stood from his computer table and walked away a couple of steps. He glanced first at the computer and then at the window. "I knew it was a bad idea going out last night. Now I feel the need to spend some time without thinking about this case."

He pouted, and with a swift move, he took his mobile phone and wallet and left to have a walk. Perhaps switching his focus to something else would have helped him gather his thoughts enough to reach his desired goal.

Chapter 22

Two days passed, Detective Lindström's suspicions of a relationship between Edward and Mr. Hopkins' death proved to be inconsistent, but the case was far from being closed.

It was clear that there was an international crime network that had killed Mr. Hopkins and had Edward on its crosshairs.

"You look more worried than usual," said Sabrina as they were on their lunch break. "Is there anything new we should be worried about?"

Twitching his mouth at her question, he turned to glance at her, "I wouldn't call them new problems, but I've had a few thoughts since Detective Lindström entered my life. Moreover, the arrival of the new customer gave me something else to be aware of."

"Do you still think he might be an undercover cop?" she guessed, wiping her mouth with a napkin.

"Maybe, I asked Mikhail to investigate him, but I still haven't heard a word from him." He shrugged his shoulders.

He took a short pause. Every time she asked something about his internal turmoil, his thoughts started to get confused in his head. He decided to change the subject, by talking about an auction coming up in Italy.

"I know, it will be in Milan, isn't it?" she replied.

"Yes, and so far, no warnings arrived from Mikhail or anyone else," he said, waving at the waitress to get the check. "The pearl, which mysteriously disappeared after Mr. Milton's death, is going to be auctioned off. It has been officially sold only once during these years. Needless to say, I want it back because I already know it wouldn't be difficult to sell it within a few months. Its recent story would surely attract several customers."

As they were exiting the restaurant, ready to return to the shop, Sabrina glanced around to ensure there wasn't anyone who could have heard what he was going to say. "Aren't you afraid if you repurchase the pearl, it might seem a bit suspicious?"

With an amused chuckle, he put his arm around her shoulder, "Is it illegal to purchase an item that disappeared more than four years ago?"

Feeling slightly derided, Sabrina shook his arm away from her shoulders. "You know what I mean! You already have the police keeping an eye on you. This would be a great chance to have them gathering in the shop like vultures."

It might have been true that it was not something he should have done yet. Nevertheless, thinking about its beauty and perfection, he felt caught in its spell or curse.

His face turned serious, and a frown creased his forehead. *There must be something real about those jinxes, or perhaps I'm losing my grasp on reality.*

They walked to the shop in silence.

By the time she'd spent with him, she had learned which was his way to cope with his worries.

He preferred to think about them alone, before asking for help or advice. She was not convinced that this was the best solution, however, she could only wait for him to knock on her door.

She knew him well enough to understand he was on the verge of a nervous breakdown, but at that moment, she had to respect his desire to be left alone.

The problem was, most of all, the nature of his business and his obsessive attachment to it.

It was doubtful whether he really enjoyed it, or it was an addiction to the adrenaline rush and to the life lived at the razor's edge.

***

Janice liked working with Sabrina because she was an easy-going person, always ready to have a light chat about almost anything.

However, when she entered the laboratory that afternoon, with her creased forehead and pursed lips, Janice realized something was bothering her. She didn't seem like the sunny person she used to know, so he avoided talking to her.

Sabrina took a deep breath. Precision was everything in her job, and she needed to focus on what she was doing. Unfortunately, the focus was what she missed the most, and as she was changing the blade of a saw, it slipped off her grip, cutting her left index finger.

235

Crimson drops fell on her overalls as she cursed her pain aloud, and the saw clattered falling on the floor. Janice stood up immediately and ran to check what had happened, grabbing the first-aid kit on her way.

"Let me see," Janice urged, putting on latex gloves to avoid touching the wound with dirty hands.

Whimpering out of frustration rather than from the pain, Sabrina let her examine the finger.

"It's not a deep cut," Janice said, relieved as she cleaned the wound with some disinfectant. "Now, let's bandage it, and everything will be fine."

She glanced at Sabrina and understood it wasn't the wound that hurt, "What's going on?"

"I guess I'm tired and stressed because of the load of work I have here and helping run the business." She tried to justify.

"Liar..." She grabbed a chair and sat in front of Sabrina, locking her gaze onto hers. "Now, tell me what's going on. It shouldn't be me to tell you how important the focus is on our job. Obviously, there is something more than stress. If you don't feel comfortable sharing your problems with me, that's fine. I would appreciate it if you would take some time to think about what you can do to solve them, so you don't get hurt further from being distracted."

Holding her hand gently, Janice lowered her gaze to the wounded finger, "It was a stroke of luck you didn't seriously hurt yourself. We all have problems, but they need to be solved. They don't disappear with a new day. Tomorrow when you wake up, they'll still be there, waiting to be solved."

Sabrina raised her eyes to her. "You're right, but I can't talk to you about it. I don't want to be bothering you with those problems. They belong to such a mess, and it would be difficult to explain to someone who isn't familiar with the story of my life. I…"

With a bright smile, Janice hushed her. "Don't say anything more, and don't try to explain. I understand we keep things for ourselves, and I don't ask you to tell me everything. What I want you to know is that whenever you need a friend, I'm here."

"I know, and I'm grateful for your presence. I could never ask for more than that, and I hope you don't get upset because I can't open my heart completely."

"Well, let's continue our work and try to forget your worries, at least for a few hours," Janice recommended one more time, standing up from the chair in front of Sabrina to return to her table.

Without replying, Sabrina watched her walking away. She considered everything that happened from the day she decided to move away from London to live with Edward. She knew his life was a mess, but she thought it could be restricted to his way of being, not to the whole world revolving around that shop.

There wasn't any use in talking with him—he appeared to be already overwhelmed by something nobody prepared him for. Indeed, he could have

237

stopped everything at any moment. The jewelry shop would be a success, even without dealing in cursed gems.

She placed her elbow on the table, resting her face on the palm of her hand, hoping to be inspired by the first idea to save her from getting crazy. She wondered whether his mother knew anything about that side of the business, or was she preventively kept in the dark?

Considering how she behaved, it's clear that she didn't know what was going on in the backroom or the deal every customer unknowingly signed up for. I'm wondering whether I should talk with Herman about my feelings. Overwhelmed, she discarded that idea.

She stood from the table and walked through the backroom to the shop. She hoped there weren't any customers because she felt she could no longer hold herself.

She gingerly peeked from the door. There weren't customers in the shop, and she caught a glimpse of Edward, focused on observing a gemstone through a loupe. His calm expression and the slight smile arching his lips could soothe her turbulent spirit.

She would have stayed for the rest of her life spying on him from the door left ajar. With a light sigh, she wished to regain some calm and wondered whether it was as it appeared, and he could control his emotions, or he just reached a compromise.

***

One thing Edward learned in his profession was to have eyes wherever they needed to be, and, with the time, he mastered how to sense what was going on behind him.

He smiled at the comforting sensation of having Sabrina's sight on him. He kept pretending he didn't see her until the situation became hilarious.

Unhurriedly, he placed the stone he was polishing on the desk and turned his eyes toward the door where Sabrina was hiding.

"Are you getting bored in the lab?" He asked.

"You will never stop surprising me." The door opened, and Sabrina appeared, walking to the desk. "Did you know since the beginning I was watching you?"

"Not for a little while. When I spotted you out the corner of my eye, I thought I'd better pretend I didn't see you." His voice, tender and calm, melted her heart.

His eyes lowered, and he noticed her bandaged finger. "What happened?"

With a fast sway of her hand, she reassured him. "It's nothing. I got distracted when I was changing the saw's blade, and I cut my finger. Only a scratch."

"Be careful! We can't afford to lose your skills." His hand reached her, and their fingers entwined. "I believe you had something more important than coming to watch me. How can I help you?"

"I guess I'm a bit nervous for the incoming auction in Milan," she confessed. "As far as I know, there
239

isn't any warning that came from Mikhail or anyone else. Yet, a little voice in the back of my head keeps whispering to warn you about something I can't even fathom."

A dark shadow veiled his expression, "I will have to contact Mikhail as soon as possible. I haven't heard from him in a while, and I wonder how his searches are proceeding. I need an exact idea of what I have to expect, either from the police or our competitors." Unlocking their hands, Edward began massaging his temples.

He had a headache, but not the kind which could be alleviated by any sort of medication. "Are you going to call him today?" she hesitated.

"Something I never want to experience is losing you."

"Everything will be fine, I promise you." Edward locked his eyes on hers. He would have done everything to avoid causing her any sort of pain. "I know you said you don't need me to protect you, but I will always try to keep the promise I made back in London. Although in this case, it won't be entirely up to me to ensure a positive outcome."

With a weak smile, she glanced around as the door opened and a customer came inside. Exchanging a fast, reassuring glance, Sabrina walked away.

In the backroom, she stopped to look at the environment. "There's no doubt they all belonged to the same family. Although you can recognize the personal touch of every single salesman, the general outlook remained the same." A long exhale

240

accompanied that distracting consideration. She resumed her walk to the laboratory, where she could finally focus on his project without further thinking about her problems.

***

As soon as they closed the shop's front door and engaged the alarm, Edward searched for the telephone and dialed Mikhail's number. Together with Sabrina, they retired to the laboratory, which had an independent alarm system.

With their breaths held for a reason they could not explain, they waited for Mikhail to reply to the call.

One ring...

Two rings...

Three rings...

"*Družíšče!*" The deep voice of Mikhail replied, breaking the silence of the room echoing like the peal of thunder.

"Mikhail, I was waiting for any news from you, and I don't know how I should interpret your silence." He struggled to sound in total control.

"I know, and I should apologize. The problem is that the police decided to tighten the level of confidentiality. My hackers and whistleblowers had a hard time finding any connection between Mr. Langley and the police." He paused for a moment to let his words sink in.

"Does this mean Mr. Langley is undercover and I should keep my eyes open?" he guessed, hoping this was all he needed to do to avoid any problem.

"I haven't said so," Mikhail replied unhurriedly. "I mean, it took quite a long time to verify his identity, and he doesn't belong to any law enforcement organization. Nevertheless, this isn't something you should consider relieving, as what I've found out could be more concerning."

Edward turned his eyes toward Sabrina, who had been open-mouthed and frozen in a single position for the whole time.

"I doubt he came to your shop by chance. You mentioned he wanted to know something about cursed items if I recall it correctly." He searched for his headphones to have a certain degree of freedom during the chat. Having to hold something at his ear annoyed him. Mikhail opened a drawer, grunting, in the desperate search for some headphones as he waited for his client to reply and eventually correct his statement.

"Mr. Langley came in as he was interested in a brooch he saw in the window. Yet he was looking for a different stone." Edward tried to recall what happened, hoping his memory wouldn't have failed him. "According to what he said, his girlfriend was interested in occultism and would have been more than ecstatic to receive a jewel made from a cursed stone..."

A louder growl interrupted him as Mikhail opened every drawer.

"Is everything alright?"

"Yes, I'm trying to find my headphones." Mikhail chuckled. "I always have them at hand, and now I can't find anything." Cursing in Russian, he stood from the chair and tried to search for them. It was no more a question of comfort—it was about the principle.

"Do you want to call me later?" Edward wondered, strange noises coming through the speaker like someone was robbing an apartment.

"No." A victorious gasp came through the loudspeaker. "I found them!"

"Perfect, so I was telling you about the reason why he was interested in cursed stones." Edward tried to resume the story.

"Yes, but what you don't know is that the girl in question is Anna Todorova, which probably doesn't tell you anything until I say she is the daughter of Ivan Todorov and Anushka Todorova. Now going a little more in detail, Anushka's maiden name is Kozar."

The last word was spoken slowly to ensure he'd put enough emphasis on her identity.

Edward's blood froze in his veins. "This means they're still after me. Why?"

"Because once you are on their funerary list, there's only one way to get off, and that's by being six feet underground. They probably got the ruby back, but they won't forgive the offense. I'm afraid they will use your participation in the next auction as a

243

chance to kill you. There you will be into a more vulnerable position, or at least this is what they think."

Mikhail took a deep breath as he went to sit down at his desk once again. Opening his computer, on the screen appeared the e-mail he had received from one of his associates, in which he informed him of the movements of the Kozars.

The information he'd gathered wasn't reassuring, and he feared it wouldn't be enough to ensure Edward's survival in case he participated in the auction. *Sadly, I cannot guarantee it even if he remains confined at home. They already know where he works, it won't take them long to find out where he lives.*

An almost unbreakable wall of silence seemed to have been erected between Edward and Sabrina.

Thoughts swirled in his mind. Once again, the ghost of having endangered the most important person in his life took over his soul, making impossible for him to get a hold of himself.

The gentle touch of her hand on his own startled him, and offering her nothing more than a weak smile, he turned his head to her.

Without taking his eyes off her, he tried to understand how serious the situation was. "What do you suggest? Should I increase the level of surveillance around my family and me? Would that be enough?"

"If they're on the warpath, not even God can protect you. I will do everything I can to ensure a higher level of safety. I will get you out of this mess," he commenced. "In this case, I would suggest you avoid coming to the auction in Milan. However, I know you won't listen to me."

A doubt crawled on Edward's mind. "Do you think this guy who came to my shop wanted to keep an eye on me? Is it a trap?"

"The way I see it, you're already in a trap. I think you're sharp enough to understand Mr. Langley came to you, buying the diamond as an excuse. I trust that if they find out where you live and work, they also know I am responsible for your safety. That was a statement to make you understand that they know how to find you," Mikhail replied.

Edward's eyes met Sabrina's, and he bit his lower lip. He understood he needed to talk privately with Mikhail. "I will think about it," he replied diplomatically. "I need some time to understand my situation and to figure out a solution. I'm not sure whether I will come to Italy for the auction. Either way, I need to reorganize my safety network here in New York."

He held Sabrina's hand to make her understand this would have been a decision they needed to take together. Taking a deep breath, Edward continued. "I will call you by tomorrow evening."

"I will be waiting for your call," Mikhail replied.

Chapter 23

As they ended the communication, Sabrina shook her head, "Do you still intend to go there?"

"I don't know," he admitted. "Any advice is welcome"

"The risk might be too high, and perhaps this is the right time to play safe and let someone else go to the auction on your own," she proposed, unsure that this would be enough to keep them safe. The message of the Kozars being able to reach them at any time came clear and loud.

"You're right. Even if, if we were actually in their crosshairs, this wouldn't guarantee our safety," he considered.

Sabrina averted her eyes from him and walked to one of the tables in the laboratory. With her mind focused on the recent call with Mikhail, she caressed the desk, where a couple of indentations were formed by regular use. Her forehead creased at the touch with the surface's roughness as if those irregularities interrupted the smoothness of her thoughts.

Before, she ignored how carelessly those tables were handled. She felt sorry for having ruined a nice piece of furniture and wondered whether it would have been wise to purchase a new one with the promise of increased attention and care. She closed her eyes and recognized every smell in the room. It started to feel like home. Perhaps that was why she got disappointed by the rough treatments reserved for the furniture. The fear of losing everything familiar to her, the feeling of home forced her to think that the game they were playing lost the original purpose. Perhaps, the curses they've been selling during these years had returned to them.

She glanced at Edward out of the corner of her eyes. Only those who knew him well would spot the almost imperceptible twitch of the corner of his mouth, sign of the storm brewing in his soul. For anyone else, his composed posture and elegant dress would suggest a confident man.

The way he nervously turned his wedding ring was another clear signal. "Sweetheart, we need to be together in this—you cannot carry on your shoulders all the risks and responsibilities connected to this business."

A frustrated shake of Edward's head and a grimace twisting his face revealed the reality behind a situation more complicated than she'd ever forecasted.

"I wish I could still have my grandfather here to ask him..." Edward whispered.

"Why, your father wouldn't be the same?" From the beginning, it had seemed like his grandfather's role was considered essential.

He kept his eyes on the floor, collapsing on a chair, and grabbing his head between his hands. "My grandfather used to run this side of the business more relentlessly. He had been a great dealer of cursed items. He trained me to become one and showed me all the details. However, perhaps times have changed, and nowadays, there are more risks involved in this deal. Since I have taken over this shop, the business once again switched more prominently to the dealing of cursed stones. My father played a safer route of the typical jeweler, relegating the cursed stones and items to the back corner."

Sabrina grabbed a chair and sat in front of him. "So, there's no use asking your father."

Before she met Edward, she had never imagined being involved in any ethically dubious business. Her family's legality, integrity, and moral standards were kept in high regard. Obviously, this didn't apply to the Sherwood family. *Morality isn't included in law codes, but...*

She felt deeply conflicted. On the one hand there were the teachings she had received since her childhood, the values in which she had been believing, on the other, that business in clear conflict to them, but that fascinated her because of the possibility of fully understand the human mind and how superstition influences it. Not to mention the adrenaline rush it gave her.

"What are you thinking?" Edward asked.

She remained silent only when there was something profoundly bothering her. He feared that she felt more concerned because of his business and family history, and he realized she was probably making the most critical decision in her life.

"I don't know how to put it in words—it's something I should solve within myself," she finally said, gathering all her strength. She knew that she couldn't keep on delaying the confrontation between her principles and the reason why she didn't keep her distance from Edward.

Let's face it, she thought, *I'm on my own, and this decision is entirely up to me. I had already embraced this dark side when I suggested the test at school. I also married the man who incarnates this shady business, and I'm admittedly excited and intrigued about it. It's like playing the innocent when I carry the same shame on my conscience.*

She brought a hand close to her lips and, clenching her fist, she bit one finger. The silence in the room was complete except for the sounds coming in from outside. With the time going by, they faded away, leaving each other's heartbeats almost perceptible.

"I know I'm a master in indecision—I can never make a choice without being devoured by doubts and regrets. Nevertheless, this time I need to gather all my courage, cast aside my uncertainties, and recall the reason why I'm here now," she commenced, trying to shut down that beast restraining her every choice. "I'm with you in this business, and if we want to reach our retirement alive, we need to work together. To do so, you need to trust and stop trying to protect me. You won't be able to do it."

"You're right," Edward said. "We will need to have another talk with Mikhail. I'll call him tomorrow morning to ask him the best course of action. But now, it's better to go home and have dinner."

His proposal came as a relief. She was already yawning, she would have gone to bed without eating, but the rumbling of her belly reminded her that she wasn't always in charge.

Closing the laboratory door made her feel more detached from the problems she left closed between the perimeter of her workshop.

***

Lars was still focused on the case of Mr. Hopkins' death.

It was clear that the young Sherwood had nothing to do with it, and the suspects of that Russian bratva found more ground.

Nevertheless, after months of fruitless research, it would have been natural to conclude this was one of those cases destined to remain unsolved.

He raised his head to look at the clock on the other side of the wall. The hands of the clock moved to 5:30 pm, but according to his level of tiredness, he would have sworn it was midnight.

He stood from his chair and decided to talk with Lucy Morgan, a detective that had been recently transferred from another department to help him with his investigations.

When he reached her, she had already switched off her computer and was getting ready to leave.

"I'm sorry, Morgan, but I need to have a chat with you about the Hopkins case." The corner of his mouth twitched, in a contrite expression, knowing he was dragging her into his misery, where private life had no meaning.

"Well, I already switched off my computer..."

"I know, but you can come to my office. I'll try to make it brief, but you know, the sooner we put the puzzles together...." He tried to explain.

"...the sooner we will have another case to take care of," she finished the sentence as she followed Lars to his office. "There's no end to this when it comes to working with you."

The years he'd self-isolated himself to pursue his job, rather than finding a balance, suddenly dropped their weight on his shoulders. Spending time chasing bad guys without seeking a compromise to achieve his own happiness didn't feel right anymore.

Perhaps she's right. For me, it's not a question about finishing or solving a case before hoping to have some time to build my personal life. For me, it has always been a question of jumping from one case to the other, he thought, *I'm not sure I know how to engage in relationships.*

The day he was forcibly taken out from his misery for his colleague's anniversary flipped a switch in his mind. He understood he needed more than a promise to himself—he needed a commitment. *Before I lose my sanity.*

251

When he opened the door of his office, for the first time he felt like as he was in the wrong place. There was his jacket, his personal items, and yet something made him uncomfortable. He stayed disoriented on the threshold, as if he was undecided whether to enter or not, under the surprised gaze of Morgan.

"Are you sure everything is fine?" She asked, pushing him inside. She threw her purse on a chair with a nonchalant gesture and sat in front of his desk. She didn't take her jacket off, hoping it wouldn't require her to get rid of it and stay there after hours.

Lars sighed and went to sit at his desk. "A short time ago, when I still suspected Mr. Sherwood of having killed Mr. Hopkins, I spoke with Mr. Orlov. He is in charge of Mr. Sherwood's safety, during his travels abroad. According to his version, after the auction in Moscow, two members of the Kozar family threatened Mr. Sherwood to hand them the ruby he had legally won. Then, I got in touch with Interpol, asking for more information about the Kozars, and their involvement in Mr. Hopkins' murder. So far, I only discovered that Mr. Orlov, in his youth, was arrested for crimes attributable to the Kozars." As usual, he paused, to make sure he had the attention of his interlocutor.

I wonder why they were so interested in that ruby. Was it only a question of honor? If so Mr. Sherwood and his family may still be in danger."

"I can't answer these questions, but I discovered something. Do you remember the case of Mr. Jason

252

Milton's death, about four years ago? And the supposedly cursed pearl that mysteriously disappeared?"

"Sure, I carried out the investigation. What is the news? Did you find it?" he wondered.

"As a matter of fact, yes." She grinned. "The pearl will be sold again in Milan, and I bet Mr. Sherwood will participate. If this is so, you can be sure that would be a chance the Kozars won't let slip from their hands."

"I agree, but we can't do anything, Milan is *slightly* out of our jurisdiction. However, I'd like to know what his intention is. Tomorrow I will pay him a visit. Lars resolved.

Morgan stood from her chair—time was passing by fast, and she still had many things to attend to outside her job.

"Where are you going?" Lars wondered.

"It's quarter past six—I have been in this office since seven in the morning. I have a life to live. We can talk about it tomorrow. After a good sleep, we will prepare a clearer plan on how to keep an eye on him." She grabbed her purse from the chair where she had thrown it.

Pouting, he glanced at her. "Fine! Tomorrow morning at half past seven, we will start again from where we interrupted this evening."

***

As soon as he switched on his computer, Mikhail saw an email from Edward. With a smirk, he went to get his morning coffee before reading it.

For him, there wasn't any other chance to wake up without it. Maybe it was the fact of not having fulfilled a whole night's rest in a long time.

The sun hadn't risen yet, but he felt like he couldn't rest any longer. He gave a fast glance outside the window as the city was still sleeping. Everything was far from his concern from his apartment's level, and nothing wrong appeared to happen in the street. "That's true until you go to look closer. There in those little corners of the main roads, under the bridges...In the less wealthy areas, where the kids are too often left unsupervised, the hands of those demons reach them far too easily, and they are lost...forever."

He exhaled as if to suppress those kinds of thoughts so early in the morning. Those were the thoughts forcing him to recall a hurtful past, which led inexorably to the memory of Sergey's death.

With a grimace, he shook his head and turned to pour his coffee into a mug. "Let's get focused on the messages I've received, and in particular, the one from my best customer, *Družíšče* Sherwood."

The smell of the freshly brewed coffee brought a smile to his face, and after the first sip, Mikhail placed the mug on the desk and opened his email.

As he read it through, he realized Edward decided to participate in the auction. "So, *Družíšče*, you want to test your luck?" He tapped his fingers on the desk, thinking about the possibility of opening up in his mind. "I tell you something, my friend, this can give me the chance to get even with the Kozars once and for all," he mumbled, still staring at the computer screen.

A wild idea started to take form through the fog in his mind. He needed some time to think about it, and looking at the clock, he wondered about the best time to get in touch with his associates in Italy. "I must wait at least a couple of hours. Not everybody is living a life of sleepless nights."

He stood from the desk and stretched his back. The sun was rising. With a smirk, he decided to have a jog outside before the city would have woken up, and traffic would have made his jog unpleasant. Without thinking about it, he dressed and rushed out in the cool Moscow morning

***

Thousands of thoughts were keeping Edward awake that night, including the feeling of having made the wrong decision in participating to the auction. He stood from the bed, trying to not wake Sabrina.

He smiled at her as he was at the door, and never like at that moment, did he feel so in love with her.

Wearing a shirt, he went to the balcony, hoping to find some order in the chaos of his thoughts. He went through the email he'd sent to Mikhail and wondered whether he had already read it.

255

The look of the city and the traffic during the night could soothe his mind. There wasn't much difference in the coming and going of cars between the day and night hours. Only the lights changed. During the day, the sun illuminated the city. At night, the artificial lights on the skyscrapers, streets, and cars created a twilight experience.

He closed his eyes, leaned in the chair, and allowed the night noises to soothe him as a lullaby. Light steps approached him from behind, and he was too busy trying to unwind to pay attention to the light in the living room switching on.

"What are you doing outside?" Sabrina's gentle voice brought him to reality. With a sudden move, Edward turned his head in her direction.

"I couldn't rest—I hoped a bit of fresh air would have helped me to relax." The sound of a siren from a police car interrupted him. They both turned their glances in the direction of the sound, holding their breaths as if they were expecting it to come for them.

As soon as they couldn't hear it any longer, he resumed, "I can't get out of my mind the incoming auction and the risks involved."

Sabrina took a seat in front of him. "At the moment, there is nothing we can do—we need to wait for an answer from Mikhail. Once we know his plan, we will be able to have a more complete picture of the situation," she replied

"We'd better go back to sleep," Edward said, getting up and opening the door for her.

***

As he returned from his morning jog, Mikhail decided to put himself to work. Considering the time, he grabbed his mobile phone and dialed the number of Giuliano Marchesi, one of his associates in Italy.

He ran a private security agency like Mikhail's in Russia. They often cooperated when one of their clients needed to travel abroad and requested professional bodyguards on-site.

"*Buongiorno, Compagno* Mikhail!" The cheerful voice of Giuliano greeted him. Every time he heard him speaking, it was like having some Italian sun shining back on his life.

"Good morning to you, *Družíšče*. I was calling you because one of my clients is going to participate in an auction in your beautiful country," he began.

"I've heard about it, and there are a couple of items I'm interested in, too," Giuliano replied.

"I need your local backup for the occasion. This won't be a regular bodyguarding service, as my client is on the crosshairs of a local bratva, the Kozars. I bet they will take that chance to bring him to eternal peace," he started to explain. "There's more, I have an unsettled business with the Kozars, and this can be the best chance I have to get even for everything." Mikhail twisted a pencil he found on his desk through his fingers.

"Mikhail, you know we're not only business partners but also friends. I consider you almost as family, which means that you can count on my full support. However, in this case, I would ask you to reach me in Italy as soon as you can to prepare a plan of action that won't bring any of us to the cemetery."

Standing up from his chair, Mikhail started pacing around the room like a lion in the cage. The more he spent time in that apartment, the more he yearned to get out of everything and start to live his life differently. "I will arrange my departure immediately and inform you about my schedule."

"Right! I will go now to the office and put my connections to find a way to solve the problem. Take care, Compagno Mikhail."

"I will do my best," replied Mikhail interrupting the communication abruptly.

***

At seven o'clock the next morning, Lars was already in his office and impatiently waited for Morgan to reach the precinct. He couldn't sleep much during the night. His rest was frequently interrupted by sudden thoughts, ideas, theories, and more.

He went to get his morning coffee from the shared kitchen when he heard Morgan's familiar voice, kindly greeting someone on her way.

Forgetting about the coffee, he rushed his steps to the corridor. "Morgan!" He called breathlessly, "Good that you arrived early."

With a huff, she turned to look at him, "Well, good morning to you too—how kind of you to ask how I am doing this morning. Thank you. I'm fine."

Lars hated sarcastic people and her way of nagging in the early morning wasn't welcome. "This isn't the place for small talks. This is a Police Precinct, and we have important work to be done," he replied, annoyed and growling like a wounded beast.

The other officers standing by in the hall began to walk away, forecasting a storm they preferred to avoid.

To be honest, Morgan wasn't impressed—nothing could impress her, not even her superior, when she felt disrespected. Narrowing her eyes, she walked toward him. Her day was already ruined.

"We gave each other an appointment this morning at half-past seven. According to the clock, there are still another fifteen minutes. If you have something that itches, I suggest you scratch it because I get easily angry when someone tries to ruin my day already from the morning."

She was furious.

Taken aback, Lars remained for a moment frozen, not sure about what he was supposed to say. Then, like a charm that freed him from a curse, he started to chuckle, so hard that his belly started to hurt, and tears streamed from his eyes. He didn't know why, but whatever the reason, it was the most hilarious of the century.

His laughter was contagious, as also Morgan started first to giggle and then exploded like a bomb. It took some time before both of them could regain their composure.

"Oh-my-God, it has been ages since the last time I have laughed so hard," he admitted. Feeling more relaxed, he realized she was right, and he had been impolite toward her. "I'm sorry, Morgan. I should have remembered my manners."

"No harm done now—I should have also been less touchy," she replied with a smile. "How about a coffee before we can start our brainstorming?"

"I think this would be the best idea of all. I could not rest. I was constantly thinking about the case. As soon as I could close my eyes, a new idea popped into my mind, and it took forever to get rid of it. This went on for most of the night. This morning the only thing I wanted to do was to start up the day on the right foot, so to have most of the things solved by this evening."

She shook her head as she grabbed a cup from the cupboard. "You need to take it easy, or you will need a psychiatrist. There isn't any need to be so much obsessed, and you know better than me how it's important to keep your mind sharp."

He glanced at his cup, filled with coffee. The pungent smell of caffeine reached his nose, sharpening his senses before the first sip.

Slowly with their cups of coffee, they walked to Lars' office, where Morgan threw her purse on one of the chairs like the night before. Yet this time, she placed her coffee cup on the table and took her jacket off, gently folding it over the purse.

He scrutinized her and took his place on the chair in front of his desk, waiting to get started. She was a pleasant-looking lady, and only then could he notice that. Her dark hair, orderly, held by a ponytail, seemed to shine at the sunrays filtering through the window blinds.

Shaking his head, he made himself comfortable, ready to start another day and resume the brainstorming for the investigation.

"Last night, I searched around for more information about the activity of Mr. Sherwood," he said, starting up his computer. "I've had some of our officers keeping an eye on him. Apparently, he had an interesting customer lately. We've found he's engaged with an American girl holding a Russian passport. Anna Todorova, whose mother had a familiar surname: Kozar."

Morgan gasped, "Those who threatened Mr. Sherwood to get the ruby and who supposedly killed Mr. Hopkins for the same reason?!?"

"Exactly! I'm still waiting for confirmation about it. I asked Officer Sullivan to find something more about her and her connection to that family."

She remained quiet to ponder about it for a moment. Averting her gaze from Lars, she glanced outside of the window. When she noticed her sight was blocked by the blind, which were still lowered, she went to raise them up.

The sunlight blinded their eyes for a second, and the whole room got illuminated.

He inhaled deeply, closing his eyes. When he opened them again, Morgan was grabbing her jacket.

"I'm going back to my office and will try to find some information about this man. Could you please send me all the data you got about him?" She said, forecasting he would ask her where she was going.

"That's a good idea—I will forward you the dossier I have saved on my computer. Meantime, I think I might go have a chat with Mr. Sherwood."

After having forwarded the dossier to Morgan, he stood up from the desk and grabbed his jacket, ready to get into action.

Chapter 24

After the usual routine to open the shop, Edward glanced at the old clock hanging on the wall. He compared the time with his mobile phone, and with a slight pout, he realized it was a few minutes behind the real-time.

Without uttering a word, he checked whether the mechanism needed to be recharged or required the expert hands of a clockmaker. The clock was ancient—it had been in the same position since he could remember, and nobody knew when it was purchased. So far, it had been working flawlessly, and never in his memory, it needed to be repaired.

He took the key used to recharge the clock. Generally, a few turns would have been sufficient for having it running for weeks. Yet, he recalled the last time he recharged it about ten days ago.

Nearing his ear to the clock, he began smiling at the gears' regular ticking and the sound of the inner mechanism. Still, he decided to keep an eye on it if the charge would have worn out too soon.

Sabrina came from the lab, where she had also disengaged the alarm system and was ready to start the day.

"In about three weeks, there will be the auction in Milan," she announced.

Turning his glance at her, he sighed. "I know, and before booking any flight ticket or hotel, we need to wait for the answer from Mikhail. But now, let's get back to work—there are a lot of orders to be fulfilled." With a tender smile, he reached Sabrina, and, holding her hand, he brought it to his lips to kiss the tip of her fingers. "Don't be afraid—everything will be fine, and I will tell you immediately when I receive an answer from Mikhail."

Sabrina's cheeks turned scarlet at the gentle touch of his lips.

The bell on the door clanged, but the crystalline chiming sounded like the screeching sound of nails against the chalkboard. As Edward turned his face, the day seemed to darken at Detective Lindström coming inside the shop.

"Detective, what a pleasure to have you back here in my shop." He greeted with a plastered smile on his face.

"Good morning, Mr. Sherwood," he replied, walking to the desk, glancing around as if he wanted to spot something or someone hidden somewhere. "I came here because I have some questions, and I hope you can give me the answers," he began. "I know you had a customer recently who had some connections with the people who might be responsible for the murder of Mr. Hopkins."

Edward raised his shoulders, "A lot of people come to this shop, and the last thing I'm going to ask them is anything about their family ties." He pretended not to know who he was talking about.

"I know—I wonder whether you are aware of this detail. According to my sources, this person might try to get even for the missed deal with the ruby," Lars explained.

Edward remained silent, considering whether also the police believed the threat feasible. In that case, the situation might have been more difficult than he ever thought it would have been.

I might have played a too risky game. He turned his glance to the door to the back room and to the laboratory. He thought about Sabrina. *Protecting her also means not leaving her alone with the grief of my death. I should have thought about this but, maybe, it's not too late.*

"Is there anything wrong?" Lars wondered as he noticed the way Edward was glancing at his shoulders.

"N-No, I was thinking about something else, but everything is fine." His voice flickered.

"So, you don't know anything about this?" Lars wondered.

With furrowed brows, Edward wasn't sure he understood what Lars wanted to know, "What do you want me to say? What do you want to know?" His voice didn't sound sure anymore. "I need to ask you questions because you clearly know more than me. Out there, there's an entire bratva who wants me dead. Those people are not playing games. Once they consider someone an enemy, they won't give up until they killed him. You should know better than anyone that people like the Kozars aren't impressed by a jeweler like me. I'm not at the head of a criminal organization like they are!" The tone of his voice reached the level his father would consider inappropriate for a salesman in this kind of shop.

Edward closed his eyes and drew a deep breath. He should have apologized and, perhaps if there was a regular customer, he would have done so. Clenching his fists, he opened his eyes again. "I didn't know this man was related to the Kozars—how could I have guessed? I have nothing to do with them except being evidently on their blacklist. Besides this, I have no idea who they are, where they are."

"I see," Lars said. "There will be an auction in Milan in three weeks, do you plan to attend? Do you know there will be the pearl for sale that once belonged to Mr. Milton?" Lars pursued.

"Of course, I know. That's the reason why I'm going there in the first place," he nagged. "I can tell you more—I'm also interested in purchasing it if I have the chance. As I mentioned once, those are special items, one of a kind. They go around the world, and sometimes they return to the previous owner."

"Let me understand something. Why in this world have you decided to go to the auction if you are aware of a possible plan to eliminate you?" Lars asked.

"Because if I'm on their funeral list, I am already dead, and nothing can save me. They will get me whether I hide or not, and my grandfather raised me not to hide from any enemy," he replied with a flicker in his voice.

Lars thought about it for a moment, "You're right, and if an organized crime group put someone in their crosshairs, it's simply a matter of time. Unfortunately, we won't be able to protect you in Italy."

"Nobody will be able to protect me anywhere. My bodyguard service is going to be there; so far, they've managed to keep me alive, who knows they won't this time too?"

With pursed lips, Lars narrowed his eyelids. "Be careful, Mr. Sherwood—it would be a pity to have you dead." He still didn't like Edward, but not for a single moment he wished him dead.

"I will try my best, Detective Lindström."

***

A couple of days passed by, and that night, the silence in their bedroom was complete. For Sabrina and Edward, it was time to find comfort in their rest. Cuddled together as if to gather strength to fight an invisible enemy, they dreamt about their life together.

Suddenly, like the screeching sound of the witches' laugh, the telephone rang, lacerating the soft cloth of silence embedding their room.

He stood from the bed with a sudden jolt and grabbed the telephone.

"Hello," he whispered, trying not to wake up Sabrina, who turned on her side, still sleeping.

"*Družíšče*, I'm truly sorry to wake you up—I might have messed up with the time difference." Mikhail's deep masculine voice, which generally calmed him, arrived at his ears like a threatening tune, and cold shivers ran along his spine.

"Misha..." he replied, still trying to make sense out of his drowsy state. He opened the balcony door to have the chill air of the night waking him up. "What's going on? It's two o'clock in the morning."

"I know," he apologized. "Nevertheless, since I managed to wake you up, the least I can do is to give you the reason why I needed to call you."

Edward took a seat on the balcony chair and slowly his mind started to get clearer from the fog of a dream. "Never mind, I hope you got good news because I'm not sure I can handle anything else at this time."

"I'm sorry to be the bearer of bad news. In three weeks, you will be in Italy for the auction. My team will support you during your visit, but I'm not sure whether I might be able to be there myself. However, you can be sure the safety level with my cooperator will be the same I can offer, if not better," Mikhail explained.

"So, what is the problem, because there is a problem, isn't there?" Edward asked, returning in the apartment. Keeping the lights off, his eyes got accustomed to the darkness. He walked to the couch and sat down.

"My informers told me the Kozars don't care whether they got their hands on the ruby. The case isn't closed with you, so they will seek revenge for the outrage at the auction in Moscow. This is why I have intensified the bodyguarding network during your stay. Can you reach Italy earlier? If you leave one week in advance, you'll get familiar with the coordination of the operation."

Edward grunted. He had already made arrangements for the following two weeks and canceling or postponing them wouldn't be easy.

However, since there was nothing predictable with the Kozars, any further step to ensure his safety could have made the difference between life and death.

"I will reschedule my flight and will inform you about the new timetable," he finally replied.

"I will be waiting for your message—now you'd better go back to sleep. Goodnight, *Družíšče*." Without waiting for his reply, Mikhail hung up the phone, ready to communicate the result to his cooperators back in Milan. There wasn't any time to waste, and he needed to be a step ahead of the Kozars, or he would lose his best customer.

After talking to Giuliano Marchesi in Italy, Mikhail stood up, shaking his head.

"No," he said. "This is no longer a question of business. Edward Sherwood is not the only person I'm coordinating bodyguarding services for, but he is the only one with whom I established a good connection. He's one of the few people I freely call *Družíšče*, and for me, this is almost like calling someone a brother."

269

It was almost eleven in the morning, and soon he would have left to reach the restaurant where he usually had lunch. Back in the days, when his business was more tangled with the mafia circles, having a steady place or a favorite restaurant was unthinkable. As a free man who paid his dues with his own brother's blood, the fact of not having any restriction was a luxury he didn't want to miss.

Even if for them the dues are paid, for me, that is not the case. Sergey will soon find his revenge and, this time, I'm not acting by instinct like before. Now things will follow a well-defined plan.

***

Edward placed the telephone on the small table in front of the couch and remained to listen to the surrounding noises.

Once again, after Mikhail's call, the room returned silent, and tiredness seemed to invite him to return to lie in Sabrina's arms.

He knew it would have been better to reschedule the flight ticket before returning to bed. Indeed, without that step, he would have remained awake until the alarm clock would have rung.

Once again, with a slight groan, he leaned to the table to grab the phone and changed his flight schedule to Italy. As soon as he had the ticket booked and sent the message to Mikhail, he returned to his bedroom. Slowly he lay at her side, cuddling with her, in the hope of regaining the

270

sweet feeling abruptly interrupted by the telephone call.

Sabrina had noticed his absence, but she preferred to postpone all her questions to the following morning. As their bodies touched and the warmth of his body wrapped her, she smiled and fell asleep once again.

***

The morning after, before the sunrise, the alarm clock woke them up.

"Who was the asshole who called you last night?" she mumbled groggily as she stretched her body on the bed.

"I thought you were sleeping. I'm sorry if I woke you up." Edward held her tightly, kissing her forehead. "Mikhail called—he might have forgotten about the time difference."

With a grunt, she held herself to Edward's body. "I was starting to get jealous..."

"Of whom? Mikhail? You're the only human being I want to have at my side, and he's too hairy for my likings." He chuckled, spelling every word between one kiss and the other.

Nothing was more annoying than the cruel routine that didn't allow them to indulge in bed for longer during the week. There was nothing else in his mind other than spending the whole morning making love to Sabrina.

271

Knowing he had to find a way to tell her about what happened that night, Edward hesitated for a longer time in the bed, holding and kissing the only woman he could ever love.

"Hmm..." she moaned in ecstasy as their bodies fused together under the sheets. "Either you don't remember we need to reach the shop, or you have something to be forgiven for."

"I think it's a bit of both." He slightly parted from her to glance into her eyes. "Last night, Mikhail called because he wants me to leave for Italy one week in advance."

Sabrina's expression turned serious as she sprung seated on the bed. An undefinable mix of disappointment, surprise, and, above all, fear darkened her face.

She remained silent for a long minute, trying to recollect and digest what he said. It wasn't the need to leave earlier —that had also happened before. What scared her was the reason for him to go.

Although he didn't yet explain it, she knew it wasn't because in this way to visit the main tourist attractions, but to avert a threat to his safety.

"Why do you need to leave so soon? When will you...?" she mumbled as finally, she could say something from the confusion in her mind.

Averting his gaze from her, Edward held her hands. "Mikhail asked me to get to Italy earlier to get familiar with the safety organization. He's afraid the Kozars might still be looking for revenge."

"Can't you give the procure to attend the auction to somebody else? I remember once Mikhail proposed something similar," she protested weakly. "I don't want you to risk your life for this business. It's not worth it." Her voice trembled as her eyes tried their best not to shed any tears.

"Sabrina, you're right. This time, though, I believe there isn't a question of being in the wrong place at the wrong time. I'm afraid they will try to get even anyway," he said, recalling Mr. Langley. "Don't ask me how I can be sure about it, but I had the strange impression that also for Mikhail, there's more in this story than bodyguarding me. This is the time when we can settle the score with them."

"Nothing good comes out of violence, and if you're planning to kill them, the rest of the family will be after you. How are you going to settle a matter with an entire criminal organization? Promise me you will keep yourself safe, that you won't run useless risks, and you will call me at regular intervals," Sabrina replied, hurt.

With a bitter smile, he hugged her. There was nothing worse in his mind than to disappoint her. "You married a dangerous man..." he whispered, getting close to her ear.

"No, I married a stubborn ass. But I love you immensely," she replied, trying to smile.

"I will do everything it takes to ensure my safety, and I will return home safe and sound. This is a promise to you, me, and my family. I believe, besides the Kozars, there isn't anyone who wishes me

273

dead," he replied with a relaxed tone in his voice. "This is, at least, what I hope. I couldn't stand the fact of being someone else's target."

Edward tried to joke about it, but deep inside, he was also scared of what could have happened in Italy. This would be a stressful week, and he needed to make sure he would never again find himself in a similar situation.

With a long sigh, Edward stood from the bed. They lingered far too long into that discussion, and they would probably have to open the shop later than usual. Nevertheless, talking about each other's fear and concerns was necessary. It would help them both to cope with that period he would be away.

They didn't have the time to eat breakfast at home and agreed to buy something from a coffee house close by. They had hardly had time to breathe. The shop needed to be kept open, and the goldsmithing project required to be carried out to meet the deadlines.

Chapter 25

That morning as Lars reached the precinct, an urgent email from Lieutenant Stanford was waiting for him, asking him to come to his office right away.

It didn't require a clairvoyant to understand that it was connected to the case of Mr. Hopkins' death. *It has passed almost a year, and we haven't made any relevant progress,* he thought.

Reaching the office, he noticed the door was left ajar, and without hesitations, he entered.

"Good morning. Did you want to see me?" Lars asked.

"Yes, have a seat," Lieutenant Stanford invited him kindly. "I want to talk to you about the investigation on Mr. Hopkins' murder. I have received your regular reports about the case and those of Interpol about the suspects. It's clear how Mr. Sherwood didn't have anything to do with the murder. It's also clear that whoever the assassin is, we have to deal with someone who knew what he was doing and acted carefully not to leave any evidence that could identify him. For this reason, we need to place the case on hold until new clues arise. Other cases require your full attention now."

Lowering his head, Lars knew that Lieutenant Stanford was right. Besides the testimonies of Edward Sherwood and Mikhail Orlov, they hadn't any concrete evidence of the involvement of one of the Kozar family members, although they were the most likely suspects.

"I understand, Sir. I just…"

"I know, Detective Lindström, and as a member of the law enforcement, I share your desire to bring to justice whoever deserves it. We all want to make things straight, but as we all can agree, this is not always possible."

Lars drew a deep breath. "I know, I spent time and energies on this case, and now it has to be placed on hold because of a lack of evidence. I feel like I'm failing in my purpose. I know that it's not all black and white, and sometimes criminals remain unpunished for the damage they caused. Especially for murder cases, like this one," Lars stood up from his chair and pointed his finger toward the door. "There's an entire family who mourned the loss of a dear one, hoping to see one day the person who did this to them will pay for his actions. Those are the people I have sworn to protect, and every time this happens, I feel I am letting them down."

"All we can do is make sure that cases like this won't be the rule, but the exception." Lieutenant Stanford replied. "We will keep cooperating with Interpol and gather information on similar unsolved cases. We will also compare them with those cases attributed to the same criminal organization members to see whether we can recognize a pattern. Maybe one day, we will get enough data to give a name to the culprit."

Lars lowered his head and walked to the door. He glanced at Lieutenant Stanford one more time and left the room without saying any word, immersed in his own considerations.

Edward reached the airport a couple of hours before the departure. As he arrived at the gates after the security check, he roamed around, looking for a way to pass the time until boarding time.

He looked at his wristwatch and decided to send a message to Sabrina.

Immediately after he sent a text and placed the phone back in his pocket, it started to ring.

"Hello, sweetheart. How are you doing? Still at work?"

"I decided to stay a bit longer in the lab. There are some projects whose deadline is approaching, and I would like to have them done in time. Moreover, since you won't be home, I don't have any desire to be there alone," she replied, still working on a bracelet.

"I already miss you, baby. It will be a hectic trip, but I will regret not being at your side," Edward said as he glanced at the window of a shop.

"I will do my best to cope with your missing—you try to bring back yourself alive," Sabrina replied as her face relaxed.

277

As he hung up the conversation, Edward leaned on one of the soft chairs of the lounge area. He felt immediately better. His thoughts ran once again to Sabrina and to the life they'd built—he was afraid she would be too busy to miss him.

He realized that he had never felt her missing so daunting and a growing sense of fear grabbed his mind. Was he going to die during the journey? He'd never thought about death before.

We never consider any sort of accident like something that can happen to everybody, he thought. *This is true until we're struck by some unfortunate events.*

He strode to the windows and followed an airplane with his eyes as it was going to take off. The shine of the sun on the metal as it accelerated on the runway almost blinded him and, gracefully, like a bird, it left the ground.

We're so busy thinking about what will happen tomorrow, and we forget to focus on what is happening right now in front of our eyes. Nor do we realize that planning for something which eventually won't come is entirely useless.

His breath choked on his throat, he feared he was falling straight into a deadly trap.

If the Kozars have the intention to get even for the offense they think I gave them, is there any way, besides offering my life, we could agree upon?

He didn't want to die, but neither was he ready to live in fear for the rest of his life—there had to be a way to stop that madness.

Edward turned to face the lounge with a slow movement, and his eyes met the clock. He had to hurry to the gate if he wanted to leave.

As he took his seat on the plane, he sent a brief text message to Sabrina and Mikhail to inform them and question him about the possibility of coming to an agreement with the Kozars.

From the plane window, he observed the activity in the airport. His telephone beeping reminded him of two main things. First, he should have switched it off, and second, either Mikhail or Sabrina replied to his messages.

It wasn't a surprise to see he received an answer from both. But, while that from his wife touched him, Mikhail's brought him back to his considerations about how frail life can be.

'Družíšče, there is no way to come to an agreement with them. It's either your blood or theirs. I managed to free myself from other businesses. I will be the one to pick you up at the airport.

Although the latter news reassured him, the fact that the offense could only be washed with blood got him even more upset.

With furrowed brows, he switched off his phone, hoping to have at least a good flight before reaching his destination.

***

It was a sunny morning in Milan when the aircraft from New York landed at the busy airport of Malpensa. Despite the comfort offered by the business class, a sense of anticipation possessed Edward as he reached the arrival gate, and all he needed was to spot the familiar face of Mikhail. After the previous message, many questions stirred his soul, and he couldn't wait to ask him directly.

Waiting in the lobby, Mikhail impatiently stared at the crowd coming from the baggage claim to spot his client. He had arranged 'eyes' all over the hall, placed at each vantage point to have a clear vision on every corner. They already got a glimpse of Edward and were following him, ready to intervene at the first suspicious movement.

As soon as Edward entered the arrivals hall, opening up into a smile, Mikhail approached him. "*Družíšče!*" he greeted, guiding him in a hurry toward a secondary exit leading to the parking lot. "Let's hurry—the car is in this direction."

Surprised by his rushed behavior, he understood the situation didn't allow any pleasantries, there would be time once in a safe place.

For this reason, he didn't speak a word—he kept the pace of Mikhail's steps until they reached a car waiting for them. The driver kept the engine on, and several people observed the surroundings.

He reached out for his phone and sent a message to Sabrina. He almost forgot to inform her of his safe arrival at the airport and he didn't want her to worry. The phone was still muted, and he decided to keep it so. *I can't find anything more annoying than the ringing or beeping of a telephone when you try to focus on a demanding task.*

He placed the phone back in the pocket of his jacket and watched outside the window. He'd been already once in Milan for business and found it curious he traveled the whole world, but never for pleasure. He didn't remember having taken an actual holiday to enjoy his time with his wife either. The most they ever did were short trips around New York.

We should make our lives easier. I would love to travel more around the world for pleasure rather than for business and alone. Last time I remember being on a leisure trip was when I was still studying in London, and I traveled to Berlin to meet my father. He grimaced as he recalled the feelings when he received the picture from Jeff.

As to cast away that hurtful memory, he shook his head, and he forced his attention on the scenery out of the window.

After half an hour, the car turned toward an unpaved road, and soon enough, fields replaced the cement and high buildings. It was beautiful to see how luxuriant and colorful the countryside was and how relatively close it was to the city. Although he had no idea why they were driving to such a remote location, he trusted Mikhail's choice.

Being in a secluded place would probably make it easier to control the surroundings. *Eventually, it'll provide better chances for an escape plan, differently than in the middle of the city* -He shook his head- *This is ridiculous. Either we're all getting paranoid, or the threat is more concrete than I forecasted.*

281

Caught in his train of thoughts, he didn't realize the car stopped in front of an old villa.

"We arrived, *Družíšče*. This is the place where you can be sure nobody is going to find you until the day of the auction." Mikhail turned his glance at him before opening the door of the car.

As he got out, he narrowed his eyes, raising his hand to make a screen from the sun's brightness. Getting accustomed to the new light environment, he glanced at the manor and its surroundings. The birds' song carried by the slight whistle of the breeze through the crown of the trees made the place look lost from the rest of the world. The noises of the street couldn't reach them to interfere with the calm of that environment.

His body relaxed as if it naturally started to be at ease, coming at one with nature and that old building.

It didn't seem to be a hotel, rather a private residence rented for the occasion. The absence of other cars confirmed that they would be the only occupants of that place.

"Such a beautiful and peaceful place," Edward considered, turning his gaze at Mikhail.

"Come, I will show you the whole premises and your bedroom," he said as they walked toward the large door of the entrance.

Edward didn't pay attention to his words, caught in the contemplation of the majestic building.

The large and massive entrance door was finely carved, showing the care with which the owners had kept it over the centuries, protecting the wood from cold, warm, and insects.

"It's so amazing the attention for the littlest detail," he whispered.

"Then, you will love the interiors." A voice coming from the inside assured.

A man in his forties appeared from the shade of the entrance, walking calmly with an elegant stride. The dark hair combed backward, and the perfectly shaved face conferred him with an aristocratic outlook, completed by the dark blue suit.

"Pleased to meet you," he said, stretching his hand toward Edward. "My name is Giuliano, Giuliano Marchesi. I'm the owner of the place."

They shook hands. "My pleasure, my name is Edward Sherwood."

"Mikhail is an old friend, and we benefit from each other's expertise in different fields. I'm a collector and deal with antiques. I also run a security business in cooperation with Mikhail. During the years, I have developed a comprehensive network of informers on the whole national territory, which comes useful for Mikhail's business and mine alike."

"We've been lucky to meet each other, but let's now go in. You will certainly want to have a shower and change your clothes before we can talk about business and start planning your participation in the auction." Mikhail gave a fast glance at Edward.

He wasn't tired, but he needed to refresh himself after such a long journey.

Giuliano led him to the second floor, where his bedroom was arranged. "Here is your room. I hope you will find it comfortable enough. If you have any request, it will be my pleasure to ensure your stay comfortable," he said as he opened the door.

"Thank you very much for your kind hospitality—this place looks like a dream. You have one of the most beautiful houses I've ever had the chance to visit," he said as he looked around himself. His life wasn't made of extreme luxury. Since he was a kid, he was raised to think more practically and focus on necessities. Although he was living in an enviable apartment in the center of Manhattan, he realized how that villa surpassed in style what he had.

"We will wait for you downstairs. When you're ready, go back to the main hall, turn to the left and follow the corridor until you reach the garden. We will talk calmly, and we will have lunch," Giuliano proposed.

The place brought memories from the manor where his grandfather lived, particularly the room where the family's history was collected through artifacts and curiosities acquired through the centuries. After his death, Herman and other relatives inherited it as an equal share. It was used mainly for family gatherings and as a holiday residence. It was located outside the city and living there wouldn't have been practical.

Shaking his head, he tried to focus on the reason he was there, and that was far from being a holiday. The specter of being closer to death than ever returned to haunt his soul, along with the consciousness that people can't control their fate.

The following week was not as relaxing as Edward had expected. The anguish did not leave him a single second, and not a single hour passed without him wondering if he would come out of that situation alive.

Mikhail and Giuliano organized the security service in extreme detail and had him exercise with the gun he would carry with him.

***

The auction would take place the following day and Mikhail and Giuliano, for the umpteenth time, were reviewing the plan with Edward.

"Now, before entering the auction house, the security service will ask you to pass through a scanner to make sure you don't have any weapons or other forbidden items. Many precious objects will be auctioned off and surveillance will do its utmost to prevent any theft attempt," Giuliano explained as they were practicing the routine to get in and out of the building. "For this reason, I had to 'convince' one of the guards to bring inside the guns we'll be carrying. We will use them only if necessary, we don't need to attract any attention and we have to make sure that everything will run smoothly without accidents."

With a nod, Mikhail stood from the chair and walked to get some water. "Knowing the Kozars, they too will find a way to introduce weapons inside the building, therefore, we will need to be prepared for any eventuality." He took a pause and filled his glass.

"We need to think only and exclusively for Edward's safety. He will have to leave this place and safely reach the auction house. Once there, he will place his bid while we keep our eyes open. Then, we are going to get quickly out of there and make sure he gets to the airport in one living piece."

The possibility of losing his life brought his work to a different light. Thinking about Sabrina waiting at home, he couldn't bear the idea of having somebody calling her informing her about a deadly accident. *It's not worth it or fair to her. I'm not going to give up this business, but perhaps in the future, I'm not going to participate in auctions personally. Giving someone else's my proxy will provide me with a sort of protection from these risks.*

"Any problem?" Giuliano wondered, noticing the change in expression on Edward's face.

Furrowing his brows, he shook his head, "I was thinking about something else." He didn't want to explain what was going on in his heart—those were personal matters that concerned nobody else but Sabrina and him. "Let's go once again through it, shall we?"

286

He wanted to change the topic. He needed to divert the attention from his own issues.

"Sure, let's start once again from the beginning," proposed Mikhail.

***

In the evening, Edward parted from the rest of the team and was seated alone in the garden. He stared at the moon after having spoken with Sabrina. Things were going fine back in the shop—the only thing hurting his heart was being far from her.

He'd been away many other times for more extended periods than seven days. Yet, he had never felt so lonely, nor his heart had ached longing to be in Sabrina's arms.

"Is this how you feel when death is approaching?" He asked the moon.

"I can't say, but it's a good question," Mikhail chimed in, as he was coming from the house where all the others were entertaining themselves. "Why are you here all alone?"

Edward turned his gaze at him for a moment to turn it back to the moon right away. He didn't like being interrupted, and perhaps Mikhail had been rude in nosing in his inner conversation. Nevertheless, he had to admit to himself he needed someone close to him.

"I was thinking about the auction. What do we know about the Kozar family? Can you be sure they're that dangerous?" He needed to understand how it was possible they considered losing an auction such a serious outrage that he had to be washed with blood.

It didn't make sense, mainly because they had the ruby back when they caused the first accident to Mr. Hopkins.

Mikhail exhaled profoundly and sat down beside him. "I wish I was able to tell you we'll be all safe, that tomorrow will be a nice day, where you'll have the chance to get back the pearl you are looking for." He took a pause to recall his thoughts. "When I was still a young kid..." his eyes glistened. "I didn't come from a wealthy family, and in Russia, this means having everything out of your reach. I was seventeen, and at that age, you start to look around yourself and understand that you will never have the same chances as those born in better families. That goddamn age when you believe you should get everything, if not more, at any cost, even selling your soul to the devil. The Kozars gave me the chance to shine. In a short time, I didn't simply complete my education, but also earn more money than I could have done with an honest job."

Edward narrowed his eyes, "You were working for them?"

"Yes, I was. They had seen potential in me, and I got trained as a bodyguard," he recalled, turning his eyes at him. "Within a few years, I thought they might give a job to my younger brother, Sergey. I talked to the main figure of the family, pleading to help him from ending on the streets, and my pleas were granted."

“But what went wrong?” Edward sensed something terrible must have happened if Mikhail was so bitter yet scared about them. In his experience, nothing was able to inspire the slightest sense of fear in Mikhail’s soul. Nothing except the Kozar family.

“It happened during an operation. There was a rumor that someone inside the organization leaked vital information to the police. Nothing is worse than suspicion, and people were constantly pointing at each other to understand who the traitor was. When they had the proof that the source of the leak was Sergey, we all knew this wouldn't have been something to be forgiven. The penalty for traitors is death.”

“So, they killed your brother...” he whispered, feeling the intensity of the moment.

“Not really. Sergey was my brother, and there is a saying within a family that people act in the same way. Genetically, the members of a family, two brothers, will never be completely different. That was the moment when I had to prove them—I would have never made the same mistake.”

Edward gasped, but his racing heartbeat choked every word on his throat and waited for Mikhail to finish his story.

“I was called one day to present myself to the family leader. He explained to me they found out it was my brother. They said he admitted, although it wasn't something intentional.” He clenched his fist to stop the shaking of his hands. “They brought me to a room, where Sergey was tied to a chair, after having beaten him almost to death. My heart sank, and I was sure his sentence had already been spelled. I didn't know that with him, my life would have ended too. They handed me a handgun, a Baikal-442, and demanded me to shoot my own brother dead. I tried to refuse it, but I realized they would have killed me and then him. Sergey stared at me, and with the last whisper, he begged me to oblige him—he whispered he would have rather died by my hand than by the hand of a bunch of sadistic criminals. I wanted to run away or to refuse and have myself killed along with Sergey. However, when I felt the cold steel of their gun pointed at my temple, I reached his head and spewing bitter promises of certain revenge, I pulled the trigger and killed him."

Mikhail turned his gaze at Edward, who couldn't say a word. "That was the way to pay my way out of the clan. I was a free man, but my family disintegrated, and since then, I haven't seen my mother or father. Everything was broken because of me. Had I never involved Sergey into that business, he would have still been alive, and perhaps the only one dead would have been me."

He drew a long breath, trying hard to recollect his strength. "This is the reason why I can tell for sure we won't have any easy way to come out. But leave the hard part to me. Time has come for them to pay for my brother's death and the obliteration of my soul. After I can be at peace."

"What if they kill you?" Edward dared to wonder, twisting his fingers entwined.

"This is not an option." He grinned. "After the auction tomorrow, you and Giuliano will leave immediately for the airport. The rest of the team and I will keep the Kozars busy and bring them into a trap attracting them to the basements, where the old foundations of the previous building are. The auction house is connected underground with several other places through tunnels. There, far from the indiscreet eyes of the security cameras, and police, we will have the time to settle our old issues. Once our mission is accomplished, I will move back to Moscow and settle the old matters also with those who are responsible for the death of my brother."

Every word coming to his mind sounded stupid and cliché, so he preferred to remain silent. Edward reached Mikhail's shoulder with his hand and patted it.

The day after, a massacre would happen, and the only thing he was aware of was that he needed to keep far from the fire between Mikhail and the Kozars.

"Do you think they already know about your intentions? Is this something you have been planning for a long time?" he wondered about the reason why Mikhail didn't mention anything to him.

"No, this was something I decided later. The initial idea was to keep my personal retaliation separated from the auction, but then, I realized that the best way to protect you was to eliminate them all, also fulfilling my desire for revenge." He lowered his gaze. "I should have told you before about it, sorry."

Despite the bitterness of being used as bait, Edward still hoped to get out of it alive. The instinct of survival prevailed over any other feelings.

"*Družíšče*, I'm sorry." He tried to apologize. "My primary aim is to protect you, and I promise you, I will do whatever in my power to keep you alive and well. The retaliation is completely separated, but since they will try to wash the offense with your blood, I will make sure the only one that will be shed will be theirs. I hope this is enough as a reason."

Edward shook his head. "There will never be a good enough reason, but I want you to understand that I sympathize with your cause. If the same had happened to me with Sabrina, I'm not sure I could wait for such a long time before thinking about killing them."

As his forehead creased with concern, his thoughts ran to his wife. "You understand I cannot leave Sabrina..."

Mikhail didn't give him time to finish his sentence. "If one of us will have to die, that one shall be me. You have my word, and I'm not going to allow more suffering than they have already caused," Mikhail promised as his voice returned steady. "We both have someone to care for—although my loved one is dead, I still owe him the deserved vengeance. Yours is still alive, and it's my duty and personal commitment to keep you alive. It will feel like also Sergey will live on... We're not so different, *Družíšče.*"

A long pause of silence fell between them, interrupted only by the chirping of the crickets. For a moment, that seemed to last an eternity, the torment in their souls subsided and, forgetting their worries, they felt at peace.

I wish I had Sabrina with me now and live our lives in a place like this. Careless, holding each other in a night like this, listening to the sounds of nature, and finally falling asleep.

His mouth arched upward into a peaceful smile as the features of his face relaxed.

"We'd better go to rest. Tomorrow is going to be a long day, and we will need all our energies. In the late afternoon, you will reach the airport."

Edward stood from the bench. Without waiting for Mikhail, he walked in the direction of Giuliano's house to bid goodbye to the day, hoping it wasn't the last of his life.

Chapter 26

The auction was scheduled for three o'clock in the afternoon. For the whole morning, they rehearsed the plan.

The surveillance group was the first to leave, after 11:00 am, in order to place themselves in the strategic points agreed with Mikhail and Giuliano. In that way, they would have a 360 degrees view both inside the auction house and outside.

At 1:30 pm, it was the turn of Edward, Giuliano, and Mikhail. In the car, none of them spoke. The first two, in particular, had never experienced such a level of intensity, their lives did not include as high risks as they were running that day.

The quiet engine of Giuliano's car and the sound insulation from the outer world made their meditating quiet, feel daunting.

As they approached their destination, Edward's heart reached the point he thought it wanted to jump out of his chest and run away to hide.

He turned his gaze at Mikhail who was looking out the window. He was seemingly calm as if nothing significant was going to happen, but the way he held his hands tightly, betrayed his real feelings. After he had told him about his brother's death, the night before, Edward understood that the stakes were very high for him too.

I would have never been able to go on. His fists and teeth clenched tight, and his breath got shallow with the rage and fear for the limitless evil residing in the human heart. *Someone has to stop them before they reach Sabrina. I don't care if they kill me, but my beloved...*

He inhaled sharply.

The car stopped at a parking space. "Here we are," Giuliano whispered gravely. He turned his eyes to the other men, and, with a nod, they got out of the car and walked to the auction hall.

Passing the safety check, they were directed to the lower floor, where they got back their handguns to be hidden in their jackets. That was the first time Edward held a gun, intending to use it against another human. The cold touch with the metal burned literally in his hands, and he placed it immediately away.

"You'd better get used to it, *Družíšče*. You might need it to get out of here alive," Mikhail said.

After the long silence that had accompanied them on the way, Edward almost didn't recognize that voice. His lips quivered as a light electric shock seemed to run through his whole body. Never like that moment had he wished to be somewhere else. This was not facing Jeff in Sabrina's apartment. It wasn't like calming down a panicking young man who thought he had lost everything in his life and needed someone to stretch a hand in his direction.

"I don't want to die...," he whispered, with tears welling in his eyes.

295

Giuliano's arms were around him in a friendly hug that helped release the tension.

"Everything will be fine. This is a safety measure we're taking. We're not sure they will be here." Giuliano tried to reassure.

"*Družíšče*, we need to go. You must get a hold of yourself." Mikhail's voice was sharp like broken glass and cut through his soul.

Edward wasn't sure he was supposed to be grateful for that, but he was right—this wasn't the time to feel emotional. They had a mission to accomplish.

Parting from Giuliano, he took a deep breath and wiped his eyes. "You're right—let's go, be focused on the auction. I don't want to miss the pearl."

They reached the hall and sat down. They didn't want to look around the hall, which had started to fill up with potential competitors for the ownership of each item scheduled for the auction.

Giuliano was startled as his mobile phone vibrated with the incoming of a message. With a slight movement as if he didn't want to be seen taking it out, he glanced at the message. With an almost imperceptible move, he tried to look behind.

They're behind us. It seems there are more than the ones sitting here – he sent a text message on Edward's phone.

A cold shiver ran along his spine as he read the message from his silenced phone. Edward didn't move—he followed the auction.

For as long as I'm here in this hall, I should be safe, later... He didn't dare to formulate in his mind what could have happened once they were outside the building. He wondered whether there was a safe place to hide or what they would have been ready to, to quench their thirst for revenge.

Finally, it arrived at the turn to bid for the pearl. He truly hoped they wouldn't step in this. Still, perhaps Giuliano had a better idea, and immediately after Edward's first offer, he overbid him.

A puzzled grin twisted Edward's face. Then, he understood. He had to make sure Giuliano won the auction. With all the probabilities, the Kozar brothers had no idea Giuliano and he were together, therefore they would let him win.

Several people were interested in the pearl, and he bid another couple of times before giving up. He was confident Giuliano knew he was ready to pay whatever sum for the pearl.

The price started to reach a critical level, but for $350k, Giuliano was the bid winner. As the broker's hammer landed on the table declaring the end of the auction and winning Giuliano's offer, he smiled.

My father sold the pearl when I was a kid. Mr. Milton bought it for half a million. I'm expecting to earn a similar sum, if not more. He wasn't interested in any other item and needed to leave the place.

Giuliano and Edward started to walk away, but they were not alone. The two brothers stood up immediately after and followed from a safe distance, not to be noticed. A few others followed from other locations and apparently walked in a different direction, yet not to the exit.

Mikhail and the rest of the team were also prepared to intervene as soon as the situation required it.

As the auction was still going on, the corridors were relatively isolated. Returning from the office where Edward and Giuliano paid for the items, the two brothers stood on their way.

A deep silence created between them, and Edward could almost hear his heart pounding on his chest. Yet, as the younger one moved his jacket aside, revealing the handgun concealed under it, he noticed one detail that changed everything.

A ring, but not just a random one. It was that of Mr. Hopkins, which had disappeared shortly before his death.

His mind raced, and, in a blink of an eye, fear transformed into chance. The crazy desire to have back the ruby, even at the cost of tearing his finger away, possessed him.

He narrowed his eyes, offering a cold stare at the brothers. Without saying anything, slowly, he made sure they got a glimpse of his own handgun.

You're not the only ones who can play with those big boys' toys, and now I can tell you I had enough of you two. Either it is my life or yours.

He had no idea what the switch had turned on in his mind. It was probably something he had inherited from his grandfather and previous generations of

Sherwood who had based the family business on the cursed stone trade.

Giuliano followed the lead and also showed them his gun. So, everybody should have had a clear idea of everybody's intention.

A noise from behind the Kozar's shoulders caught their attention, an unmissable chance Giuliano didn't miss and pushed Edward away toward one of the secondary corridors. According to the blueprints, it should have led to another hall, the restrooms, and the exit.

"This isn't the time to play the heroes—run." Giuliano rushed, pushing him away.

The commotion increased, and rushed steps seemed to follow them. A relieving feeling took over his heart as they appeared to not be following them but instead running toward the basement. "Mikhail is leading probably downstairs, where he's set the trap. We need to run out of here!" Giuliano pulled him in the direction of the exit.

"Not without having this issue solved... I'm not going to hide for the rest of my life. I can't run away forever, and I don't want to live in fear!" His eyes shone with a glare of pure hate as he spelled his words. "Not without my ruby either..."

Giuliano glanced at him, failing to recognize in that hatred-filled person, the slightest resemblance to the man he had learned to know, in the last week. "What the fuck you're talking about? You can't win against them—let Mikhail take care of them, and let's get the hell out of here. You'll be safer at the airport." He grabbed him by the shoulders, trying to make him move in the direction of the exit.

Edward wriggled violently against him. "You go, and I will stay. I'm not going anywhere without the ring. Sabrina was right, and now it's too late to just flee."

With those words, knowing he might have not survived, he started to walk back in the direction of the noises. He needed to understand what the situation was and who was in advantage. Considering the noises, they were already reaching the basement.

"Come," he said to Giuliano, who followed him from a distance. But Giuliano hesitated, turning around himself a couple of times, grabbed by the demon of indecision. According to the plans, his task was to take Edward away to the safety of the airport. That was what they agreed from the beginning and what he thought was Edward's desire.

However, as Edward kept walking without him in the direction of the basement, he decided to follow him and offer his backup.

Slowly they moved toward the noises The depth of the basement, the use of the silencers, and the lack of surveillance system in those semi-abandoned places offered them the perfect ground to set their score with few chances to be heard, and the police alerted. They reached one of the underground escape routes, connecting the basements of two separate businesses in the same building.

Those were old remnants of ancient foundations, of which only old blueprints kept record. It would have been the best place for a massacre. Despite the reduced manpower, Mikhail and his team moved forward, pushing the two brothers and their henchmen to what was supposed to be the place to get even.

As Edward and Giuliano walked through the dimmed underground corridors, the noises got closer. The musty smell, the thickness of the air mixed with the stench of death, sharpened his senses. They proceeded along the narrow corridors, trying to avoid stumbling or walking over the corpses of the few people who had perished during the descent to that trap. The noises of voices, steps and occasional gunshot filled the gap of silence between Giuliano and Edward, who with a measured pace followed the direction of the action.

***

From his position behind a corner, Mikhail's teeth clenched. He needed to be face-to-face with the brothers before solving the issues he still had opened with the rest of the family members in Moscow. *Now or never, this is the day when Sergey will have his revenge—they will pay for his death.*

The good chance finally arrived when he had the opportunity to advance closer, after shooting one of their henchmen. "Time to get even!" Mikhail shouted as he leaned out. "Let's solve this like men."

The two brothers glanced at each other and grinned. Without a word, they came out pointing their guns in the direction of Mikhail.

"This isn't your business, Misha! We're not after you!" Yuri, the elder brother, said.

Mikhail growled in anger—*only Sergey could call me Misha*. He discarded the pistol he had in his hand and grabbed the suppressed Sig Sauer's tiny copperhead, which owned one of the bratva henchmen he killed. Mikhail checked the magazine, and with a swift, catlike move, guided by his thirst for revenge that had been brewing inside him since the death of his brother, Mikhail got out from behind a corner. He pointed the submachine gun, and with a feral shout, he fired the full round against his opponents until the two brothers lay dead on the hard, rotten, concrete floor.

He walked closer to them. "I should have done what you did to me and made you shoot at each other, but never mind, now is the turn of the rest of the family," he spat.

Knowing the danger was temporarily over and that it was time to run away, Giuliano and Edward, together with the only other bodyguard alive, Nikolay, reached Mikhail. "We need to get out of here, pronto!"

"Yes, one moment still," Edward replied, walking to the brother who wore the ring. With a smirk, he took it off and placed it in his pocket. "Now, we can go."

The silence in the car as they drove away was complete. Nobody had anything left to say. If Mikhail couldn't succeed in his plan, the retaliation against everybody else in the car would have been terrible.

Everyone was considering their own safety, but most of all, that of their loved ones. Edward feared they might harm Sabrina, especially as the mysterious customer, related to the Kozar family, knew where he could hit and hurt.

I'm not sure we will ever reach an end. Differently from what I always thought, my father made the best choice. My grandfather should have warned me about because I believe there is a whole story untold, and the darkest details of his success have been buried with him in his grave. Unfortunately I haven't listened to my father's words, and I became just like my grandfather, and one day, my secrets will be buried together with me. Edward lowered his glance to his lap. *Will that be the end of the Sherwoods, merchants of curses?*

As they reached the manor, everybody retired to their rooms, willing to deal only with their own demons. In the silence of the room, Edward considered calling Sabrina to inform her about the delay. Still, he wondered how he would cover the reason for it.

With a deep breath, he grabbed his mobile phone and dialed her number.

***

Sabrina returned from the lunch break when her phone started to ring. A broad smile appeared on her face as she saw Edward's ID caller.

303

"Hello, there! Are you already at the airport?" Sabrina's cheerful voice replied.

On any other occasion, that would have been enough to make him feel the luckiest man in the world, but at that moment, it arrived like a punch on his face—he could barely breathe. Tears welled his eyes and a lump formed in his throat. His body ached, desiring only to lie in bed, while his soul couldn't find any comfort and peace.

"Sweetheart, is everything okay?" She wondered, recognizing when her husband was on the verge of crying.

"I'm fine, baby. I miss you so much. I missed the flight, and I need to reschedule it, probably tomorrow or so," he replied. "It has been a long day, and everything has happened. However, I have the pearl, but it was quite expensive this time."

He desperately tried to change the subject and find something else to talk about, starting with good news, perhaps the only one he could offer. Then he recalled the ring he took from the hand of the youngest brother. "I brought something with me. I will need to contact Mr. Hopkins' family, as this is something that belongs to them."

Sabrina's voice brightened up, "What do you mean?"

"You certainly remember the ruby he bought, the one that disappeared into the nothingness. I found it, and I want to return it to the owners. There isn't any curse, and the ruby should at least give them some peace of mind. That's proof that Mr. Hopkins' life too found the right revenge, and his soul can finally rest in peace," he whispered. "How is everything going back home?"

"Here, everything is going fine, or at least I hope so," she hesitated. "What I mean to say is that recently I felt a bit weak. I didn't know whether it was the stress of having you far away or the whole situation that put some extra weight on my shoulders. Nevertheless, today I decided to see my doctor about it."

"What did he say? Will you need some time off? I can certainly arrange it, plus I will be back home and take care of the rest," he assured.

"I will certainly need to take it easy and have more time for myself, but the reason isn't that I'm ill, but because I'm pregnant. There's a little Sherwood who's going to inherit the family business." Her voice trembled. They never talked about having children, as their lives were far too hectic to even stop for a second and think about the possibility.

A long pause of silence filled the gap between them. Edward wasn't sure he understood what she said, and if it were, soon enough, he would be a father.

A child? Should I be happy or worried? He thought as he considered the day he had. *If this is the case, we need to reconsider the whole business and recreate a safety level, including the most vulnerable link in the chain.*

"Are you angry?" Sabrina's voice faltered.

The sound of her voice chimed like church bells, bringing him abruptly from his considerations. "O- Of course not! Why in this world would I be angry?"

"I don't know, maybe because I was expecting any sort of reaction from you more than silence."

"Darling, I am the happiest man in the world. The point was that this news arrived completely unexpected." A bright smile appeared on his face as he realized the news under every aspect.

"I understand that this might not be the best time. We are going through a challenging period, and I also understand the risks posed by those criminals that are after you, but maybe we can figure out an escape route." She didn't want to give up her pregnancy. Still, she also had to admit that having a child while being in the crosshairs of a mafia family wasn't exactly what she hoped for in her future.

"That was also my main concern, but I would never ask you to get rid of it. We can work this out—there must be a way out." He took a short pause, that day entered in his personal book of records for being extremely challenging, physically and emotionally. That was the day when first in his life was involved in a shooting, risked his life, and had the news of becoming a father. "Perhaps you should call my father and see if they can reach you or if you can reach them until I return." He wiped his face with his hand, trying to think clearly.

"That's what I thought because there's more," she added. "Do you remember that customer connected with the Kozars?"

His blood froze on his veins—the fact that he had reached the shop as they were supposed to murder him brought his soul to another level of fear.

"Did he come in? What did he want? Did he threaten you?" His voice startled.

"He didn't come in, but I saw him stopping by in front of our shop. He watched the items on display on our window, and then he raised his eyes to look inside the shop as if he was looking for someone. Then, without entering, he resumed his walk," Sabrina explained.

"I'm afraid I can't assure your safety from this moment on. Not at least until this story is going to be over." Trying to be concise, Edward explained what happened back at the auction.

Mikhail interrupted him entering the room at that same moment without even bother knocking at the door. "*Družíšče*, are you talking to your wife?" He asked unceremoniously, growling like an angry beast.

Jolting to turn in his direction, the phone fell to the ground. "Yes...I thought you had already left. What is going on?" He asked.

Mikhail paced toward him and grabbed the phone from the floor, "Sabrina?" He asked to make sure she was still online. On another occasion, Edward would have protested more violently. Still, in that situation, he was sure he had a good reason to behave in such a rude way.

"Y-yes...what?" She muttered.

"Within a few minutes, three people will enter the shop. One of them will take your place at the desk. Meanwhile, the others will drive you to a secured location. Is there someone else working with you?" Mikhail tried to talk slowly and calmly to make sure she understood what she needed to do.

"Janice is working in the laboratory." Sabrina's voice trembled.

"Tell her a new employee is coming, as you need to reach Mr. Sherwood for closing an important deal." Mikhail kept his voice steady. "Much probably there isn't any need for you to even hide. After I murdered Yuri and Aleksander, I'm sure that they will lose interest in killing you and wish rather wash the offense with my blood. Nevertheless, I prefer not to risk anything. Did I make myself clear?" Mikhail concluded.

"Of course, I will talk immediately with Janice. Can I speak to my husband?" She asked.

Without replying, he handed the phone to Edward, displeased by that intrusion in his private life. It didn't help to know that the situation required fast action and offered no room for politeness.

Edward waited to be alone once again in the room and locked the door to ensure that nobody would interrupt them again. She was the most important person in his life. He didn't appreciate any meddling when he was with her, whether on the phone or personally.

"Sweetheart, I'm so sorry for the trouble I'm causing you. I feel like I can't give anything but worries when instead, I promised to protect you and make you happy." He felt like he would have never engaged in any sort of relationship. His life was far too messy and bringing someone else into his chaos had been unfair.

"Ed, that day I married you, I knew perfectly what your life was like. I was aware of the risks involved. Despite that, I still said yes, and you want to know why? Because when you look at me, when you hold me in your arms, I feel loved. You're not supposed to protect me—I can do that by myself. Neither do I need you to decide for me. I did it already."

Those words gave him the same feeling of a stone that fell from his heart. Probably, he didn't deserve a person like Sabrina, or perhaps they deserved each other more than they could even understand. They were alike in many aspects, and those slight differences didn't bring them apart. They were the little details that spiced up their life together.

"I love you...," he whispered.

"So do I, but now I need to go—the men Mikhail was talking about are coming. I will call you."

That said, they quit their conversation, praying with all their strength that it wasn't going to be a goodbye.

Chapter 27

Sabrina left with the two men who came to get him from the shop. She didn't have any time to get any luggage from home, and they assured her she would have a chance to get clothes and everything she would need once they'd arrived at safety. The only document she was allowed to gather was her passport.

Unaware of where they were heading, all she knew was that they had reached a private airport. "I need to understand where you're bringing me," she insisted, breaking the wall of silence built between them.

Joshua, one of the men sent by Mikhail, offered her a freezing glance—visibly annoyed by that request. "We've been asked to secure your location. This means it should be far from your workplace, and the one Mr. Sherwood is now. We cannot reveal it now, and we're going to use a private aircraft to make sure nobody can track your position," he explained.

The other man, Brandon, remained silent as if he couldn't hear anything of what Joshua said. He paced at Sabrina's side, observing what was going on around him as they kept walking in the direction of a two-engine plane.

"The chosen location is quite remote, but we made sure you will have enough supplies for the time we'll need to spend there," Joshua added as they got inside the plane, ready to leave.

Without replying, Sabrina sat down and fastened her seat belt. It was now clear that her questions were destined to remain unanswered, at least for the moment. Perhaps she didn't even need to know everything right away.

Knowing where I'm going now won't have any meaning. The only important thing is to keep safe and pray that also Edward will.

The plane left for a not-so-comfortable flight, and as the ground became farther to be concerned, Sabrina drew a deep breath. She wasn't sure whether she would have been safe, but her soul felt better about being far from the ground.

***

Mikhail asked Giuliano, Edward, and the bodyguard team's only survivor to gather in the breakfast room. That was the time for explanations, as none of them had any idea about what was going on. Everything resembled a nightmare, from which nobody seemed able to wake up.

With a grave expression, Mikhail glanced at them all. "I know I need to apologize, and I want you to know that the last thing I wanted was to put any of your lives in danger. We planned everything in a way that Giuliano and Edward would have left the place immediately, leaving my team and I to deal with the Kozars."

A long pause of silence fell between the people in the room. Giuliano wanted to explain that he tried his best to get him out of there, but unexpectedly

Edward insisted on returning and having things solved from his part too.

He lowered his gaze, feeling the responsibility of the casualties on his shoulders.

"*Družíšče*, I don't know the reason why you returned, that was indeed an irresponsible and stupid move from you. Nevertheless, it's also true that your intervention created the right diversion that gave Nikolay and I the right advantage, so no harm done."

Shyly, Edward peered at him, keeping his head lowered, like a child caught in mischief and waiting for punishment. "I'm sorry. You see, I didn't mean to do any harm, and probably I haven't even thought about the implications my decision would have had. One of the brothers had a ring with the ruby I acquired at the auction in Moscow. I sold it to Mr. Hopkins, and when I saw it on his finger, I thought the family deserved to have that back, knowing that their loved one had been revenged. I know it's a stupid idea, but for once, I didn't think about me and my personal gain, and that was an important moment in my life."

Giuliano smiled and placed a hand on his shoulder. "It was a nice thought, but also a stupid one." He turned his glance at Mikhail. "What's next?"

"I'm leaving right away for Moscow. I know where I need to hit to stop all the madness. The elder member of the family will have to pay for his sins. I don't know whether I will get out of their place alive, and if this means saving yours, my life will also have finally gained meaning. Besides, I died already many years ago." He hit his chest with his fist. "Nikolay will be in touch with you as soon as he considers the situation cleared."

Giuliano stood up, followed by Edward, tears in his eyes. "Take care, *Compagno* Mikhail. You have been more than a business partner—you have been family, and as such, I need to know whether there will be a time to meet again or a grave where to mourn your loss."

Edward reached Mikhail's hand, shaking it. "I'll never forget you, Misha. If you can, don't get killed."

With a brief hug, Mikhail and Nikolaj greeted Edward and Giuliano and left.

***

A couple of days had passed since Mikhail left with a flight booked from a private company, and since then, the other two men remained in the mansion and kept their distance. In the evening, Edward had left the house to reach a lonely spot in the garden. His soul was restless, waiting for some news from Sabrina to confirm she came to a safe location or from Mikhail to confirm the nightmare was over.

The night was calm, and the chirping of the grasshoppers gave relief to his distressed soul. He sat down to admire the starry sky and be alone with his thoughts.

The last time he was in that same spot, it was right before the auction. He was with Mikhail, and he hoped he could have returned home soon.

313

He missed Sabrina and was sure his life wouldn't have been the same ever again.

However, that was the way Sherwood's shop was running. Although his father tried hard to be different from the rest of the family, he could not step away from the side business that distinguished their shop from all the others. It was their signature.

Edward lay on the grass and stared at the sky. He hadn't heard from his father for a long time and wondered whether he should have given him a call to make sure nothing had happened to them.

The possibility of having them as a target was fairly remote, also because of the level of safety and the bodyguarding network, his father still kept protecting his family. He glanced at the clock, and with a quick grimace, he decided that whatever he had in mind, it was supposed to wait until the morning after.

It was already half past midnight, and although he wasn't drowsy, he decided to return to his room.

A beep coming from his telephone informed of the incoming message. He increased the pace of his steps back to the house as he grabbed the phone to read it.

A smile appeared on his face to confirm that Sabrina reached a safe location, though complaining about the area's remoteness. "You'll be fine, babe, and soon we will be back home together and start to build the life for our baby," he whispered as he typed his reply.

A second message followed the first one, which was perhaps the one he was waiting for more than anything else as it came from Mikhail.

> *"Družíšče, as you read this message, you should know that we were able to keep ourselves alive. This also means that you will return home and be reunited with your wife soon enough. Yet, I want first to make sure personally that nothing will threaten your or your beloved ones' life. I will be back at you soon, it has been a pleasure working with you, and I hope to meet you in better times."*

Relieved by that message, he typed a fast reply to confirm its reception.

The whole house was immersed in the most complete silence. The lights were switched off, as all its guests were supposed to be already sleeping in their rooms.

It was unnatural for the mansion to be so silent. Even when Giuliano was the only occupant, there was at least music or the chatters of the service personnel or even an unexpected guest for dinner.

For the last few days, the two guests hardly ate anything sharing the same table.

The personnel refrained from talking as if a funeral was taking place, and a respectful quiet had to be kept.

Every comment was exchanged as a whisper or with an agreeing glance. The gravity of the silence was like a curtain heavily falling upon those who entered the house.

The ticking of Edward's steps on the marble floor resounded through the corridor as he approached, almost blindly, his room. The moonlight from the windows illuminated the long hall with a bluish silver tone. The white light curtains gently moved by the night breeze lent a ghostly appearance to the environment.

Yet, also the ghosts were waiting in their corners for something to happen, something able to frighten them too.

With a light click and a creaking sound of the hinges that needed probably to be oiled, the door of Edward's room opened. Carefully, he closed it behind him and switched on the light.

The richness of the room's decoration regained the festive look as the warm yellow light of the chandelier pervaded every corner, bringing to life the color of the paintings on the walls and ceiling.

"This house is a museum," Edward considered aloud. For a person like Giuliano Marchesi, it couldn't be any different. His family collected items for generations. The care for the details and the taste for what's beautiful were inherited from father to son.

"I would like to live in a place like this, but in Manhattan, this amazing beauty would be wasted. These interiors belong to something that deserves them like this mansion, immersed in the peace of the natural environment, far from the bustling city, and connected with its roots."

A smile appeared on his face, contemplating the possibility of moving one day to live in a similar house, in a place full of history far from the city.

"We might purchase an estate here in Italy and spend our holidays here. It could be a great place to retire once we decide to step out of the market."

He lay on the bed, glancing at the paintings on the ceiling, listening to the silence surrounding him, and allowing his thoughts to run wild.

Groaning, he stood from the bed as if grabbed by a thought. He reached his jacket with long strides, where he kept the item he had purchased at the auction.

His hand searching the pocket met an object of a different shape from the jewel box where the pearl was stored. Furrowing his brows, he grabbed it, and with questioning eyes, he inspected it.

He was surprised to find an item he didn't consider anymore. In his hand, there was something dangerous like the deep red pigeon blood Burmese ruby, flashing through the thick frame of a blood-stained golden ring.

Carefully, he took from the other pocket a handkerchief and gently removed the bloodstains. He polished the stone and the frame thoroughly.

"We, the Sherwoods, are goldsmiths, jewelers, and stone dealers. For centuries, we've sold not simply

317

jewels—we created and sold dreams... Be warned, when you enter my shop, remember to be careful what you ask and pay for, as a curse can only turn into a nightmare."

EPILOGUE

The fair weather invited Sabrina to stay on the porch. She was reading a book as her eyes, every now and then, raised, admiring the rippling of the surface of the lake as birds reached it looking for food. The pine trees mirroring on the water and the fresh smells coming from the forest soothed her senses and made her feel at peace with the world.

The silence, the peace, and the sensation of safety were something she'd been longing for a long time. That place that, in the beginning, she had found boring with its remoteness, over time, it had been starting to seem her the best place to live in. If Edward had been there, then everything would have been perfect, and she couldn't have asked for anything else.

If only Edward could be there with her, she was certain to know perfection.

It was past 3:00 pm when her attention was caught by noises she thought she'd forgotten—the grinding of the wheels on the unpaved road and the engine of a car.

The guards patrolling the area and surveilling the surrounding of the house didn't raise any alarm, so, she didn't worry.

Yet, curious to know who the unexpected visitor was, she walked toward the front of the house.

319

The black suburban shining in the afternoon sun, stopped in the yard in front of the cottage. Sabrina, bringing a hand to her forehead to protect her eyes from the sun, remained watching the doors of the car opening.

For a moment, she couldn't believe her eyes—she was sure it was a dream or a mirage, as the man who came out from the rear seat was really Edward.

He smiled at her, and at that point, with tears welling her eyes, she understood the nightmare was over, and their lives could go on the way they knew before.

Almost sobbing, she held herself to him as he embraced her tightly in his arms. "I've been missing you so much!" he whispered.

"There was a time when I feared I would never see you again," she replied, parting from him.

"Obviously, you don't know me enough, I could never let you alone. Moreover, I couldn't forgive myself for having never met our child," he said, turning his glance at her belly. "How is he doing?"

"He? I think it's going to be a girl!" she giggled. "The baby is fine, and so am I, although I tend to get easily tired, but I guess that is normal."

They walked back inside the cottage and went to have a seat on the couch. There were so many things to be said, and they kept staring at each other's eyes as if none of them had any idea from where to start.

"During these two weeks, I had the time to reconsider what has happened and the way I recklessly have been carried out the family business. I'm not proud of the lies I have told you or the reason why I lied to you." He lowered his gaze, avoiding looking into her eyes. "I was sure that keeping you unaware of what I was doing would have kept you safe. But then I realized the level of threat I had exposed you and myself to, and just how wrong I was. Nothing could have given you the safety I wished to grant you more than stop playing like nothing can touch me."

Sabrina smiled and placed a hand gently on his. "I've never told you, but I was aware of most of the things you tried to keep between you and Mikhail. In the beginning, I was hurt, but I also had the time to reconsider our life together and the way we lived it so far. We've been both acting irresponsibly, but now we need to think about our actions more carefully, as we're not anymore alone. Our child will need to be protected."

"I was considering taking over the mansion of my grandfather. Living in Giuliano's villa in Italy made me think about the beauty of that place and how I'd like my family to be surrounded by that same beauty. Concerning my job, I might follow the same example as my father. I can return to focus more on the regular shop and production of jewels, rather than risking my life around cursed pearls or gemstones." He shook his head.

Sabrina looked at him. She knew that was a promise that, although he would have kept, it wouldn't make him happy. "You know what I think instead?"

"What?" he narrowed his eyes as if he tried to guess what was going on in her mind.

"I think about that room in your grandfather's mansion. You know the one where all the portraits of the previous business owners. Those are your heritage, and we would short-change them by quitting the activity that makes the Sherwood Jewelry famous. I also know we would close an important choice to our child, whether to follow in it or not. I'd say we keep dealing with those items, but let's keep the business safe. There must be a compromise we can reach, isn't it?" Her bright eyes looked into Edward's, leaving him speechless.

"There must be a way, and together we will find it." He held her hand in his own, keeping his eyes on hers.

"That's the reason why we're together. We're not that different from each other, after all. And perhaps it's not only you who has been called to serve the curse. We've been chosen to do this together and keep the legacy going on."

"I love you immensely," he whispered.

Just a few weeks before, all seemed to fall apart, and then in the quiet of the countryside, in a place that seemed out of the world, it returned to make sense. Everything was harmony and beauty. In their hearts now, there was the certainty that a curse is never one-sided. Like the reflections on the surface of a pearl, its light scatters in every direction. So the curse will reach the person who receives, the one who delivers it, and those who watch in awe, waiting and holding their breaths.

Without another word, they stood from the chairs. As the sun started to set, they left to return home, where they would rebuild their lives and create a safe nest for their growing family.

THE END

I hope you enjoyed reading this novel as much as I did writing it. This was a standalone, but I believe you might enjoy reading my new series of police procedurals set in Rome. In the gorgeous setting of the eternal city, Police detective Maurizio Scala is called to solve intricate mysteries and dark crimes to give justice to those he'd sworn to protect. You can find the first book of the series here: The Year of the Mantis – A Commissario Scala mystery (Book 1)

Follow me on:

Facebook: https://www.facebook.com/PJ.Mann.paperpenandinkwell

Twitter: https://twitter.com/PjMann2016

Website: https://pjmannauthor.com

ABOUT THE AUTHOR

Paula J. Mann lives a double life. She is a geologist by day and a novelist by night. She's best known for writing psychological thrillers and dramas, like her debut novel 'A Tale of a Rough Diamond.'

She also writes historical fiction, like Aquila et Noctua, and paranormal suspense like 'Thou Shalt Never Tell.'

Traveling is another passion, and she shares her experiences on her blog together with whatever topic raises her attention: http://paperpenandinkwell.blogspot.com.

BIBLIOGRAPHY

Books in Italian:

Inganno fatale – Dove tutto ha inizio Vol.1

Inganno fatale – Insonne Vol.2

Inganno fatale – Il patto con il Diavolo Vol.3

L'anno della Mantide – le indagini del Commissario Scala Vol.1

I Segreti delle Persone Perbene – Le indagini del Commissario Scala Vol. 2

Books in English:

Thrillers:

Deadly Deception – Prelude (Vol. 1)

Deadly Deception – Insomniac (Vol. 2)

Deadly Deception – The Devil's Deal (Vol.3)

A Tale of a Rough Diamond

The Ghosts of Morgan Street

The Man from the Mist

<u>The Year of the Mantis – A Commissario Scala mystery (Book 1)</u>

<u>The Secret they Hide – A Commissario Scala Mystery (Book 2)</u>

Historical fiction:

<u>Aquila et Noctua</u>

Paranormal suspense:

<u>Thou Shalt Never Tell</u>